The Scandalous Summerfields

Disgrace is their middle name!

Left destitute by their philandering parents,
the three Summerfield sisters—
Tess, Lorene, and Genna—and their
half-brother, Edmund, are the talk of the
ton…for all the wrong reasons!

They are at the mercy of the marriage mart
to transport their family from the fringes of
society to the dizzy heights of respectability.

But with no dowries, and a damaged
reputation, only some very special matches
can survive the scandalous Summerfields!

Read where it all started with
tempestuous Tess's story

Bound by Duty
Already available

Read Edmund's story

Bound by One Scandalous Night
Available now

And look out for the rest of
the family's exploits, coming soon!

Author Note

In my author note for *Bound by Duty* I said that I'd based The Scandalous Summerfields mini-series on my mother and her sisters and brother. Not their life stories, mind you, but as inspiration. Edmund Summerfield, the hero of this book, represents my uncle Ed.

My mother was very close to her sisters, but her brother was older and never quite a part of that close-knit group. We'd see my uncle Ed at least once a year, but it was always for brief periods—an afternoon visit, an evening meal—always shared with lots of family. As a result, I did not know Uncle Ed very well. What I do remember about him, though, is his infectious laugh. When my uncle laughed, everyone laughed with him.

The only similarity between my uncle Ed and my hero Edmund is that both were somewhat separate from their close-knit sisters. In Edmund's story I wanted to explore what it might be like to be *in* a family but not really a *part* of it. Edmund has dealt with this sense of being separate his whole life. Like so many of us, he pretends it doesn't matter to him, when in reality he yearns to feel he belongs—as we all do.

Sometimes where we truly belong is not entirely clear to us, but I believe everyone has such a place. Will Edmund believe it as well?

BOUND BY ONE SCANDALOUS NIGHT

Diane Gaston

First published in Great Britain 2016
By Mills & Boon, an imprint of HarperCollins*Publishers*
1 London Bridge Street, London, SE1 9GF

Large Print edition 2016

© 2016 Diane Perkins

ISBN: 978-0-263-26311-4

Printed and bound in Great Britain
by CPI Antony Rowe, Chippenham, Wiltshire

3011 8119082422

Diane Gaston always said that if she were not a mental health social worker she'd want to be a romance novelist, writing the historical romances she loved to read. When this dream came true she discovered a whole new world of friends and happy endings. Diane lives in Virginia, near Washington, DC, with her husband and three very ordinary house cats. She loves to hear from readers! Contact her at dianegaston.com or on Facebook or Twitter.

Books by Diane Gaston

Mills & Boon Historical Romance

The Scandalous Summerfields

Bound by Duty
Bound by One Scandalous Night

The Masquerade Club

A Reputation for Notoriety
A Marriage of Notoriety
A Lady of Notoriety

Three Soldiers

Gallant Officer, Forbidden Lady
Chivalrous Captain, Rebel Mistress
Valiant Soldier, Beautiful Enemy

Linked by Character

Regency Summer Scandals
'Justine and the Noble Viscount'
A Not So Respectable Gentleman?

Mills & Boon Historical *Undone!* eBooks

The Unlacing of Miss Leigh
The Liberation of Miss Finch

Visit the Author Profile page
at millsandboon.co.uk for more titles.

To the memory of my uncle, Edward Gelen,
with his shock of white hair and infectious laugh.

Chapter One

Early hours of June 16th, 1815—
Brussels, Belgium

Brussels was in chaos.

Bugles blared in the streets, their sounds echoing off the huge buildings of the Grand Place, repeating, over and over the call to arms. All officers and soldiers must report for duty!

For battle.

Wellington had learned that Napoleon and his army crossed into Belgium and were marching towards Brussels. Wellington's soldiers needed to mobilise quickly to stop him.

Lieutenant Edmund Summerfield of the 28th Regiment of Foot wound his way through townspeople of all shapes and sizes and well-dressed gentlemen and ladies still waiting for carriages to bring them back from the Duchess of Richmond's ball. Everywhere men were shouting, women wailing, children crying. Soldiers in uniforms of all colours rushed to and fro. British and Hanoverians in red, Belgian and Dutch in dark blue, British light cavalry in light blue, Rifles in dark green, Highlanders in plaid kilts. The array of colours mimicked a carnival, but the mood was tense, a tinderbox that with one spark could turn to riot.

Edmund forced himself to remain calm. He shifted his bag from one shoulder to the other and wished his head were clearer. He'd spent the evening in a tavern, drinking and playing cards with fellow officers too low in rank and importance to be invited to the Duchess's ball. The bugle's repeated call, still resounding through the tension-filled air, had sobered him greatly.

He pushed his way to the curb of the rue du Marais. Horses, wagons, carriages, men and women dashing on foot, blocked his way. Through the kaleidoscope of colour he spied a vision in white across the street, an angel amidst the tumult. While he watched, a man in labourer's clothing grabbed her around the waist. She beat on the man's arms with her fists and kicked his legs, but this man, rough and wild-eyed, dragged her with him.

Edmund bounded into the busy street, heedless of the traffic, narrowly missing being run down. He made it to the other side and chased after the man abducting the woman. Her shimmering white gown made it easy not to lose sight of her. The man ducked into an alley between two buildings. Edmund reached the space a moment after.

'Let me go!' the woman cried. Her blonde hair, a mass of curls, came free of its bindings and fell around her shoulders.

The man pinned her against the wall and took the fabric of her dress in his fist.

'Vous l'aimerez, chérie,' the man growled.

'No!' cried Edmund. He pushed his bag like a battering ram at the man's head.

The man staggered and loosened his grip.

Edmund dropped his bag and slammed his fist into the man's jaw, sending him sprawling to the cobbles. 'Be off with you! *Allez! Vite!*'

The man scrambled to his feet and disappeared into the dark recesses of the alley.

Edmund turned to the woman. 'Did he hurt you? *Vous a-t-il blessé?*'

She looked up and the light from a street lamp illuminated her face.

He knew her!

'Miss Glenville!'

She was Amelie Glenville. Her brother, Marc Glenville, was married to his half-sister Tess.

Her eyes, wide with shock, looked past him.

'Miss Glenville?' He touched her chin and made her look at him. 'Do you remember me? I am Tess's

brother, Edmund. We met at your parents' breakfast two days ago.'

Her face crumbled. 'Edmund!' She fell into his
arms. The beautiful Amelie Glenville fell into his
arms. Who would believe this?

When Amelie entered the room that morning, for
one heady moment he'd been caught in the spell of
her unspoiled beauty. Fair of face. Skin as smooth
as cream. Cheeks tinged with pink. Eyes as azure
as the sea. Hair, a mass of golden curls, sparkling
in the light as if spun from gold. Lips lush and ripe
for kissing. Innocent. Alluring.

And smiling at him during their introduction.

The next moment, though, he had been introduced to her fiancé, a most correct young man, a
Scots Greys cavalry captain and son of an earl. Reality set in and Edmund had instantly dropped her
from his mind. Even if he wanted to court some
young woman—which he did not—a viscount's
daughter like Amelie Glenville would never do for
a bastard like him.

And here she was embracing him.

'What are you doing here?' he asked her. 'Why
are you alone?' She'd obviously been to the Duchess of Richmond's ball. Her white gown must have
been lovely before it had been so roughly handled.

She drew away and tried to sort out her clothing.
'Captain Fowler left me here.'

The fiancé? 'Left you? Why?'

She huffed. 'We had words.'

'He left you because of a quarrel?' No gentleman, under any circumstance, would desert a lady on a city street in the middle of the night, especially not on a night like this. 'What about?'

'It does not matter,' she snapped.

She sounded more angry than alarmed, at least. That was fortunate. Did she even realise what had almost happened to her?

'And I have no idea how to walk back to the hotel,' she continued in a peeved tone. 'Could you direct me?'

Good heavens! The man had abandoned her without her knowing the way back? 'I think I had better escort you.'

She rubbed her arms.

He shrugged out of his coat. 'Here, put this around you.'

'Might we go back now?' Her voice wobbled a bit. 'It is the Hotel de Flandre.'

She'd be better off staying angry. 'I remember what hotel it was.'

He picked up his bag and offered her his arm, which she readily accepted and held with an anxious grip.

They stepped from the relative quiet of the alley back into the cacophony of the street.

'Hold on tight,' he cautioned, and she squeezed his arm as people bumped against them, the soldiers hurrying to battle, the others to somewhere safe.

What on earth had possessed Fowler to abandon her on such a night? This was not an afternoon stroll through Mayfair. It was after one o'clock in the morning, and the soldiers on these streets would soon be facing battle; the townspeople, possible occupation by the French. She'd already discovered what could happen to a beautiful, unescorted woman when emotions were so high.

She was lovely enough to tempt any man. Even him.

But he must not turn his thoughts in that direction.

'Do you not have to go to your regiment?' she asked as a company of Belgian cavalry rode by, the horses' hooves drumming on the stones of the street.

He did need to reach his regiment as soon as possible, but why stress her with that knowledge? 'I am more in fear of what my sister and your brother would do to me if I left you alone on the street. My sister would draw and quarter me. Your brother would probably do worse.'

'Why would they ever know, unless you told

them?' she retorted peevishly. 'I have no intention of speaking a word of this night to anyone.'

So much for trying to use levity to counteract this nightmarish episode.

'Then blame my conscience,' he said. 'I would think very ill of myself if I abandoned you.'

'Unlike some gentlemen,' she muttered.

'There will be plenty of time for me to reach the battle.' He hoped. 'I doubt Napoleon will disturb his sleep.'

Fine words, but who knew how close Napoleon was to Brussels? Edmund had heard varying accounts. One thing was certain, though. Men would fight soon. And die.

He concentrated on getting her through the crowd without further mishap. The streets cleared a bit when they reached the Cathedral of Saint Michael and Saint Gudula. It rose majestically into the night sky, its yellow stone glowing against the black sky. Men would be stopping at that Gothic church for a few prayers before battle, Edmund would wager. It could not hurt to pray a little.

Pray not to die.

Edmund shook his head. *Don't think such thoughts*, he told himself, but he'd seen too many battles on the Peninsula, seen too many good men die while he survived. Soldiers always talked of having only a finite number of battles in which to remain unscathed before it was their time to die.

Miss Glenville swiped her gloved fingers across her eyes. Was she weeping? If only he could have prevented this ghastly night from happening to her. She was too lovely and unspoiled to have been so roughly treated. To think what that ruffian had in mind to do to her made him tighten his hand into a fist.

He needed to distract both of them from their thoughts. 'So what did happen with Captain…Captain Whatshisname?' He only pretended to forget.

'Fowler.' She spoke the name as if it were a term of contempt.

'Captain Fowler.'

'We quarrelled and he walked away and left me.' She turned her head away.

The scoundrel. 'What sort of quarrel would make a man abandon you?'

The doors of the cathedral opened, revealing the glow of candlelight inside. A man in uniform emerged, head bent. Edmund hoped the man's prayers would be answered.

He turned again to Miss Glenville. 'Tell me what you and Captain Fowler quarrelled about.'

She swiped at her eyes again. 'I certainly will not.'

He persisted. 'Is that what is making you weep?'

He feared it was the other man's mistreatment of her.

'I am not weeping!' she cried. 'I am angry.'

Anger was better. Good for her.

Better for him, too. He was caring too much, caring about never seeing a beauty such as Amelie Glenville again if he lay dead on the battlefield.

'It is really none of your business, you know,' she snapped.

'No doubt,' he persisted. Ungentlemanly of him, but it distracted him from morbid thoughts. 'But you say you will not speak of this, say to your brother or my sister. You should talk about it with someone, since it is plaguing you so. I am unlikely to say anything to anyone.'

After all he might soon be dead.

'Why would I talk to you?' she responded in an arrogant tone.

He'd almost forgotten. He'd been talking with her as if she'd consider him her equal. 'Yes, wise not to tell the likes of me.'

'The likes of you?' She sounded puzzled.

Need he explain? 'Surely the scandalous details of my birth were whispered into your delicate ears.'

'What has that to do with it?' she asked, then smiled wryly. 'But you are correct about the details of your birth being whispered in my ear.'

He gave her a smug look.

'Your sister told me more about you,' she went on.

He laughed. 'What did she tell you? That I was a horrid boy who teased her and played pranks on her?'

'Did you?' She glanced at him but quickly glanced away.

This was better. Who would guess that he'd think talking about himself was desirable? It kept them both from more painful thoughts, though. 'Tess could not have informed you of my wayward activities in the army. My sisters know nothing of that. Their ears are delicate, too, you see.'

She batted her eyes at him. 'Wayward activities? Are you some sort of rake? I have been warned against rakes.'

'Oh, be warned, then,' he joked. 'I am a shameless rake.'

'Are you?' Her voice lowered almost to a whisper.

Had he gone too far in this bantering? Had he reminded her of the ruffian who'd accosted her? 'You are quite safe with me, Miss Glenville.'

She glanced at him again, and her good humour fled. She turned away. 'Yes. Safe.'

If only he really were a rake, he thought. He would steal a taste of her lips and take the memory with him into battle.

They walked in silence until they reached the

Parc de Bruxelles, its main paths lit by lamps. The *parc* looked almost as busy as it did in the daytime, but now other couples were not leisurely strolling on the paths. They were either hurrying into the shadows or clinging to each other.

'Shall we cross through the park?' he asked. 'It will be safe enough tonight. Or would you prefer we walk around it?'

'We may cross the park,' she responded.

She was still lost in her own thoughts. Edmund wanted her to talk to him again. Seeing so many sweethearts clinging to each other affected him. How many would be torn apart for ever? He supposed they were trying to grab one more moment of feeling alive. Perhaps that was what she and Fowler quarrelled about. Perhaps Fowler asked her for more than she could respectably provide. Soldiers leaving for battle often wanted one last coupling with a woman.

As they walked through the park, he heard faint sounds of lovemaking coming from behind the shrubbery. Surely she had noticed, too. Surely she could hear the sounds.

'I have a suspicion that your Captain Fowler might have asked for liberties,' he tried to explain. It did not excuse Fowler's abandoning her, but maybe it would help explain his behaviour toward her. 'Men often want a woman before battle.'

She stopped. 'You think he propositioned me?'

Now he was not so certain. 'That was my guess, yes.'

Amelie kept walking. He really could not be more wrong. Fowler had not propositioned her. But he had left her.

'He put you in danger by leaving you,' the lieutenant went on. 'That was unforgivable.'

Could he not talk of something else? Anything else?

Was it possible to grow older in an instant? Because that was how it felt to Amelie. One moment she was young and in love; the next…

'Unforgivable,' she repeated. But his leaving was only part of his unforgivable behaviour.

Not that it mattered to Fowler.

They continued across the park, heading to the gate on the other side. As they reached it, another couple entered, a plainly dressed young woman and a tall, red-coated infantryman.

The young woman halted. 'Miss Glenville?'

Amelie stared at her. 'Sally?' She glanced back to Edmund. 'My maid,' she explained.

'Oh, miss!' the maid cried. 'Are you back from the ball? There is to be a battle, and your father wants to leave early in the morning for Antwerp. I have packed for you. Must I come to you now? I—I hoped for a little while longer.' Her words came out in a rush.

Next to Sally a young infantryman stood at attention, eyeing Amelie and Edmund warily. But when he gazed at Sally his countenance turned soft and worshipful. Amelie envied her so acutely the pain was physical.

She glanced from the maid to the infantryman and back. 'Of course, you must have as long as you like, Sally. In fact, I do not need you at all tonight. I will manage quite well without you.'

The maid grasped Miss Glenville's hand in both of hers. 'Oh, thank you, miss! Thank you so much.'

The maid pulled on the infantryman's arm. The young man bowed quickly to Edmund, and the couple disappeared into the park.

'He is, I believe, an old friend of Sally's,' she said, as if she owed Edmund an explanation. 'Amazing that they met here in Brussels with all the soldiers here, but, then, your sister and I met my brother in this park the first hour we arrived. And a friend of yours with him, as I recall. And a friend from London, as well.' Now she was babbling.

'Such lucky happenstance,' he remarked.

Not as lucky as she had been that Edmund had happened to be across the street when that horrible creature attacked her. She could still feel the man's hands gripping her, smell his unwashed skin—

She buried her nose in Edmund's red coat. Its scent—his scent—banished the memory.

'You were very kind to your maid,' he said.

She shrugged. 'How could I refuse her? It was her one chance, perhaps.'

It was a chance she would never have. When Fowler first paid her court, she had woven joyous dreams of living happily ever after in her very own fairy story, but she learned that real life was not a fairy tale. It was more often filled with lies, deception, painful words and grave disappointments.

At least Sally might be able to capture a few moments of joy. Amelie hoped the girl would have many such happy moments.

Amelie would not.

'I commend your liberal attitude,' Edmund said.

She was startled. She'd been lost in her own miseries.

He grinned.

She blinked and really looked at him for the first time this night.

He was taller than Fowler. More muscular, easy to see now that he was without his coat. The hair beneath his shako was as dark as night, his thick brows the same hue. His lips were finely formed as if some master sculptor had created them; his chin, strong and shadowed by what was probably a day's growth of beard that made him appear more like the rake he claimed to be. His smile robbed her of breath.

When she'd met him two days ago, she'd immediately felt taken with him. He'd appeared so handsome in his regimentals, the bright sunlight from the windows making his red coat even more vibrant, his smile even more dazzling. He'd looked then like a fine man, a strong soldier, a brother Tess could be proud of. Even with her head full of Captain Fowler as it had been, she'd thought how nice it would be to know Edmund Summerfield better and how sad it was that his birth made him even less acceptable to society than her own family.

What did birth matter, though? Fowler's was as respectable as one could be, but he'd behaved abominably, walking away without a second glance, leaving her utterly alone just because—

Edmund's smile faded. 'Your Captain Fowler must not have appreciated you.'

Tears stung her eyes. 'No, he did not. Not at all.'

To her surprise, he put his arms around her. She knew he meant only to be comforting, but, his strong arms wrapped around her, his muscular body flush with hers, other emotions were stirred. It gave her a hint as to what she so desired, what she could never have. She knew that now.

She did not pull away from him. This might be the only time a man's arms held her.

Edmund released her and they resumed walking.

'So what was it that caused the words between you and Captain Fowler?' he persisted. 'If it was not him propositioning you.'

'I do not wish to say,' she responded. 'Not to you.'

She felt him bristle. 'I forgot. One must not confide in a bastard.'

'It is not because you are a bastard,' she shot back. 'It is because you are a man.'

He nodded, and an amused look came into his eyes for a moment but vanished as quickly. He lowered his voice. 'That is precisely why you should talk to me. I am a man. I may be able to explain the actions of another man, perhaps explain the actions of both of the men who hurt you tonight. It may ease your mind.'

She felt the tears threaten again. 'Nothing will ease my mind.'

They reached the entrance of the hotel just as a throng of Belgians, obviously full of drink, filled the pavement, blocking their way. One of the men seized Amelie's arm, jabbering in French, and tried to pull her away from Edmund. His uniform coat fell off her shoulders and her heart raced in fright.

It was happening again.

But Edmund grabbed the man's clothing and

shook him. The man lost his grip on Amelie. Edmund lifted him off the ground and thrust him into the crowd, knocking several other men down. They jumped back to their feet and came after Edmund, who took hold of Amelie, picked up his coat and charged into the hotel in one swift movement.

The men did not follow them into the hotel.

'There,' he said. 'You'll be safe in here.'

She was beginning to wonder if she would ever feel safe again. Napoleon could be knocking at the door by morning. Men in the street seemed to feel entitled to do as they pleased, and even men who had once professed love could speak words that wounded more grievously than a sword.

'Will—will you escort me to my room?' she asked.

He put an arm around her, but, again, it was meant only in sympathy. 'Directly to your room, and I will see you safe inside.'

Chapter Two

Under ordinary circumstances it would be scandalous for Edmund to walk a young, unmarried woman up hotel stairs in the wee hours of the morning, but this night no one would pay them any heed. Even if someone noticed them, it would not change what he must do. He must escort her all the way to her room. She'd had two brushes with danger and that was quite enough. He would see her to safety or be damned.

'Do you object to me calling you Edmund?' she asked as they climbed the stairs. 'It is how Tess refers to you, so I think of you as Edmund.'

To hear her speak his name felt intimate to him. They'd spent mere minutes together, not more than an hour, certainly, but, somehow, it seemed right that she call him by his Christian name.

Besides, all this hour he'd been thinking of her as Amelie.

He smiled again. 'I do not object, but that means I must call you Amelie, you know.'

'Would that be so hard to do?' she countered, somewhat uncertainly, he thought.

He pretended to need to think about it. 'I suppose I could manage it. We are somewhat related, one could say. By marriage.'

They reached the upper floor where her hotel room was located.

'Since we are now so familiar, *Amelie*,' he emphasised *Amelie*, 'there is no reason not to tell me why you and Captain Fowler quarrelled.'

'Would you stop pressing me on the subject?' she snapped. 'I have no intention of telling you. It is very private.'

'But we are somewhat related.' He added, *'Amelie.'*

She lifted a finger to her lips, and he fell silent. They were near her parents' rooms, where he'd breakfasted with her two days before.

She knocked softly. 'Maman, Papa, I am back.'

Footsteps could be heard from behind the door. She gestured for him to stay out of sight.

Her mother opened the door a crack. *'Dieu merci!* I was worried.'

'No need to have worried, Maman,' she said.

Of course, she'd only been abandoned once and nearly abducted twice!

'We are leaving Brussels,' her mother said. 'Your father has arranged for carriages to take us to Antwerp very early. Your maid will wake you at five.'

'I will be ready.' The door opened wider, and she leaned in for her mother to kiss her on the cheek. She kissed her back. 'Try to sleep, Maman.'

She waited a moment after the door closed, then indicated to Edmund to follow her again.

When they reached her hotel-room door, he extended his hand for her to give him the key. He unlocked the door, opened it and stepped aside for her to enter.

She hesitated, though. 'Will you check the room for me?' she asked in a nervous voice. 'I am a little afraid to enter it alone.'

He crossed the doorjamb. A fire was lit in the fireplace, but the room was dark and full of shadows. He found a taper on the mantel and used it to light the lamps. The room brightened a bit.

He carried one of the lamps with him throughout the room, not believing there was anyone hidden and ready to jump out and attack her, but wanting to reassure her of that fact.

'There is nothing to fear here,' he told her. He placed the lamp on a table and placed the key into her hand. 'Lock the door after I leave.'

She took the key and stared at it for a moment before looking back up at him. 'Must you go to your regiment immediately?'

It would be a two-hour ride, at least. 'I have time,' he said.

Her shoulders relaxed in relief. 'May I offer refreshment?'

'Do not go to any trouble.'

'It is no trouble.' She pulled off her gloves, and he noticed her hands shook. 'I think Sally hides a bottle of sherry in here. Shall I pour you some?'

He'd prefer brandy. 'Sherry? Why not?'

She found the bottle and two glasses. 'Please sit, Edmund.' She poured his glass and one for herself, a large one, which she gulped down.

He waited for her to sit first. She lowered herself into a chair and poured herself another glass.

She was still distressed from the night's events, he thought, and Edmund wondered how he'd be able to leave her until she was comfortable again. Why he should feel this responsibility foxed him. She was once merely a pretty face—a beautiful face—to him. Now, perhaps because he'd rescued her, she'd become someone whose welfare mattered to him.

He watched her gulp down the second glass of sherry. 'You should talk about what happened to you tonight.' He spoke in a low voice. 'The sherry won't be enough.'

She quickly put down the glass. 'I suspect there is not enough time. You must leave for your regiment.'

His brows rose. 'A moment ago you were anxious for me to stay; now you want me to leave? Which is it, Amelie?'

Her glance darted to the door before focusing on her lap. 'I do not want to be alone right now.'

'Then talk to me,' he persisted.

She looked up at him and snapped, 'Why are you so sure talking will help me?'

'I have three sisters.'

The challenge left her eyes, so that must have been explanation enough.

'The—the attacks from those horrid men.' The distaste showed on her face. 'It was frightening, but what more can I say except that?'

'Then talk about what is most unsettling you,' he said.

'I am certain you do not have enough time for that!' She huffed.

He raised his brows and spoke with humour. 'Is it so long of a story?'

Her glance darted back to him. She smiled.

He pinched the stem of his glass.

By Jove, she was temptation itself when she smiled.

Was it possible that talking could calm her? Amelie doubted it very strongly, but, if he left, she would be alone—and likely alone for the rest of her life. Why not tell him?

Courage was necessary. Her trust in men had been shredded this night, and Edmund Summerfield was certainly a man.

'You will not tell anyone? No matter what?' she asked.

He looked directly into her eyes, his expression serious. 'Upon my honour.'

His words resonated inside her. From her brother she knew men did not say such words lightly. At least, *honourable* men did not.

Edmund delayed his duty to his regiment to bring her safely off the streets of Brussels. There was honour in that.

She was stalling and he was waiting patiently, no longer pressuring her to speak, no longer using humour to cajole her.

But to speak it aloud meant facing it, did it not? Facing what she had done. Facing the truth she had learned in return. Opening her bleak future to herself.

He sipped his sherry.

She tossed him a defiant look and poured herself a third glass, but this time she did not gulp it down.

She took a breath and took the risk. 'You know, of course, that Captain Fowler and I had just become betrothed—'

He nodded.

She could not sit still and speak of this. She stood and paced in front of him. 'My brother procured invitations to the Duchess of Richmond's ball, you know, my first ball given by a duchess. I was in raptures about it. Captain Fowler was my escort. I thought nothing could be better, especially when Wellington himself arrived! Wellington! At the same ball.'

Even though Amelie's father was a viscount, it did not mean they were invited everywhere. Because of her mother. Not only was her mother French, her mother was also a commoner and, after the Revolution, her family had become active in the Terror, beheading friends and relatives of the British aristocrats.

Consequently Amelie and her parents were barely tolerated by the *ton*. It was only because of Edmund's sister, the one who'd married an elderly earl, that she'd been invited anywhere last Season. That was how she met Captain Fowler. She thought he had not minded about her scandalous family. At least he'd told her so.

Edmund broke into her reverie. 'The ball ended early, I heard.'

She collected herself. 'Yes. I was much affected when Wellington announced that Napoleon was marching towards Brussels. I—I knew it meant

Captain Fowler would ride into battle. I knew it meant I might never see him again. I begged my parents to allow him to walk me back to the hotel instead of riding in their carriage. I wanted to be alone with him.'

She glanced at Edmund, who continued to watch her from his chair with eyes that merely waited for more but showed nothing of what he thought.

She turned away from his gaze. 'You thought he propositioned me. You thought he might have taken advantage, saying, *give me something to remember you by*, or something like that.'

'Men think about last chances when they know they will go into battle,' he said in a quiet voice.

She swung back to him. 'Not only men! I thought of last chances, too! I begged the captain to come to this room and make love to me.'

His brows rose.

'Are you shocked?' she asked.

'Surprised. Not shocked.' He lifted his glass to his lips.

Her voice turned shrill. 'Does that make me wanton? Does that bring shame on me, on my family? Is it so very bad that I spoke those words to him? That—that I wanted…the lovemaking?'

He placed his glass on the side table and rose, coming to her and holding her by the shoulders. 'This is what the quarrel was about?'

She nodded.

He guided her back to her chair and sat her down.

Tears pricked her eyes, but she refused to let them fall. 'He said that no respectable woman would ever think such a thing. That I was wanton. Shameful. That I was no better than Haymarket ware. That I must have more of my mother's common French blood in me than he had supposed.'

She burned with anger all over again. True, her mother was the daughter of French merchants who had worked to guillotine aristocrats, but her mother had no part in that. Her mother was the dearest creature in creation. Amelie tried to slap Fowler across the face for speaking of her so.

It had enraged him.

Her throat tightened with the memory. 'Fowler said he was finished with me and that he was certain some man on the street would pay me for what I was offering.' He'd said more, as well.

'Damned prig.' Edmund said.

She looked up into his face. 'Is it not I who deserves censure?'

She was not well bred, obviously, she thought to herself. Otherwise she would not have made such a proposition to Fowler. Or maybe she'd merely been a silly romantic, who believed love conquers all. *Amor vincit omnia.* She'd learned the phrase in Latin.

He reached over and put his hand on her chin and made her look at him. 'What you felt was the most natural thing in the world.'

She averted her gaze. 'Other young women like me do not say such things to men.'

Perhaps it was her mother's blood that made her crave a man's touch. Even Edmund's hand heightened her senses.

Edmund shook his head. 'Do you not suppose other young ladies at the ball said the same to the men leaving them?'

'The captain said not.'

He leaned back. 'The captain is a fool.'

She reached for her glass of sherry again and drank the remainder.

He pointed to the glass. 'What else are you not telling me?'

She was feeling a bit giddy. 'Nothing.' Except what was hardest to face. She picked up the bottle. 'There is just a little more left. You may have it.' She refilled his glass and tried to summon her courage to continue speaking.

'Fowler broke the betrothal,' she finally said.

'Fortunate for you,' he countered.

She bristled. 'Fortunate? Fortunate?' She jumped to her feet and strode over to the window. 'It is easy for you to say such a thing, but it shows your complete lack of understanding!'

'Enlighten me, then,' he said.

She could not even listen to him. Her voice rose. 'Do you know what he said to me?'

'Tell me.'

'He said he had made a terrible mistake asking me to marry him, that he'd done so only because of my dowry.' She'd never guessed that fact. 'He said his parents were against me, but he'd learned that too late. He'd thought himself trapped, he said.'

'Heed me, Amelie.' His voice turned low and firm. 'You are exceedingly lucky not to have married him.'

She knew that now. The thing was, she'd thought Fowler loved her. She'd been convinced of it. She'd seen nothing in him to suggest he was not head over ears in love with her.

'He threatened me,' she went on. 'He said that if I told anyone that he broke the betrothal, he would spread the news about what a wanton hoyden I was.'

Edmund's countenance darkened. 'The blackguard!'

His outrage surprised her. And warmed her.

But he still did not comprehend. She'd been fooled. So easily fooled. That was the most distressing part. One moment she'd believed Fowler blissfully in love with her; the next he had abandoned her on the dangerous streets of Brussels.

Amelie leaned her head against the cool pane of

the window. 'What is the use to talk about this? It does not change anything.'

'What would you change?' he asked. 'Surely you do not want him now.'

'No.' The sadness crept in to her voice. 'I do not want *him*.'

Again he did not understand. The moment she realised she had been utterly misled by Fowler, she also realised she could never trust any man. How could she know if a man truly loved her? She could never marry without knowing.

'But—you see—' she tried to explain. 'It is unlikely now I shall ever marry.'

He rose and walked over to lean against the wall next to the window. 'You are spouting nonsense.'

She lifted her chin. It was not nonsense. 'I must face the reality of my situation. I am too scandalous—my family is too scandalous. Who would wish to marry me? Except, perhaps, for my dowry. If I can be fooled so easily, how would I ever know if what a man wanted was me or simply my dowry?'

'Ah, I see.' Edmund nodded. 'Fowler wanted your money.'

'I do not want a man who only wants my money!'

'Of course you do not,' he said soothingly.

She swung away from him. 'Oh, stop it!'

'Stop what?' He sounded surprised.

'Stop speaking platitudes.' She huffed. 'I knew talking to you would do nothing for me!'

He seemed to ignore her outburst. 'Did you not have several suitors before Fowler?'

'I did not!' Only Fowler.

He'd been the perfect suitor, she'd thought. The man she'd dreamed of finding, she'd thought. So respectable. The younger son of an earl. In a fashionable cavalry regiment. She'd fancied herself so in love with him, when his regiment was sent to Brussels, she convinced her parents to follow him here. He'd seemed happy she'd come. Their betrothal made her parents happy. Made her happy.

Edmund took a step closer. 'Forget Fowler. Do not let what happened with him decide the rest of your life. You will find a man worthy of you.'

'Worthy of me,' she repeated sarcastically. 'I shudder at the thought. What sort of man is worthy of a hoydenish ninnyhammer with a family who is accepted nowhere?'

He touched her chin again and made her look into his eyes. 'I see only a beautiful woman with pretty manners, who, I suspect, thinks more deeply than anyone gives her credit for.'

He was so close to her now she could see the individual hairs on the stubble of his beard. She felt her face flush, but she was unsure if it was because he was so close or because of his words. 'Now who is talking nonsense?'

He stepped back and crossed his arms over his chest. 'Be truthful, Amelie. You know you are beautiful, do you not?'

She used to think so. At least her family said so. Her maid said so. And men on the street sometimes looked at her, but Fowler had also said she was beautiful. Was that another lie? 'How do I know if being told I was beautiful was simply empty flattery?'

He leaned close again. 'I have no reason to flatter you, and I say you are beautiful.'

This time it felt as if all her skin had blushed.

She dared to meet his eye. 'Do you truly think so?'

He came even closer, so close his lips were an inch from hers. She felt his breath on her face and the heat of his body.

'I truly think so,' he murmured.

Chapter Three

Edmund stepped back.

Heavens! What was he about? He'd nearly kissed her, and now she looked bewildered.

'Forgive me,' he said.

'For what?' she whispered.

'For coming too close.'

Her brow creased in confusion. 'I thought you were going to kiss me.'

He could not meet her eye. 'That would be pretty shabby of me.'

She turned back towards the window. 'I suppose it is something you would not want to do.'

Should not do, was more the piece.

'That was one thing Fowler must have been honest about,' she spoke more to the windowpane than to Edmund. 'He never kissed me. Except on the cheek like my brother might do.'

Edmund had not felt like kissing her like a brother.

'He obviously did not want to.' She released a long sigh. 'No man has wanted to kiss me.'

'It is more likely that they wanted to, but refrained,' he said.

She whirled around. 'And you? Did you want to, but refrained?'

'I am really not a rake, Amelie.' Although he'd nearly behaved like one.

She turned away again. 'I wish you were.'

He was uncertain he heard her correctly.

She glanced over her shoulder. 'Are you shocked at that? I did proposition a man tonight, after all.'

He'd tried to treat her like his little half-sister Genna instead of the alluring creature she was at this moment. He'd promised her she was safe with him.

She laughed drily. 'I would certainly hate to think that the only men who wished to kiss me were those ruffians in the street who tried to have their way with me.'

'They would have done more than kiss you, Amelie,' he said. 'If you yearn for love, they were not offering it.'

She turned back to him. 'Do you know what distresses me the most about never marrying?'

'You must not give up on marriage.' How could any man fail to see the merit in her?

She whirled around again, halting his speech. 'It

distresses me that I will never know a man's kisses. I'll never know the lovemaking that passes between men and women. Husband and wife.'

'You will,' he said.

The lamplight reflected in her eyes, filling them with fire. 'Will you kiss me, Edmund?'

Every muscle and sinew in his body yearned for him to taste her lips. 'No, Amelie. It would not be wise.'

Her eyes filled with tears, making them look even bigger. 'I suppose it would be distasteful to kiss me, would it not?'

'No, Amelie, it would not be distasteful.' It was a struggle not to crush his mouth against hers.

'Then you are repelled because I am so wanton in the asking.' Her voice strained, as if she was trying to stifle a sob. 'Like Fowler.'

He moved closer to her. 'I am anything but repelled by you, but I am not the man for you. You must wait—'

'For whom?' she cried. 'Why can you not be the man who first kisses me? You've been my friend this night.'

'A friend, but not your equal,' he tried to explain. 'Remember, I am nothing but a bastard and you are the daughter of a viscount.'

'And what does that signify? You are the son of a baronet and I am the daughter of a French commoner,' she countered. 'Why is any of that an impediment to a kiss?'

'My sister is married to your brother.' He was grasping at straws.

She gave him a speaking look. 'You are not kissing your sister and I am not kissing my brother.'

How could he convince her? He must not cross that line with her, and he was very close to doing so. Something had changed as they'd talked. She'd somehow become important to him.

She turned back to the window. 'Listen to me.' Her voice filled with pain. 'I'm standing here begging you to kiss me. How pathetic a creature I am! No wonder Fowler wanted to rid himself of me.'

Her pain pierced through him like the sabres he'd soon be facing.

He put a hand on her shoulder and turned her around to him. He cupped her cheeks in his palms and tilted her head to him. Leaning down so his lips merely hovered over hers, he asked again, 'Are you very certain you want a kiss?'

'Yes,' she rasped.

'It may not be wise, but I will comply.' He closed the short distance between them.

A satisfied sound escaped her mouth. She wrapped her arms around his neck.

Her lips parted and his tongue touched hers. Her

lips were soft and warm, and her mouth tasted of sherry.

It was as if a spark had touched off a firestorm. Desire flashed through him, engulfed him. He pressed his body against hers.

Her fingers dug into his hair and she ground herself against him. He was powerfully aroused. Imagine her believing herself unlovable. She was everything a man could desire. She'd affected him as no other woman.

But she was not for him.

She deserved what she'd thought she had in Fowler. A respectable aristocrat who loved her, not a bastard taking advantage of her vulnerability.

The rumblings of heavy wagons and the clap of horses' hooves reached her window. A reminder. Where he must go. Who he was—a lowly lieutenant from an infantry regiment, without name or fortune. This would change some day, he vowed. He'd earn his fortune, some day, somehow, but he was still a bastard and not for her.

He released her and eased her away.

'What?' She looked dazed.

He tried to smile. 'There now. You have been kissed, but if we do not stop, we may commit a more serious indiscretion.' Being alone with her in her hotel room, kissing her, was indiscreet enough. 'Besides, Napoleon beckons. I need to go.'

She nodded. 'You must go fight a battle. I do understand.' She backed away from him. 'Thank you for saving me. Thank you for—for the kiss.'

His grin came naturally. 'It was my pleasure.'

She smiled in return and their gazes held.

'Best I take my leave.' He crossed the room and retrieved his coat. She followed him and helped him put it on.

Standing behind him, she put her arms around him and rested her cheek against his back. 'I do not want you to leave me.'

He did not want to leave her either, but his resolve was weakening by each moment he stayed.

He turned around, still in her embrace. 'Will you be all right?'

She looked up at him, her jaw firmly set. 'I shall have to be.'

The lamplight made her skin glow, and the tumble of curls around her face shone like a halo. He tried to commit her face to memory, a memory to soothe him on the battlefield, a reminder of who and what he fought for. If he survived—*if* he survived—who knew if he would ever see her again? Could he bear that?

She rose on tiptoe and placed her lips on his, unschooled and tentative.

Desire slammed into him again. He put his fingers into her hair and held her in the kiss, savouring it like a man feasting on his last meal. Her soft curves pressed against him once more. Good God. He was on fire, wanting all of her, craving to ease the need that threatened to consume him. He picked her up, and she curled her legs and arms around him. Without heed of what he was doing, he carried her to the bed, prominent in the room, even though he'd not allowed his gaze to stray in its direction.

'Yes,' she murmured against his lips. 'Yes.'

Amelie knew what Edmund wanted. She was not so green a girl not to know what could transpire between a man and a woman, why young ladies like herself were carefully chaperoned. What difference did it make now, if she were chaperoned or not? She was not destined for marriage or respectability. Fowler had taught her that.

But ever since she'd met Fowler and fancied herself in love with him, she'd felt that urge to couple with him. She'd savoured every touch of his hand. She'd felt frustration when his lips touched her cheek and not her mouth. She'd realised that she was a woman who wanted the bedding part of marriage. She'd thought she wanted it so much with Fowler that she dared to ask him to make love to her before he went to battle, lest he be killed and she never know his embrace.

Of course, that all died in an instant when he rebuffed her.

The thing was, the urge for lovemaking was even stronger with Edmund. Why not indulge it? She was unlikely to have another chance.

He sat her on the bed and captured her mouth again. She savoured the delight of it. To touch her tongue to his was so incredibly intimate, and it sent sensation shooting through her. It was as if her body had come alive for the first time.

His hand slipped to the sensitive skin of her neck and moved down to cup her breast.

Oh, my! How could a touch in one part of one's body be felt so acutely in another? His hand on her breast ignited sensation in her most womanly place. It made her want more, much more. It made her want him to touch her skin all over and even to touch that—that most private of places.

She must be wanton. There was no other explanation. What was she to do with these feelings for the rest of her life? The least she could do was indulge them this one time. There could be no unwanted consequences the first time, she'd heard the maids say. When else could she do this without anyone knowing?

Edmund would not tell. And, even if he did, who would believe him? No one knew they were together. No one would ever know.

But Edmund suddenly broke off the kiss. 'Amelie, we cannot do this. I won't do this.'

She was bereft. And a little wild. To have those sensations aroused and so abruptly denied was like dousing a raging fire with a bucket of water.

Except this did nothing to extinguish the flames inside her.

She pushed him away and leapt from the bed. 'Then stop! And be gone! And do not tease me so. Do not pretend you want me and then just stop! You are worse than Fowler! At least he told me right away he did not want me!' Her emotions were running away with her mouth, and she could not stop herself. 'Does no man want me? Not even when I offer myself? What is wrong with me? Am I really as detestable as Fowler said? Not even as desirable as Haymarket ware—'

He seized her by the shoulders. 'I did not say I did not want you!'

She pressed herself against him again, putting her arms around him. 'Then make love to me, Edmund. This may be my only chance. I want to know love at least once. Show me, please. Please!'

How was he to resist her?

He kissed her again, a long and tender kiss that showed all the yearning he could no longer disguise. He wanted her with every fibre of his being.

He wanted this one last moment of beauty and joy before facing cannon fire, blood and death.

When his lips left hers and tasted of her neck and shoulders, she sighed. 'Yes. That is glorious. Yes.'

His hand slipped beneath the neckline of her poor battered dress, now ripped and dirty from the violence of the street. He savoured her smooth skin and the feel of her nipple as his palm scraped against it.

She writhed with his touch and twisted around, presenting her back to him. 'Unbutton my dress. Please, Edmund.'

Somehow his fingers undid at least a dozen tiny buttons. As soon as they were free, she pulled her dress over her head. He took off his boots and coat.

She presented her back to him again. 'My stays.'

He untied the laces of her corset, loosened them and pulled her corset down so she could step out of it. He stripped off his trousers and drawers and added them to the puddle of clothing on the floor. He lifted her onto the bed and, as he climbed after her, she pulled off her shift.

She was naked and as beautiful as any goddess could possibly be. Her breasts were full, high and firm; their nipples dark rose. Her waist was narrow, but her hips a pleasing balance. Was she perfection? What had he done to deserve such a gift? Perhaps it meant he would meet his end. If so, he was thankful for her.

'Do—do I please you?' she asked, her voice small.

He allowed his gaze to luxuriate over her. 'Very much.'

She smiled and gazed upon him. His chest bore more than a few scars, gifts from the Battle of Albuhera, but she did not seem to notice. Her eyes widened as she gazed farther down, but, then, she would not have seen a man fully aroused before.

Edmund could have taken her quickly and roughly and eased the almost painful desire coursing through him, but his mind still functioned well enough to remember she was a virgin. He had no wish to hurt her. He wanted to show her pleasure. He wanted to show her all the delights of lovemaking, to show her she was meant to have pleasure from it. Most of all he wanted to reassure her that she was worthy of love.

He settled beside her and kissed her again, on the lips, on the tender skin beneath her ear, on the long column of her throat. He caressed her breast and relished the feel of it beneath his fingers. He scraped her nipple with his palm, and she moaned in response. He explored her with his hands and lips, and she writhed beneath his touch.

Her skin was as soft as rose petals beneath his rough hand. He fancied she was like some special flower, pampered into blooming in a hothouse, protected from all harshness. A lonely flower, apparently, and one who wished only for someone to love her. He was not the man for her, though, not a low-ranking, baseborn son of a failed father with no name and no one to recommend him.

He could but try to show her what love could be between a man and a woman. He could show her the delight and the satisfaction.

'I am going to touch you,' he warned. 'So I won't hurt you.'

He slid his hand down her body.

'Yes, yes, touch me,' she whispered, placing her hand on his and guiding it to the moist place between her legs.

He eased his fingers inside her and gently stroked and stretched her. The feel of her aroused him further, but still he held back to make certain she was ready for him.

'Just do it,' she cried. 'I want you to.'

He could not hold back now. He rose over her and entered her, moving as slowly as he could manage, when all his body wished to do was to rush to the climax.

Amelie marvelled at the sensations he created in her. To feel him joined to her was glorious, but each stroke left her urgent with need. This was beyond her expectations, yet her whole body seemed to be screaming, *More! More!*

She was glad it was Edmund showing her these delights. He was kind and strong and...skilled. Even she, with no experience at all, could tell he knew exactly how to please her. Fowler had left her and Edmund had not. She felt safe in Edmund's arms in a way she could never be in Fowler's.

The pleasure Edmund had already given her had been remarkable, but she knew there was more. She needed more. She needed to rush to some destination, though she did not know what it was. The closer they came to it, the faster they ran. She wanted—needed—to reach this place, but, at the same time, she did not want these sensations to end. It was like riding in a racing carriage, powerless to stop, but giddy with excitement, even so.

He moved faster and she moved with him, seeking more.

Suddenly the sensations exploded inside her, flooding her with waves and waves of pleasure, over and above all she'd experienced so far. He thrust one more time and tensed inside her. Was he spilling his seed? It must be so.

He relaxed on top of her, covering her with his body and his weight. How had she suddenly turned to butter, melting beneath him, with no will to move?

He rolled to her side, breathing hard, an arm flung over his face.

'I—I did not know it could feel like that,' she murmured.

He turned to face her. 'It doesn't always.'

She furrowed her brow. 'Did I disappoint you?'

He reached over and toyed with a lock of her hair. 'No, Amelie. You did not disappoint. Anything but.'

She released a breath. 'Good, because it did not disappoint me either. It was quite the most wonderful thing I have ever experienced. I shall remember it always.'

His expression softened, then turned sad. 'A memory,' he murmured. 'A fine memory.'

She smiled. 'Yes. And I thank you, Edmund. You have given me more than I knew to desire.'

He turned his head away, and it felt as though he'd run a far distance from her.

Amelie rose on to her elbow. 'What is wrong, Edmund?' *Why leave me now?* she wanted to add.

He sat up and the lamp illuminated his bare chest crisscrossed with scars. He'd soon be in battle again, she remembered.

'It was not well done of me,' he said.

She blinked in surprise. 'Not well done?' Nothing could have been better.

He looked down on her. 'Do not let this stop you from seeking a proper marriage, Amelie. No matter what people say, men cannot tell who is a virgin and who is not. This need not spoil your future.'

She sat up. 'I told you. There will be no marriage for me. This was my only chance—to—to feel that.' Only now, how was she to bear that she would never feel such sensations again?

'You will find a man worthy of you, I am certain,' he said. 'Do not let this one night stop you.'

She did not care about the rest of her life, only of this moment with him. She was glad he'd been the one to show her such delight. She could not imagine making love to any other man. How had she ever believed she'd want this with Fowler?

She did not wish to argue with Edmund about it though, not when he was bound for battle. 'I am glad I shared this with you, Edmund. Truly I am.'

He seemed to wince in pain with her words. He rubbed his face and glanced around the room before meeting her eye again.

'Do you know how to take care of yourself?' he asked.

She had no idea what he meant. 'Of course.'

He relaxed. 'Good.'

She peered at him. 'Are you regretting this, Edmund?' She did not want him to regret it. She wanted it to be a lovely memory for both of them.

He stared into her eyes. 'I am not regretting it for me.'

She flushed with happiness. 'Then might we do it

again? Just one more time before you must leave?'
And face Napoleon's army.

One more time could not hurt, could it? It would
still be like the first time, would it not? No consequences?

He pulled her down on top of him for a kiss that
sent the sensation surging through her again and
sent any doubts about consequences scattering in
the wind.

Edmund felt no reluctance in making love to
Amelie this second time. His guilt belonged solely
to the first event, did it not? At least he told himself so. Told himself to savour this unexpected opportunity to experience again the pleasure of her
body, the sweetness of her spirit.

Whoever finally won her love would be fortunate indeed.

But to Hades with that man, tonight she belonged
to him and this sweet memory of her would always
be his alone. When he left here, he'd go to where
his horse was stabled. He'd ride hard to where his
regiment was billeted and then, when dawn came,
they would march toward Napoleon's army.

To battle.

Edmund had cheated death many a time before. If
this was the time luck would fail him, at least he'd
die knowing this lovely creature had wanted him.

Had loved him.

He pressed into memory the feel of her skin under his hands, the luxury of her breasts, the taste of her kiss. He rejoiced in her unschooled but sensuous response under his touch. When he entered her again, she felt familiar, as if they'd belonged together for an eternity.

It was a gratifying illusion when the eternity of death was a distinct possibility.

Each moment of lovemaking drove the thought of death from his mind. To Edmund, Amelie represented life. With each stroke his resolve grew. He would live. He must live.

Life was full of possibilities.

His spirits soared as she moved with him, building their need, anticipating their release. He rode the passion to its culmination and, just as if they'd had an eternity to attune themselves to each other, they reached the heights together.

Edmund burst with joy. This was life! He would live for this!

When he lay in languor with Amelie in his arms, they did not speak. He simply enjoyed the comfort of lying next to her, the warmth of her body warming him. Her breathing turned soft and even. She slept the deep satisfied sleep of a woman well loved.

He slipped out of the bed and dressed as quickly and as quietly as he could. It must be nearing three in the morning. He'd need the rest of the night to ride to his regiment. He folded her clothing and searched the room for paper and pen, finding both on a small writing table in the corner.

Dear Amelie,
I shall remember this night with great fondness and gratitude. I hope you remember it without regret. Do not lose heart. Do not let one night or one man take away your dreams. You possess everything any man could desire. One day you will make some lucky gentleman a wonderful wife.
Best regards always,
E.

He folded the paper and placed it next to her on the bed. Then he moved quietly around the room extinguishing the lamps.

All except one candle. By the light of that candle, he took one last look at her. One last image to burn in his memory.

He picked up his bag, blew out the candle and walked out the door.

Chapter Four

Three months later, September 1815—London

'Edmund? Edmund Summerfield?'

Edmund, just stepping out of Horse Guards onto the parade, turned.

Marc Glenville quickened his step to catch up to him. 'I thought that was you.' He extended his hand to shake. 'How are you, Edmund? What a surprise to see you in London.'

Edmund was surprised as well. It was September. He thought everyone would be in the country hunting birds, not in London. He'd not written to any of his sisters that he would be in England, because he expected to return to Brussels in a week or two, and he assumed they would not be in town. Who could have thought he would run into his half-sister Tess's husband?

Amelie's brother.

He accepted the handshake. 'I arrived a few days ago.'

He'd come into town to settle his affairs in person. He'd planned to write to his sisters from Brussels after he returned. Better to inform them by letter afterwards than tell them ahead of time what he intended to do.

'Tess will be delighted you are here,' Glenville said. 'Where are you headed?'

'Back to my hotel.'

'Are you staying at Stephen's Hotel?' Glenville asked.

It was a good guess. Stephen's Hotel catered to army officers and, even though Edmund was not in uniform, Glenville would assume he would stay there.

He nodded. 'I am.'

Glenville clapped him on the shoulder. 'Come have a drink with me first. It is but a short walk to Brooks's.'

Edmund could think of no excuse. 'A drink would be welcome.'

As they started to cross the parade, Glenville gestured to Edmund's leg. 'How is your injury?'

'Mostly healed.'

A French sabre had sliced into Edmund's leg at Waterloo. He still limped a bit when he first rose in the morning, and it still pained him at night. He'd helped Marc carry a grievously wounded Fowler back from the battlefield, despite his own injury. Fowler, the supposed fiancé who had abandoned Amelie on the streets of Brussels—although Edmund had said nothing to Glenville about that. Fowler had been wounded in the ill-fated Scots Greys' cavalry charge. Would Glenville have brought Fowler back to Brussels if he'd known how reprehensibly he'd treated Amelie? Edmund did not regret saving Fowler, though. Even a cad like him did not deserve to die on that battlefield. Too many of them died undiscovered, and none of them deserved that fate.

How strange was fate? Edmund's life had become entwined with Glenville when he married Edmund's sister. Had Glenville not met Edmund, he might have walked by Edmund at Waterloo and not asked him to help bring Fowler back to Brussels. Care of Edmund's leg might have been delayed. The wound might have festered. He might have lost his leg. Or his life. Many of the wounded died for lack of immediate care.

Fate also entwined him with Fowler, a man he'd preferred to have known nothing of. But he would not for all the world have missed his brief time of knowing Amelie. What if he'd never met her? What would have happened to her if he'd not noticed her on the streets of Brussels that night, had not been there to save her from that brute who'd meant to molest her? What if he'd not walked her back to the hotel, not made love to her?

How the memory of that night had sustained him! During the hard fighting at Quatre Bras. All during the rain-drenched night after that battle. During tense moments of inaction at Waterloo.

After his injury.

Knowing that Amelie, with all her warmth, beauty and passion, was still in the world had been and still was a comfort. Spending those precious hours with her had been like touching light. He'd become more resolved than ever to make something of his life, to succeed where his father had failed, to prove to his departed mother that her sacrifices had not been for naught.

How had Amelie fared? What memories did she hold about that night? Regret? Shame? He fervently hoped not.

Of course, he could simply ask Glenville how Amelie was.

'How is Tess?' he asked instead.

Glenville's expression turned soft. 'Tess is wonderful.'

Edmund nodded in approval. Tess deserved such a man to love her.

'And your family?' he went on.

'My parents are getting along very well.' Glenville spoke this with some surprise.

'And your sister?' He tried to keep his tone even.

'Amelie?' Glenville rubbed his forehead. 'Amelie has had it rougher than the rest of us. Fowler, you know.'

Edmund was surprised. 'Fowler died, didn't he?' That should have been the end of it for her.

When last Edmund saw Fowler, he'd been barely clinging to life—but still alive. Glenville and Tess had taken him back to England to his parents. Edmund had stayed in Brussels to be cared for by Lady Summerfield, his half-sisters' mother, and her lover, Count von Osten. Even though that lady had run away from Edmund's father and abandoned her children years before, Edmund had searched for and found her. He'd stayed with her and the count in Brussels both before the battle and after.

'Fowler lived,' Glenville said. 'But there is no thought of marriage between him and Amelie now. His parents said he was in no condition to marry and that it was best to break the engagement. Amelie never speaks of it, but there is no doubt she's been changed by all this.'

Was the change due to Fowler? Or was Edmund responsible? It had been nearly three months since that night together. He'd hoped she'd rebounded from both.

He and Glenville continued walking past Carlton House, the grand residence of the Prince Regent.

Glenville suddenly halted. 'I have a better notion than going for a drink! Come to dinner tonight. My parents are at the country estate, but that will give you and Tess more of a visit. We have no plans for the evening. I will go home directly and send word to you at your hotel if by some chance we must withdraw the invitation, but I can think of no reason you should not be very welcome.'

If Glenville's parents were in the country, Amelie would be with them. There was really no reason not to see Tess now that she knew he was in town. He could tell her in person what he'd planned to write in a letter.

Besides, he missed her. And Genna and Lorene. Might they be in London, too?

'Dinner. Name the hour and I will be there.'

'Come at seven,' Glenville said. 'We are at my parents' on Grosvenor Street. Third house from the corner adjacent to the square.'

Edmund had not spent much time in London and none in the fine houses around Grosvenor Square, but he knew where Grosvenor intersected with Bond Street. 'I will find it.'

Glenville smiled. 'Excellent! Tess will be happy to have a nice long visit with you.'

At a little past seven, Edmund sounded the knocker at the third town house adjacent to Grosvenor Square.

A footman opened the door, and Edmund gave him his name. 'This way, sir.'

Edmund followed him to the door of the drawing room, where he was announced. As Edmund stepped into the room, Tess was already on her feet, rushing towards him.

'Edmund!' She flung herself into his arms for a hug. 'What a nice surprise.' She immediately pulled away to look at him. 'How is your leg? Marc said it was healed. Is it? Does it pain you still?'

He smiled at her, surprised how pleased he was to see her. 'My leg is healed. Nothing to worry over, I assure you.' He gazed at her sparkling hazel eyes, her shining chestnut hair. 'You look even more beautiful than in Brussels, Tess.'

She blushed. 'I am happy. That is the reason.'

Her husband approached. 'How good you could come on such short notice. I am delighted we will have the evening together.'

Glenville and Tess stepped aside.

From a chair near the fireplace, another woman stood. 'Hello, Edmund.'

Amelie! He caught himself before he spoke her name aloud, bowing instead. 'Miss Glenville. Good to see you again.'

A memory of holding her in his arms, feeling her soft skin against his palms, her lips against his, slammed into him. He'd missed her, although why he should miss a woman he'd only spent a few hours with would make no sense to anyone.

Except to him. Those hours together had had an impact that would never leave him. She was the inspiration for him to dare to make himself a success.

She looked as beautiful as ever, but thinner. Paler.

'You must call me Amelie.' Even her voice seemed altered. Softer. Tenser. She made an attempt at a smile.

Tess pulled him towards the sofa, near Amelie. 'Come. Sit. Marc will pour you a glass of claret. You must tell me why you are in London and why you did not write to us that you were coming.' She gave him a scolding look.

He glanced at Amelie, who sat again, before turning to Tess. 'I assumed you would be in the country.' He assumed they all would be in the country.

'Marc had some work to finish,' Tess said. 'And Amelie came for a visit.'

Marc poured the wine and handed a glass to him and one to Tess. 'That was why I was at Horse Guards.'

Edmund tore his eyes away from Amelie. 'Work brought you to Horse Guards?' What sort of work at Horse Guards did a viscount's heir perform?

Glenville smiled. 'Indeed.' But he did not explain.

It appeared Edmund and Amelie were not the only ones to keep secrets.

'But why did you come to London, Edmund?' Tess asked again.

He took a sip of his wine and took one more glance at Amelie before facing Tess. 'I sold my commission.'

Her eyes widened. 'You are no longer in the army?'

'I sold out.' He gestured to his clothes. 'That is why I am not in uniform.' He met Tess's gaze, but wondered if Amelie even attended to his words. 'Napoleon is defeated. The war is over. Without the war, there is no future for me in the army. Regiments will disband, I fear. There will be fewer and fewer opportunities to advance.'

And who would promote a bastard when there were plenty of aristocratic sons wanting the higher ranks? When fighting in Spain, he'd been passed over for field promotions. Captaincies had been given to men with fewer skills and less seniority.

'But what will you do?' Tess asked.

He could not resist a glance at Amelie, who sat

primly, eyes lowered, hands folded in her lap. 'I plan to return to Brussels.'

'Brussels? With Mama?' Tess's voice rose.

Tess and her sisters had not known their mother was in Brussels, let alone that Edmund had corresponded with her for several years and stayed with her when his regiment was sent to the area. Because of Edmund, Tess and Lady Summerfield had forged a reconciliation, albeit an ambivalent one. Unlike Edmund, Tess had not forgiven her mother for abandoning them.

But this was not the time to discuss Lady Summerfield.

'There are fortunes to be made on the Continent, now that the war is over,' he said instead. And Count von Osten had a talent for finding them.

'You sound like Papa,' Tess accused.

Their late father had always chased an easy fortune, finding instead only debts and failure. When his half-sister Lorene sent him money to purchase a captaincy, Edmund had been surprised there had been any money left to inherit. While Edmund recuperated in Brussels, he used that money, not to purchase an advancement in the army, but to make the very sort of investment his father might have made. Except, unlike his father, Edmund made good profits from taking the risk. Now that he'd sold his lieutenancy, he had even more money to invest.

'I'll do well enough, Tess,' he assured her. 'Besides, I only have me to worry over.' Not a wife, three daughters and a bastard son, like their father.

'No more talk of money,' her husband said cheerfully.

'Then tell me of Lorene and Genna,' Edmund said, glad to change the subject. 'Are they in London, too?'

Their sister Lorene had married a very old man, a reclusive earl who lived near their village in Lincolnshire. She'd married him for his money, which seemed unlike her. Edmund had never met the man.

'Lord Tinmore has retired to the country.' Glenville's voice rang with contempt. 'He has filled Tinmore Hall with guests who are invited for the bird shooting.'

'Guests?' Edmund said. 'I thought he was an old recluse. Was that not what was said of him when we were growing up?'

'He probably has invited his eligible gentlemen friends in an effort to get Genna married off,' Tess responded. 'He is eager to be rid of her, I think.'

'How old is Genna?' Edmund asked. 'Is she not too young?' His eyes darted to Amelie again. How old was she? he wondered. Had she been too young? He'd not given that a thought that fateful night.

'She is nineteen now.' Tess rolled her eyes. 'Plenty old enough, but she professes to be against marriage. She sometimes vows never to marry, but it is unlikely Tinmore will allow her that choice.'

Edmund was alarmed. 'Surely he will not force her!'

Tess exchanged a look with her husband, who answered, 'I fear Tinmore is capable of almost anything.'

'What of Lorene?' Edmund asked. Could he take care of both Lorene and Genna if it became necessary? 'Does he treat her ill?'

Tess shook her head. 'He is indulgent of Lorene as far as I can surmise. She wants for nothing, but he wants Lorene all to himself, not shared with her sisters.'

Edmund curled his fingers into a fist. 'You will tell me if he mistreats either of them.'

'We will not let them be mistreated,' Glenville said emphatically.

The butler entered the room to announce that dinner was served. Tess took Glenville's arm. There was nothing for Edmund to do but offer to escort Amelie. Her graceful fingers wrapped around his offered arm.

'How are you, Amelie?' he asked in a lowered voice as they trailed behind Tess and Glenville.

She raised her blue eyes to his for a moment but

quickly averted them again. 'I am well enough, I suppose.'

She appeared altered, though, not full of sparkle and happiness like when he first met her in Brussels. She was different than when he'd made love to her, as well. She seemed…worried.

In the dining room she was seated next to him, and he was aware the entire time of her closeness. He found himself wanting to see the expressions on her face to gauge how she was feeling.

There were so many questions he wished to ask her. Was she ill? Was she still affected by Fowler's behaviour in Brussels? Did she ever think of the night they'd spent together? If so, did she remember it as he did? As a transforming experience? Or did she feel regret, remorse, or worst of all, shame? Should he have left her at the hotel door?

He hardly attended to the conversation at the table, hardly knew what he'd said to anyone. He'd talked about his investments, his plans to travel to wherever a fortune could be made. He and Glenville debated what countries that might be and also what the end of the war might mean to the economies of Britain, France and the rest of the Continent. If only he could remember what they concluded. A part of his mind had fixed on Amelie and would not let go.

* * *

Amelie made a show of eating, although she mostly pushed food around her plate. She'd not had an appetite of late. Would he notice?

She'd forgotten how handsome he was. Out of uniform in a beautifully tailored coat and trousers that showed his muscular legs, he was an impressive sight.

Was he glad to see her? She could not tell. There was no way to talk to him alone, and she dared not reveal that she knew him a great deal better than Marc or Tess could ever imagine. Perhaps his reticence to even look at her was to help keep their secret. She hoped so. She hoped it was not that he disliked encountering her again.

After dinner he and Marc did not linger over brandy. Instead they all returned to the drawing room for more conversation.

She'd thought she might never see Edmund again, thought he'd return to the army and be sent somewhere far away, but here he was and now she needed to make a decision. To speak to him now, to tell him of her—situation—or to have him find out later, perhaps in a letter from Tess.

It had bothered her greatly that he would find out after the fact and not hear it from her own lips.

He was here now, though. This might be her only chance.

But how to speak to him alone?

She could not think of any excuse to do so. He seemed not to pay her much mind, so would likely miss any hint she could try to send him to let him know she wanted to see him alone, with no one around. Just her and Edmund.

Eventually she excused herself, saying she was going to bed. Instead she put on her cloak and sneaked outside. She'd stand in the chilly September air until he walked out the door.

She waited in the stairs that led from the street to the servants' entrance, hoping none of them opened the door and caught her there. The wind and damp seemed to find their way to her hiding place, making the minutes ticking by move even more slowly. How easy it would be to simply turn around and re-enter the house and tell herself she'd tried. He might stay for hours, might he not? Could she wait so long? Her feet, still in her dinner slippers, felt like ice, and her ungloved fingers trembled as they sought warmth in the recesses of her cloak. How long had it been? She tried to listen for the chiming of clocks, but all she could hear was the wind, an occasional carriage rumbling by or the chattering of her teeth.

Finally she heard the front door open, and she

emerged from her hiding place, stepping into the light cast by the rush lamps.

He turned at the sound of her footsteps. 'Amelie! What are you doing out here?'

'I—I wanted to see you alone,' she managed.

He took hold of her arm and walked her back into the darkness. 'Tell me truthfully, Amelie. How do you fare? Your brother said you were not doing well. Are you ill?'

'I'm not ill,' she said.

'Do not tell me you are still affected by Fowler.'

She almost laughed. 'Certainly not.'

'Then is it what transpired between us?' He sounded distressed. 'If so, I am so sincerely sorry—'

'It is not that,' she broke in. 'At least not precisely.'

'You must not allow that night to change you. You are still beautiful. More beautiful, in fact. There is no reason you cannot marry—'

She cut him off again. 'There is a reason, Edmund! A very important reason. That is why I contrived to see you alone. There is something I must tell you.'

'What is it?' His voice was tense. She could not clearly see his face.

Her heart pounded painfully in her chest. She took a deep breath and said words she'd never until this moment spoken aloud.

'I am going to have a baby.'

Chapter Five

The air was knocked out of Edmund's chest.

A baby.

He knew efforts to prevent a baby were anything but reliable, but he'd ignored that. He'd allowed his passion to overtake him.

'You might wish to ask if the child is yours,' she said stiffly. 'I assure you it is. And I am certain I am carrying a child. I have not had my courses since—since that night. I am sick every morning, fatigued all day, and I feel…altered. No one knows. Of course, they will discover it soon enough.'

'A baby,' he whispered.

She lifted her chin. 'Do not fear. No one knows of our meeting that night, and I will say nothing. You will be safe from blame. I am perfectly aware I was the cause of this.'

'No.' He knew who was to blame.

She took a breath. 'Well. There it is. That is why I wanted to see you alone.'

She turned to leave, but he seized her arm. 'Do not tell me such a thing and then leave.'

'There is no more to say,' she told him. 'I ask nothing of you.'

'Nothing of me?' he repeated. She wanted him to have no part of it?

Her eyes flashed. 'I'll not get rid of it, if that is what you are about to say.'

He still gripped her arm. 'I was not about to say that.' He was about to ask her why she wanted him to have no part in a child they created together, why she did not see what they must do, even if she disliked it.

'I do not yet know what I will do,' she went on. 'Perhaps my parents will send me to France. I have relatives there. I've never met them, but perhaps they will be accommodating.'

He released her and paced in front of her, talking more to himself than to her. 'You would give the baby away? Or pay someone to care for it?' She preferred that?

She shrugged. 'I do not *want* to do either of those things, but I cannot imagine my parents allowing me to keep the child. Think of the scandal I would bring on them.'

He came closer. 'There will be scandal, no matter what.' But he knew the right thing to do.

'You need not worry about that,' she said.

He need not worry? He'd been born to scandal. He never worried about what people thought of him.

Except for one person. He cared what Amelie thought of him, and it seemed she wanted nothing to do with him.

He was so close to her now his body flared in response to her, betraying him as it had that night in Brussels. He again remembered how it felt to lie next to her, how it felt to be inside her.

It wounded him that she did not want him to take responsibility for the child, but what did that matter? She must see there could be no other way.

He began pacing again. 'I can provide for the child.'

'Money is no issue,' she said. 'I have an inheritance, and my father can easily pay.'

'I am not speaking of money.' He was speaking of what must be done.

She cleared her throat. 'I have no more to say. I—I thought it my duty to tell you. I truly ask nothing of you—'

Before he could protest, before he could tell her what he thought they must do, no matter how distasteful to her, she turned and rushed down the servants' stairs and into the house.

She left him standing on the pavement. Alone.

* * *

Amelie closed the door and ran up the servant's staircase to her bedchamber, fighting tears.

There. She told him. She'd done her duty to him and assured him she would not use the child against him. No one would ever know it was Edmund's child; no one but her. At least she could console herself that he would be free to live his life, to build his fortune, to have his adventure, like he'd spoken of at dinner with so much energy and passion. She would do nothing to stop him, nothing to spoil his happiness.

She tore off her cloak and flung herself on her bed.

If only he had not looked so handsome. If only he had yelled at her for being so foolish as to allow a baby to be conceived. If only he had not roused in her those wanton feelings. Goodness! Merely having his hands gripping her arms made her recall how those hands felt against her naked flesh. Even in her predicament, she'd yearned to couple with him again, to feel that intense ecstasy that he created in her.

Well-bred young ladies did not feel such things. Well-bred ladies did not get themselves with child. They married for social advantage for their families and procreated to beget heirs, not because they craved a man's touch and the thrill he could create. This was her downfall, certainly. If she had not been so wanton, she would not be in this fix, but she was determined she would not ruin his life along with her own.

It was some consolation that she'd assured him of that fact.

Edmund returned to the Grosvenor Street town house at ten the next morning. As he announced himself to the footman attending the door, Glenville walked down the stairs.

'Edmund!' Glenville was, of course, surprised to see him. 'You are back so soon. To what do we owe this pleasure?'

Edmund had come to call upon Amelie, but to say so now would only cause Glenville to ask questions. He might as well provide the answers first.

'A moment of your time?' he asked.

'Certainly,' Glenville said, still sounding puzzled. 'Come to the library. Would you like some refreshment?'

'No,' Edmund handed his hat and gloves to the footman. 'Just a word with you.'

Glenville gestured for Edmund to follow him. The library was behind the drawing room, in the back of the house. If the drawing room was designed to impress and entertain, the library was intended for comfort and solitude. It was lined with books and filled with comfortable chairs.

Glenville lowered himself into one of them. 'Please have a seat.'

Edmund remained standing and debated how to start.

Might as well charge ahead. 'I came to ask for something which, no doubt, you will be unprepared to hear.'

Glenville's brows rose.

'Actually, it is not something I think you can grant, but I owe you the courtesy of hearing it from me.'

'And this is?' Glenville asked.

'I would like to pay my addresses to your sister.'

Glenville's eyes widened. 'Pay addresses?'

'Court her,' Edmund went on. 'Marry her.'

Glenville shook his head in bewilderment. 'But you do not know her!'

Edmund knew her better than Glenville could guess, but he could not explain. He'd promised to never speak of that night to anyone.

'It is true we have not been in each other's company—' he began.

Glenville cut him off. 'Not above twice! Once in Brussels and last night.'

Three times, actually. 'I would still like to speak to her.'

Glenville stood again and walked over to a far corner of the room. He turned. 'Do not get me wrong, Edmund. I think you are a fine man. I am proud to be connected to you by marriage, but I do not think this will work.' He paused. 'Your suit is—is just not…' His voice faded.

'Not acceptable because I am a bastard?' Edmund finished for him.

Glenville lifted his hands. 'That is of no consequence to me, but I cannot see my father giving his permission.'

'I will have to speak to him, of course,' Edmund said. 'But first I would like to speak to your sister.'

Glenville frowned. 'Are you thinking she will accept you, because her betrothal to Fowler fell apart? She is still young. My parents will expect other suitors.'

Better than he, a bastard with uncertain prospects, though perhaps not once the pregnancy was discovered. 'I am well aware that she might deserve a better suitor than me.'

Glenville shook his head. 'I still cannot wrap my mind around this. What makes you think she will accept you? She spoke hardly two words to you last night.' He frowned and peered suspiciously at Edmund. 'Are you experiencing financial difficulties? Because Tess and I would be glad to help you—'

Edmund straightened. 'I am not after her dowry! Believe me, money does not enter in this at all.'

Glenville sputtered. 'This is hardly making any sense!'

'What is your objection to me speaking to her?' Edmund pressed on. Even a decent gentleman, like Glenville, could not help but wish for a better man than Edmund for his sister's husband, apparently. Edmund was disappointed, but not surprised. 'I am perfectly willing to withdraw if she should refuse me.'

Glenville's expression, however, seemed filled with kindness. 'I do not object to you speaking to Amelie, Edmund. I do not object to you at all. I am merely taken aback.'

'That is all I ask,' Edmund said. 'To speak to her.'

'By all means. And I wish you well.' Glenville walked to the door. 'Wait here. I will send her to you.'

He left the room, and Edmund pressed his fingers against his temple. No one would think this viscount's daughter should marry a mere bastard. Even Edmund did not think himself worthy of her. Her marriage to him would cause talk. More talk when a baby was born too soon, but this was the respectable solution, the honourable choice.

A few minutes passed before the door opened again.

Amelie walked in. 'Edmund?' She looked surprised and less than happy to see him. 'What are you doing? My brother said you wanted to speak to me.'

She also looked unwell.

'Are you ill?' he asked, taking a step towards her.

She halted him with her hand. 'Mornings are bad for me. Tell me what you are about, though. My brother looked uncertain. You did not say anything to him about—about—?'

About Brussels? 'Never,' he responded. 'I gave my word.'

'Well, my guess is that my brother is going to pound me with questions after you leave. Why would you wish to speak to me? Marc and Tess are going to want to know. When the truth comes out about—about me, this might make them think you were involved.'

'I *was* involved,' he said. 'I *am* involved. Stop talking and listen to me.'

She clamped her mouth shut and crossed her arms over her chest.

'You ran off last night before I could make plain to you what we must do—'

Her eyes flickered, but she did not move.

'There is only one solution, Amelie. We must think of what is best for the child, not for you or me.' He was not coming to the point. He took a breath. 'We should marry. Marry me, Amelie.'

'Marry?' She looked shocked.

He hurried on. 'The baby will have my name instead of no name. He or she must never know the scandal of being a bastard or of growing up not knowing who his parents really were. The child will be able to grow up respectably.'

'You cannot truly wish to marry me!' she cried.

He'd never dreamed it to be possible. 'You cannot wish to marry me, but our wishes cannot matter in this. We must do this for the baby.'

'For the baby,' she repeated, glancing away.

He strode up to her and placed his hands on her shoulders. 'I know what it is to grow up a bastard. It is an albatross one must carry all one's life. It is the fact against which everything else one does is judged. I do not want that for our child. I cannot allow what I have done to so burden a child.'

'It was *my* doing, Edmund,' she said sadly. 'You should not have to pay the consequences of what I have done.'

'What *we* have done,' he corrected. 'I accept my part in it.' Indeed, he knew he bore the lion's share of the guilt. 'But the child. He or she should not have to pay the price.'

In so many ways Edmund had been lucky. He'd not been abandoned to the streets of the Rookery.

His mother had loved him. His father had acknowledged him and raised him as a gentleman, sent him to school and purchased his commission. But, even so, never, in any situation, had he been allowed to forget he was a bastard.

'What say you, Amelie?' he went on. 'Will you marry me?'

Amelie glanced away, at war with herself.

The idea of it made her immediately feel safe, when before she'd been consumed with fear. To face this problem with Edmund at her side dispelled the fear.

She winced inwardly. How awful of her to think of her baby as a problem. Edmund was right that they should think of the baby, not as a problem, but as a child who would grow into adulthood. What they decided right now would affect the rest of the child's life.

But marrying Edmund would affect *his* life, too. Could she rob him of his future? All his wonderful plans?

She walked over to a chair and lowered herself into it.

She lifted her gaze to him. 'Yes, Edmund, I will marry you.'

A relieved smile crossed his face, and he sat in the chair adjacent to hers. 'We are in agreement, then.'

'What shall we do now?' she said.

'We should marry right away,' he said. 'I will procure a special licence.'

'Yes, right away,' she murmured. 'People will still talk when the baby comes early.'

'But not so much. All is forgiven if we are married.' His tone was subdued.

They were both resigned to a fate neither would have chosen. They sat in silence together while the mantel clock ticked away.

'Marc and Tess will want to know what we discussed here,' she said finally.

'We will talk to them together,' he said. 'If you desire it.'

'Yes. I do agree.' They might be strangers discussing how to reach a destination.

'What do they know about that night in Brussels?' he asked.

'Why, nothing,' she responded, more energy reaching her voice. 'My family still believes I walked back to the hotel with Captain Fowler.'

'You did not tell them he broke the engagement?'

'There was no reason to,' she explained. 'Especially when he was injured. When his parents wrote that he had to withdraw from the betrothal because of his injuries, it was easy to accept it and say nothing.'

'You were not sorry?' Now his voice showed some emotion.

'Not at all.' She'd be pleased never to face Fowler again. Ever. 'Although I was sorry he was so grievously hurt in the battle.'

'Your brother thought I was daft to ask to court you,' he said with some humour.

'You told him you wished to court me? He did not say so.' No wonder Marc had acted so strangely. She could not help but laugh. 'He must think we are strangers!'

He smiled and her heart seemed to flip in her chest. When Marc told her Edmund was here, Amelie resolved not to think of how handsome he was, nor how skilfully and kindly he'd made love to her, but both thoughts came rushing back.

She felt the colour rise in her face and suddenly she felt awkward with him. 'Perhaps we should speak to Marc now.'

'Certainly.' He stood and offered his hand.

She put her hand in his, relishing the strength of his grip and the masculine roughness of his skin, as she'd relished touching his body that night in Brussels.

That scandalous night that had changed both their lives.

They walked out of the library and into the hall,

where Staines stood in attendance. 'Mr and Mrs Glenville wish for you to go to them,' he said.

'Where are they?' she asked.

'The drawing room.'

As they walked to the drawing room door, Amelie glanced at Edmund. 'Are you certain of this?'

'Very certain,' Edmund replied.

She nodded and Edmund opened the door. Marc and Tess immediately looked up and left their seats.

Tess walked up to Edmund and gave him a hug. 'What are you about, Edmund?' she asked at the same time.

'Did Marc tell you why Edmund wished to see me?' Amelie asked her.

Tess nodded. 'Marc said… Well, it is nonsensical.'

'I have accepted him,' Amelie said. 'We will marry as soon as possible.'

'What?' Marc's voice grew louder.

'You do not know each other!' Tess cried.

Marc gripped Amelie's arms. 'Amelie, do not be so hasty—'

Edmund broke in. 'I realise I am not the husband you would choose for her.'

'I already told you it is not that,' Marc insisted. 'It is that you have no real acquaintance and—and our father is not likely to approve.'

Amelie's spirits dropped. 'I had forgotten. Papa must approve who I marry until I come of age.'

'I had not considered this,' Edmund said. 'How old are you?'

'Edmund, you do not even know how old she is!' Tess cried. 'You know nothing of each other!'

'I am nineteen,' Amelie answered.

'Good God,' murmured Edmund, but as if to himself. 'Nineteen. Same age as Genna.'

Marc looked from Edmund to Amelie. 'Why do you not wait? What is the haste about marrying? You need time to know each other. And if you wait until you are twenty-one, it will not matter if Papa approves or not.'

Amelie glanced at Edmund. He raised his brows.

'We do not have the luxury of time,' Amelie said.

Edmund looked at her.

She met his eye. 'I might as well tell them.'

'Tell us what?' Tess asked.

'They will know soon enough,' Amelie went on.

'Know what?' Tess's voice turned impatient.

Amelie took a fortifying breath. 'We cannot wait, because—'

'Are you certain of this?' Edmund asked her.

She nodded.

'Certain of what?' Tess's voice grew shriller.

Amelie faced both her brother and sister-in-law.

'I am certain we need to marry quickly, because I am carrying Edmund's child.'

Her statement was met by a stunned silence.

'No,' Marc said in a low voice.

'Edmund's child?' Tess shook her head at Edmund. 'It cannot be. This is all a hum. You have not been together.'

Edmund spoke quietly. 'We were together, Tess. Obviously. The night of the Duchess of Richmond's ball.'

'No,' she insisted. 'Amelie left the ball with Captain Fowler.' She swung towards Amelie. 'Is this Fowler's baby?'

'No!' Amelie and Edmund cried in unison.

Amelie's face flushed. 'Fowler abandoned me that night, Tess. He left me alone on the streets of Brussels. I do not know what I would have done if your brother had not found me and escorted me back to the hotel.'

'I dare say you would have been better off!' Glenville's nostrils flared as he turned towards Edmund. 'You seduced my sister?'

Amelie stepped in front of Edmund. 'He did not seduce me. It was my doing. All of it.'

Edmund pulled her back. 'Do not try to put a better face on it, Amelie. I seduced you.'

'No! Edmund!' Tess cried again. 'You would not do such a thing to an innocent girl. You would not!'

It pained Amelie to see Edmund lowered in Tess's eyes.

'I *did* do it, Tess,' Edmund said. 'I *am* responsible.'

Amelie broke in. 'No. The fault is mine.'

But no one listened to her.

'I do not know how he convinced you,' her brother growled. 'But he took advantage, of that I am certain.'

No. *She* had taken advantage!

Edmund looked Marc directly in the eye. 'I accept my responsibility and my duty. For your sister's sake, I will do the honourable thing.'

Marc's eyes flashed. 'Honourable. There is nothing honourable in what you have done. This will cause our family more scandal.'

'I cannot change what happened,' Edmund said. 'But I can do what is right now.'

Marc swung to Amelie. 'You still need Papa's approval, you know. He will never give it.'

'He will give permission,' Tess said dispiritedly. 'What other choice will he have? There will be a baby.'

'I will speak to your father in person,' Edmund said. 'I will explain.'

Marc shook his head. 'He will not believe you. He'll toss you out. Your story is too far-fetched.'

'But it is true!' Amelie cried.

'It sounds like a cock-and-bull story,' Marc said, 'even if it is true. Papa will never believe Edmund if he travels there alone with that tale.'

'I do not believe it!' cried Tess. 'Not of Edmund.'

Edmund gave Tess a quelling look but glanced back at Marc. 'Then come with me. He will believe you.'

'Go with you?' Marc still looked as if he'd rather accompany a pen of swine.

Why couldn't her brother be on her side about this?

'He will believe you.' Edmund repeated, keeping his gaze steady.

Amelie interrupted. 'Neither of you have to go. I will write Papa a letter.'

Edmund turned to her and gently touched her arm. 'No letter, Amelie. I must face your father. It is the only way.'

It was good of Edmund to offer, but Amelie was certain he would be treated very ill.

Marc's shoulders fell. 'Edmund is right. This is not news for our parents to read in a letter. Papa is more likely to approve if Edmund tells him like a man.'

It pained Amelie that she'd caused her brother to be so angry at Edmund. Before this Marc had held him in high regard.

Her brother straightened. 'It is but a six-hour ride. We can be at Northdon House before nightfall if we leave soon.'

'I should accompany you,' Amelie said.

'No!' Edmund cried.

'Absolutely not!' her brother added.

At least they agreed on that idea.

'Not in your condition,' Tess added. 'You must take care, or you will endanger your health.'

Six hours on horseback could not be good for the baby.

Edmund turned back to Glenville. 'I can ride the way I am dressed, and I do not need a change of clothing, but I need to hire a horse.'

Marc started for the door. 'I'll send Staines to the stables to tell them to saddle my horse and to hire one for you.'

Tess followed him. 'I will tell Cook to pack you some food.'

Amelie and Edmund were alone in the room. Her insides were churning, not only from the morning sickness, but also from the stress of this encounter. The stress of everything.

She turned to Edmund. 'My brother blames you. My father will blame you, too. It is I who should tell him what really happened.'

He looked down on her. 'What really happened was I took advantage of you. Let it go at that, Amelie. That night in Brussels I should have seen you safely to the hotel and left you there. That fact cannot be disputed. I must accept their anger just as I must accept that our marrying is what we must do.'

'But it is my fault,' she said in a small voice.

He touched her arm and attempted a smile. 'I have faced men in battle lunging at me with swords and shooting pistols. I've had cannon balls miss me by inches. Facing your father will not be so difficult nor so dangerous.'

She was not so certain.

She placed her palm on her abdomen to quiet her roiling stomach. 'Marrying me changes things for you. I am so dreadfully sorry.'

His gaze seemed to harden. 'We simply do what we must, Amelie. That is how we manage. One task at a time. The first task is your father's permission.'

Chapter Six

It took no more than an hour before Edmund and Glenville were on the road to Hertfordshire, where the Northdon country estate was located. Glenville rode a few paces ahead of Edmund, clearly having no wish to converse with him. Glenville's displeasure was palpable, and Edmund could not blame him. Edmund would react the same—worse, in fact—if a near stranger had violated any of his sisters.

Edmund let Glenville decide when to stop and rest the horses, when they should quicken the pace and when they should slow. Why quibble about such trifles? They rode past crumbling Roman ruins and pretty villages with houses all in a line next to the road. They passed through busy market towns and quiet villages where the few people in the street took notice and eyed them with curiosity.

Edmund had too much time to think, and that was not a pleasant circumstance. *Turn off your thoughts*, he told himself. *Numb your mind as you used to on long marches in Spain.*

The sun was very low in the sky when they rode through a pretty village that time appeared to have forgotten. The houses and shops looked as if the War of the Roses had been fought the day before. Edmund knew they must be close. The village was called Northdon.

Soon he spied a large Palladian house in the distance, its white stone gleaming in the waning light. Northdon House, no doubt. At its grand wrought-iron gate, Glenville dismounted and opened it.

As they approached the house, Glenville said, 'Let me do the talking.'

'No.' This time Edmund must be in charge. 'I tell him.'

'Let me do the talking up to that point, then,' Glenville said anxiously.

Glenville's presence was greeted with happy excitement. Both his parents ran to greet him. There were hugs and kisses and exclamations of pleasure showered on him before Lord and Lady Northdon even seemed to notice Edmund, who was greeted with greater reserve but kind civility.

They all retired to a drawing room.

As soon as Lord and Lady Northdon were seated,

Edmund faced them. 'We have come because I have a very important matter to discuss.'

Lady Northdon looked worried, Lord Northdon apprehensive.

Edmund took a breath. 'I will not mince words. Your daughter and I must marry. She is carrying my child.'

'Mon Dieu!' Lady Northdon cried.

Lord Northdon's face grew red with rage. 'You did what to my daughter?' he said after.

'She carries my child,' Edmund repeated.

'You ruddy bastard!' Northdon charged at him.

Glenville held him back.

Edmund stood his ground. 'I accept your anger, sir. I understand it. But what is important now is for us to marry quickly and avoid as much scandal as possible. To accomplish that we need your permission.'

'No!' Northdon cried, his son still holding his arm. Northdon shrugged him off but faced him. 'Amelie does not wish this, does she, Marc?'

'It is what she wants,' Glenville answered.

'It cannot be!' his father cried.

'Ma pauvre fille,' whispered Lady Northdon. 'Is she in good health?'

Edmund answered her. 'She is sick in the mornings and greatly fatigued.'

'You know this?' Glenville looked surprised.

Edmund turned to him. 'She told me.' He faced Lord Northdon again. 'Do we have your permission?'

'I would rather kill you,' Northdon snapped.

'Then your daughter will have an illegitimate child.' Edmund kept his voice as even as possible. He was used to people hating him because of his birth. This was not much different. 'I wish to prevent that.'

'You have to give permission, Papa,' Glenville said. 'It will be best for Amelie.'

'Marriage to this—this bastard cannot be what is best for her.' Northdon spat out the word *bastard*.

'He is the child's father,' Glenville pressed. 'You must allow them to marry.'

'Give your permission, John!' Lady Northdon became more agitated. 'Remember Lucien! I will not lose my daughter the way we lost Lucien.'

Who was Lucien?

Lord Northdon's shoulders slumped, and he suddenly looked old and feeble, which he was certainly not. 'Yes, Ines,' he said in a weak voice. 'Not like Lucien.'

A pall came over the room, as thick as smoke.

When Lord Northdon finally raised his head, his eyes were filled with pain. 'Please get him out of my sight before I change my mind and kill him.'

'Come.' Lady Northdon took Edmund by the arm. 'You must be hungry.'

Lady Northdon was still a beautiful woman, although her features, so like Amelie's, were pinched with stress and unhappiness. The crisp sunny September day had been rendered bleak—by Edmund. If only he could simply remount that horse and ride far away from all of them.

But that would not safeguard his future son or daughter.

Lady Northdon led him to a smaller drawing room, one with many windows and furnished with a table and chairs. The breakfast room, Edmund thought.

'I will have Cook prepare some food. Someone will bring it in a moment. Please enjoy your repast and wait for me here. I will come back for you.'

It seemed expedient to agree. 'As you wish it, *madame.*'

A few minutes later, a servant brought him a tray.

He ate the warm bread and cold meat, downed a cup of tea and waited. Finally Lady Northdon returned carrying a letter.

He stood.

'It is the permission. Signed and sealed.' She handed him the folded paper.

'Merci, madame.' He took the letter and slipped it into a pocket inside his coat.

She looked up at him. 'Treat my daughter well, *s'il vous plaît.*'

He met her eyes. 'You have my promise.'

She held his gaze for a moment before gesturing for him to follow her back to the hall. He assumed he was taking his leave. At least he was not leaving the house through the tradesmen's door.

On the way he asked, 'Who is Lucien?'

She paused and turned towards him. 'My son. My first son.' Her words were strained.

'Why was he spoken of today?' he persisted.

She averted her gaze. 'He was killed in a carriage accident on his way to Gretna Green.'

'I see.' Gretna Green. The village in Scotland that was close to the border and a frequent destination for hasty, unlicensed weddings. He did not ask Lady Northdon to explain further. He had no desire to cause her more pain. She'd been an ally, albeit a reluctant one. He was grateful to her for it.

She turned and continued to walk to the hall. 'Say nothing of your situation to anyone,' she said, as if they'd not just spoken of her dead son. 'We wish no one to know, not even the servants. Let them guess, if they must, but no one must know.'

'I give my word.' He never intended to speak of the reason of his marriage. Scandal was best dealt with by a closed mouth.

They reached the hall, where a footman handed

him his hat and gloves. The man crossed the hall to the door ready to open it and, Edmund supposed, eject this unwanted visitor.

'Your horse will be ready for you outside,' Lady Northdon said.

He bowed to her and spoke quietly. 'Thank you for the refreshment. You did not have to be so kind.'

She shrugged. 'I am French. We expect these things to happen, no?'

He smiled inwardly. She sounded like Amelie.

Lady Northdon went on. 'Lord Northdon and I will travel to London as soon as we can arrange it. In two or three days, I expect.'

He reached out his hand. 'I will keep my promises, *madame.*'

She hesitated before accepting his handshake. *'Bon voyage, monsieur.'*

Edmund walked out the door to his waiting horse. He'd ride to the village and take lodging in an inn there before heading back to London in the morning. After a wash up and a change of clothing, his first stop in London would be Doctors' Commons and the office of the Archbishop of Canterbury.

For the special licence.

That evening Amelie had no desire to eat, but she sat in the dining room with her sister-in-law, pushing at her food and trying to force some of it into her mouth. She and Tess had avoided each other all day. Amelie loved and esteemed Tess as if she were the sister she'd always dreamed of having. Now, though, she'd surely lost Tess's good opinion. She'd known it ever since Edmund's unexpected arrival and his quick departure with Marc.

Where were they at this moment? she wondered. Surely they'd seen her father by now. How had her father reacted? Had he given his approval?

The question consumed her mind and had done so all day.

Never had Amelie dreamed marriage would be a possibility, a way to salvage some respectability for the family after her impulsive night with Edmund. He'd rescued her again, just as he had on the streets of Brussels. Just as his lovemaking had rescued her sense of self-worth after Fowler had dashed it to the pavement.

What if her father refused his permission for the marriage, though? Would they elope to Gretna Green?

Gretna Green. The name always made her think of Lucien. Of how he died and of how her mother and father had shouted at each other afterwards.

They'd only so recently reconciled, in Brussels where Amelie's vision of her own marital happiness had been shattered. What if her problem made them fight each other again?

Her problem. Her *baby*, she meant. Babies were supposed to be happy events, were they not? How awful that hers had become a problem to get through. She glanced down at her plate, but instead saw in her arms a baby swaddled in soft blankets and Edmund smiling down at the tiny being. Her heart thrilled for a brief moment.

Was this what other women felt when they knew they were carrying a child? Was it possible or merely more of her fanciful thinking?

She glanced up at Tess, who picked at her food just as much as Amelie had. What were Tess's thoughts? Amelie dared not ask, not with the footman in the room serving the meal. Perhaps Tess was quiet because she did not want to speak with her. Perhaps Tess had a disgust of her behaviour, like Fowler had been disgusted of her. Perhaps Marc despised her as well, her brother, whom she loved with all her heart.

Tears pricked her eyes. She blinked them away.

Enough of this self-pity. She'd been bold with Edmund in Brussels, and, if nothing else, being bold had exhilarated her. She could confront Tess. Find out where she stood with her.

'I have an idea,' she spoke into the silence of the large dining room. 'Let us take our tea in Maman's sitting room. It will be so much more comfortable than the drawing room.' Where the silence would bounce off the walls.

Tess looked up. 'If you like.'

Amelie turned to the footman. 'Staines, would you bring the tea to us there?'

'Yes, miss.' He took her plate.

'And dessert, too?' She glanced over at Tess. 'Shall we have our dessert there, too?'

Tess nodded.

They left the table and walked in silence to the sitting room. Amelie busied herself lighting the candles so there was no need to talk. Staines and another footman soon brought the tea tray and the small cakes Cook had baked for dessert.

When they left, Amelie gathered her courage. 'Speak plainly to me, Tess. I fear what you must think of me.'

Tess looked at her with surprise. 'Of you? I am so angry at my brother, I cannot think of anything else. How could he do that to you? Seduce you like that. Ruin your life?'

'It was not Edmund's doing. It was mine.' Amelie took a sip of her tea. 'I wish you and Marc would understand that.'

'Nonsense.' Tess gave her a reproving look. 'We do not hold you at all responsible. You did not know what you were about, but Edmund did.'

This was too difficult to believe. Was all the blame to be borne on Edmund's shoulders?

'You must think ill of me, though.' Amelie tried again.

Tess leaned over and put a comforting hand on Amelie's. 'Not at all. I am worried for you, though. You do not look at all well. We must devise a way for you to see a physician without anyone finding out why.'

'I am a little sick to my stomach and very fatigued,' Amelie admitted. 'And I have not been able to speak a word of it. Why my maid does not question it, I cannot tell, although Sally seems very distracted these days. I do not know what is wrong with her.'

'Well, it is good that she has not guessed,' Tess responded. 'I have no doubt the servants will discover the truth, but perhaps they will keep the family's confidence. By the time you show, you should be married and perhaps no one will bother to count the months.'

No one had much bothered with her before all this. Perhaps they would not think about her and Edmund at all.

Amelie picked up one of the cakes and tried taking a little bite.

Tess went on talking. 'I did write to my sisters. They must know what Edmund has done.'

'Oh, Tess. Did you have to do that?' Now his other two sisters would be angry at him. Why could Tess not have let them think Edmund *wanted* to marry her?

'Of course they must know,' Tess said, although she sounded uncertain now. 'They are my sisters.'

Tess's older sister Lorene had married a very old man. Married him for his money, people said. Amelie had met Lord Tinmore once. He was as intimidating as he was ancient. Tess's younger sister Genna was Amelie's age. Amelie and Tess had attended some entertainments in their company. Unlike Amelie, Genna seemed to enter any party with confidence, as if she did not care a fig about whether anyone spoke to her or danced with her. She never wanted for partners.

So, in addition to everything else, Amelie would probably ruin Edmund's relationships with his sisters. He would despise her even more for it, would he not?

After leaving Doctors' Commons, Edmund walked directly to Grosvenor Street to see Amelie. Staines, the same footman who'd attended the door before, gave him entry and bade him wait in the drawing room while he went to find Amelie. This room was becoming familiar. Its arrangement of chairs, tables and sofa. The porcelain figurines on the mantelpiece. The portraits of Lord and Lady Northdon hanging on the walls.

At least the portraits were not red-faced with anger at him, nor aching with remembered pain because of him.

Amelie entered the room. She was still pale, making her blue eyes seem even larger and her hair more golden. She stole his breath.

'Edmund? You are back so soon? Is Marc with you?'

He was not about to tell her that he had been sent away alone.

'He stayed behind.' And Edmund had no idea when Glenville would return.

She merely stared at him, eyes wide in the unasked question.

'Your father gave his permission,' Edmund assured her.

She released a relieved breath, but her brow then creased in worry. 'Was it very bad for you?'

His cheek flexed. 'Not intolerable. Your mother was kind.'

Her expression softened. 'Did I not tell you she was the dearest creature?'

No use telling her of the pain his presence caused, nor the memories he had provoked. 'She was all that.'

She bit her lip. 'Are you still resolved on the matter? Because I would not fault you for withdrawing your proposal.'

It was the very thing that nagged at him—the impulse to simply vanish. 'Is that what you wish me to do?'

'I could not blame you for it,' she said. 'I have made everything miserable for you and you seem to accept it in a way I cannot.'

He raised his brows. 'So it is not what you wish?'

She did not meet his eye. 'It is the best solution. The right thing.'

Which was not precisely saying it was what she wanted. Well, it was not what he wanted either, was it?

She took a breath. 'Forgive me. You must be very fatigued. Please do sit, Edmund.'

He shook his head. 'I will not stay. I merely came to tell you that I have applied for the licence. It will take a few days. The archbishop's clerk said they must write to my parish.' More time for him to change his mind. 'But I will call upon you as soon as it is ready.'

A line formed between her eyes. 'You are welcome to call before that.'

Not by anyone else in the household, he'd wager. 'I am not so certain of that.'

'What do you mean?'

He should not have spoken. 'Your parents are returning to London. I do not think they welcome me.'

'I see.' She looked confused, however.

He took a step towards the door. 'I might as well
take my leave.'

'No!' Amelie cried. 'Do not go.'

He turned, surprised she would wish him to stay.

She averted her gaze but spoke in a low, quiet
voice. 'Do not leave me, Edmund. I have no one to
talk to about this!'

It had not occurred to him that Amelie would
want him to stay. Would she not resent the sight
of him like everyone else in her family? The truth
was, his emotions were still in turmoil, and this
room simply could not contain them.

He stared at Amelie. 'Would you like a walk in
the park?'

She smiled. 'I would!'

Soon they were strolling through Grosvenor Gate
onto one of the footpaths that crossed Hyde Park. It
was late afternoon, but the weather was fine. It was
actually a fine day for a walk in the park and, to
Edmund's surprise, the tension inside him calmed.

Because he walked with Amelie.

Much like that night in Brussels, it seemed as if
they'd known each other a lifetime.

Edmund broke their silence. 'You know I fully support you talking to me.'

'What?' She looked puzzled.

'You said you wished to talk to me. You know I believe you should tell me everything.'

'Oh!' Understanding dawned on her face. 'Like the night in Brussels.' She smiled. 'You made me tell you about Fowler.'

Her smile made her even more beautiful.

'I did not make you,' he said. 'I encouraged you.'

'Encouraged me, then,' she responded.

'So talk to me now.' She was not alone, he wanted to assure her. Now, as inexplicable and as fraught with tension as it was, they belonged together.

She hesitated a moment, then her words came out in a rush. 'I—I want you to know how grateful I am that you will marry me.'

He did not deserve her gratitude, not when he'd created her problems. 'I am not certain gratitude is what you ought to be feeling.'

'No one else will believe it is my fault and that is so unfair to you. I know it is my fault.' Her voice was firm.

'Let us not return to that topic, Amelie. It does not concern me that I am held to blame.' He accepted his blame. 'What else is on your mind?' Something he could change, he hoped.

She did not speak for several steps. 'I also feel

so ashamed. I only thought of myself. You thought of the baby.'

'Your situation was different than mine. It cannot compare.' He could leave and resume his life with very little consequence. She could never do that.

'I want so badly to think of the baby the way you do.' She sighed.

At times the idea of the baby struck him like a cannonball in the chest. A little life made from that sensuous night they had shared, a little person who would truly belong to him, the line of the triangle that joined him to Amelie for ever.

Because he was a bastard, his connections to family were always fractured in some way. His mother was not married to his father. His sisters were only half-sisters. But he, Amelie and the baby made a family. A proper family.

The emotions around that were too acute to be discussed.

'Perhaps if we made plans, it would help.' So much easier to talk of practicalities.

'Plans?' she asked.

'Such as where to live.'

'Oh.' She fell silent again. 'I have not thought be-yond—beyond anything.'

'I had planned to return to Brussels.' Although he'd intended to remain in Brussels only a short time. He'd toyed with the prospect of seeking his fortune in the Colonies or in the new United States of America, but he would not take Amelie into such uncertainty. 'We could live quite well in Brussels.'

He felt her body stiffen. 'I must go where you wish, Edmund. I do understand that.'

But she did not want to go to Brussels. 'Speak the truth to me, Amelie.'

She took several steps before speaking in a low voice. 'I—I had hoped to remain near my mother. With the baby—'

He'd forgotten. She was so young. He must not take her from everything and everyone she loved and needed.

'Would you prefer to stay in London?' He could continue managing his investments from here in London.

'Oh, yes!' But her voice lost its excitement. 'Our town house is so small, though. There is hardly enough room for Marc and Tess.'

Edmund had no intention of living in the Northdon town house. 'We would lease rooms of our own.'

'Could we?' She smiled. 'That would be perfect!'

It would suffice.

The Serpentine came into view. They walked towards it.

The rippling water of the Serpentine, the green

grass and trees added to the ease of talking together. Edmund was glad of it.

Or was it being in Amelie's company that soothed him?

She pulled on his arm. 'Look, Edmund.' They walked closer.

A nanny and two very small children, a boy and a girl, stood at the edge of the water throwing pieces of bread to a gaggle of geese who swam towards the easy food. Edmund did not know how to gauge the ages, but both looked barely out of leading strings.

The little girl threw a piece of crust and squealed with delight when the geese fought over it.

The boy pulled away from the nanny and toddled towards the grass and pulled out a clump. He held it in his little fist until he reached the water and threw it in. Half the geese swam for it, but they quickly lost interest.

The nanny dashed over to the child and brushed his hands clean.

'Is that what we will have, Edmund?' Amelie asked in wonder. 'A sweet creature like those darling children?'

The little boy turned back to grab more grass; the nanny followed.

'No. No more grass,' she admonished.

At that same moment, the little girl reached for the ducks and lost her footing.

Edmund dashed over and scooped up the child before she fell in the water.

'Oh, my goodness!' cried the nanny as she rushed over.

'No harm done,' Edmund said.

The child, oblivious of her close call, merely squirmed around and wrapped her pudgy arms around Edmund's neck.

The little girl's skin felt smooth as finest silk, and she smelled like sweetness and innocence.

Edmund glanced at Amelie.

She wore a look of wonder that perfectly mirrored his own emotions.

Soon he would be holding his own child, *their* child, a child he and Amelie created together.

His heart soared with joy.

Chapter Seven

Two days after Edmund returned to London, Marc Glenville sent word that Lord and Lady Northdon had also arrived. No invitation to the house had been included, however. That rebuff stung, like so many of the slights he'd endured his whole life. Were they trying to keep him from Amelie? If so, it was wrong. He and Amelie needed the time together. He called upon her every day.

They went out each day and visited the sights of London, places he'd never had the opportunity to see—the Tower, Westminster Abbey, the Egyptian Hall. They were easy in each other's company. That was an encouraging sign.

Her family remained an impediment. Her father avoided encountering him when he called and if her mother appeared, she acted civilly, but nothing more. Amelie avoided speaking of them.

* * *

Today Edmund would not see Amelie. Instead he would use the day to discharge several errands that needed doing. First and foremost was to check on the special licence. It had been seven days since his first visit to the office of the Archbishop of Canterbury, and he presumed they would have received the necessary information from Lincolnshire by now.

He went to Doctors' Commons first thing.

'The information has not yet arrived,' the Archbishop's clerk said in a snooty tone.

The clerk knew of Edmund's father and knew Edmund was the bastard son. No doubt that had played a major factor in the delay.

'What is the delay?' Edmund demanded.

'I am certain I cannot say,' the clerk responded. 'Come back tomorrow. Or the next day.'

No doubt the man would make no effort to discover why.

This was ridiculous.

Edmund left the office and went immediately to Bow Street. He hired a man to travel to Lincolnshire to procure the necessary documents. He ought to have done so in the first place.

From there he stopped at the Exchange to meet with the stockbroker he and Count von Osten used.

The investments Edmund made had the potential of rather quick profit. He aimed to grow his funds enough in order to leave Amelie's dowry entirely untouched, and he was well on his way to achieving his goal. His guiding principle in investing was to think of what his father would have done and do the opposite. So far that strategy had worked exceedingly well.

After the Exchange he walked back to his hotel. When he entered and turned to the stairway to climb to his room, the hall servant called to him. 'Lieutenant Summerfield!'

Edmund had given up explaining that he was no longer Lieutenant Summerfield.

'There is a gentleman to see you,' the servant said. 'He awaits you in the parlour.'

The parlour was off the hall and was a place where one could receive visitors or simply sit comfortably to read or write letters. Who would call upon him except Lord Northdon or Glenville? He did not relish receiving either of them.

Edmund thanked the servant, crossed the hall again and opened the parlour door.

An elderly man sat in a chair facing the door. He did not rise at Edmund's entrance but raised his brows, 'Summerfield?'

'Yes,' Edmund said uncertainly.

'I am Lord Tinmore.'

Tinmore? His sister Lorene's husband.

'Has something happened to Lorene?' Edmund asked. Why else would this man call upon him?

'My wife is in excellent health.' Tinmore acted as if Edmund's question had been an impertinence.

'I am glad to hear it,' Edmund replied, more puzzled than ever.

Tinmore flushed. 'I'll have no sarcasm, young man!'

How the devil could he have offended Lord Tinmore? He'd never seen the man before this moment.

Edmund glared. 'Are you in a position to dictate to me, sir?'

'I most certainly am!' Tinmore cried.

This was madness. Edmund attempted to stifle the animosity this man had instantly aroused in him. 'You have an advantage over me, sir.' Edmund struggled for a civil tone. 'You know why you have called upon me, and I haven't the slightest notion.'

Tinmore pursed his lips. 'A clever man might guess.'

'There you have it.' Edmund lifted his arms. 'I am not clever.'

Tinmore pointed to a chair adjacent to the throne-like one upon which he sat. 'Sit.'

Edmund had met men like Tinmore in the army. Colonels or generals, typically, consumed by their own importance. Defiance was the only way to earn their respect.

'I'll stand,' he said.

Tinmore flinched as if surprised his order had not been instantly obeyed. 'Very well, I will get to the point.'

At last, Edmund thought.

'My wife tells me you have left the army and that you have got a respectable young woman with child, Glenville's sister.'

How the devil did he know?

Tess.

Tess always told Lorene everything, even when they'd been little girls. Why did Lorene tell Tinmore, though?

Edmund straightened. 'You have not yet told me why you have called, sir.'

'Did you think I would not react to this? Leaving the army. Debauching an innocent. What have you to say for yourself?'

This was the outside of enough. Edmund took a step closer and spoke in his most menacing voice. 'I fail to see why my actions are any affair of yours.'

'Of course it is my affair!' Tinmore shot back. 'I provided you money for your captaincy, not for you to sell out and sully the reputation of the family.'

Edmund felt the blood drain from his face. 'You provided the money?'

'It was at my wife's request.' Tinmore's expression turned smug.

Lorene implied that the money had been from their late father's estate. Edmund had used these funds for his investments in Brussels, investments that had yielded immediate returns. That money had been the seed from which he would grow his fortune.

'I certainly did not provide the money for you to leave the army,' Tinmore went on. 'Now look at you, about to bring scandal to the family—'

Edmund held up a stilling hand. 'Your money will be returned. With interest. If you would be so kind, please furnish me with the name of your man of business and I shall see it done.'

'Because of you, Lady Tinmore and I have returned to London—'

Edmund interrupted him again. 'Then I will see you receive my bank draft at your town house.' He bowed. 'That ends your involvement in my affairs. Good day, sir.'

Edmund turned and walked to the door.

'Come back here!' Tinmore called to his retreating back. 'I am not finished with you.'

Edmund was finished with him, though.

Edmund did not return to his hotel room. Instead he strode out of the hotel again and made his way swiftly to Curzon Street, asking a man on the street to direct him to Lord Tinmore's house. He trusted he could walk more swiftly than Tinmore could return either by carriage or on foot.

Edmund intended to speak with his sister before her husband returned.

He was admitted to the hall and was left waiting there until the footman announced him. Both Lorene and Genna appeared on the stairs and hurried down to greet him.

'Edmund!' Genna cried, flinging herself into his arms. 'I have been pining to see you!'

Lorene was more reserved. 'What a lovely surprise. Shall we sit in the drawing room? I'll order tea.'

'I will not stay long enough for tea,' he said. 'I need only a few minutes of your time.'

'We have a lot to ask you!' Genna said with good humour.

A lot he had no intention of answering.

The Tinmore town house was more opulent than Amelie's family's house on Grosvenor Street. They crossed a large hall to a drawing room twice the size of the Northdons'. Its furnishings were elegant, but slightly outmodish, remaining in the neo-classical style of a bygone era, all pale colours, Roman themes and intricate plasterwork.

As soon as they were alone in the room, away from servants, Edmund faced Lorene. 'Did the money you sent for my captaincy come from your husband?' He was too angry to mince words.

She blushed. 'Yes.'

'That and Tess's and my dowries, although he got out of paying Tess's dowry,' Genna added.

He could not focus on that statement at the moment.

'Why did you say it came from our father?' he demanded.

'I did not say so precisely,' Lorene prevaricated. 'I said I found some money that belonged to you. I did not say that it came from Lord Tinmore.'

'It is why she married him,' Genna broke in.

'Genna!' Lorene cried.

Genna tossed her a glance. 'Well, it is. You married him because our father left us no money for dowries. You did it so we would not have to become governesses or ladies' companions.'

Edmund swung back to Lorene. 'Were things so bad?'

Lorene, more petite and fine-boned than Genna or Tess, glared at her sister. 'It was the best decision I could make, and I think it is churlish of you to be annoyed about it!'

Edmund took her by her shoulders and turned her

towards him. 'Why did you not tell me?' he asked
in a softer voice.

She raised her eyes to him. 'What could you have
done, Edmund? You could not have supported us
on a lieutenant's pay. It barely supported you.'

If he had not devised ways to make money elsewhere, he'd have been hard-pressed to even keep
his horse.

'I will return the money to Lord Tinmore,' he
continued. 'So this need not be between us any
more.' Nor between Lorene and her husband. Tinmore could not hold it over her head as he'd held it
over Edmund's.

'Can you afford to return it?' Lorene looked sceptical.

'Yes, I can afford it.'

'Of course he can,' Genna commented. 'Miss
Glenville's dowry should be a large one.'

It was Edmund's turn to glare at Genna.

'What about that, Edmund?' Lorene asked in a
scolding tone. 'Tess wrote us about Miss Glenville.
I cannot believe you could be so shabby. She was
such a pretty girl. Look what you have done to her.'

Amelie was still pretty. Beautiful, in fact.

But he was not about to discuss this with Lorene and Genna. 'We are to marry, yes, but her
dowry has nothing to do with my repaying Tin-

more.' He kept his tone even. 'That is all I wish to say about it.'

'I just hope there is not too much talk,' Lorene said.

'Yes, how awful for the Summerfields to be the topic of gossip and scandal,' Genna said with sarcasm.

Edmund heard a carriage outside. Luckily it did not stop but reminded him that he intended to leave before Tinmore returned.

'I must go,' he said.

'When will we see you again?' Genna asked.

'I do not know,' he admitted. 'Soon, perhaps.'

'I hope so.' Lorene added, 'We should talk about this marriage, Edmund.'

Not if he had any choice in the matter. 'I will see you are kept informed.'

'I'll walk you out.' Genna stepped forward and clutched his arm.

Lorene followed them into the hall, where Edmund collected his hat and gloves. Genna walked out the door with him.

'How do you and Lorene fare here?' he asked Genna as soon as they were outside.

'Under Tinmore, do you mean?' She released a breath. 'He delights in ordering everyone about, that is for certain.'

'Does he mistreat you?' If so, the man would answer to Edmund.

'Not mistreatment, not really,' she said. 'Lorene never complains about doing his bidding, and I hardly ever do as he says. I am certainly not going to marry someone just because he wishes to be rid of me as soon as possible.'

Genna. Always obstinate.

He placed a kiss on her forehead. 'You will tell me if you need me.'

She waved a dismissive hand. 'I am able to take care of myself.'

He smiled at her. 'Then tell me if Lorene needs me.'

'That I will do.'

A carriage appeared at the end of the street.

'That is Lord Tinmore's carriage,' Genna said. 'I prefer to go in before he sees me.'

He squeezed her hand. She hurried into the house, and he walked in the opposite direction of the approaching carriage. He, too, preferred that Tinmore not see him.

Amelie rested on a chair in her bedchamber, her feet on a stool. She'd managed some tea and toast. Nonsensically, on the days she'd spent in Edmund's company, the morning sickness had been barely noticeable.

Her maid, Sally, entered the room, carrying some freshly laundered, folded clothing. Sally walked slowly as if every step was an effort.

'Are you feeling unwell?' Amelie asked her.

'Just a little weary, miss,' she replied.

Poor Sally. The young soldier she'd spent time with that night in Brussels had not survived the battle. It had been very hard for her.

'Well, rest today,' Amelie told her. 'I do not require much of you.'

'Thank you, miss.'

There was a knock at her door, and Sally answered it.

Staines, the footman, appeared in the doorway. 'Miss Summerfield asks to see you, miss.'

'Miss Summerfield?' Why would Tess's sister call upon her?

Perhaps Tess was out.

Amelie did not have the energy to go down to the drawing room. 'Ask if she minds coming up here and show her up.'

'Very good, miss,' Staines said.

'And send up some tea?'

He nodded.

'Do you need me, miss?' Sally asked.

Amelie gave her a reassuring smile. 'Not at all. Tell anyone who questions you that I ordered you to rest. '

'Thank you, miss.'

* * *

Sally slipped out of Miss Glenville's room and wearily climbed the stairs to the small attic room she shared with Mrs Glenville's maid. She took off her shoes, sat down on her cot and buried her head in her hands.

What was she to do?

She touched her belly. There was no question now. She had Calvin's baby inside her. All that was left of him. His body had lain among the dead on the Waterloo battlefield. She could not bear to think of it.

He hadn't meant to abandon her. That night before he left for the battle he promised to marry her, but now he was gone.

What was she to do?

Lady Northdon would sack her, she was certain. The only family she had left was her sister, and she was in service, too, not in any position to help. Calvin had a cousin somewhere, but why would Calvin's cousin take her in, even if he believed that she carried Calvin's child?

She lay her head on her pillow and tried to slow her racing heart. Sometimes she could not even breathe she was in such a panic about what would happen to her and her baby. Would she be forced to take the baby to the Foundling Hospital? To abandon all that was left of Calvin? How could she bear to do that? But how could she live with the baby? She would lose her position here, and who would hire a ladies' maid with a bastard child?

Staines knocked on Amelie's door and announced Miss Summerfield.

'Hello, Miss Glenville!' Miss Summerfield breezed in, taking off her hat as she walked in the room. 'I am so delighted you are at home.'

'Did you want to see Tess? Is she out?' Amelie assumed that Tess was Miss Summerfield's first choice to visit.

'No!' she said cheerfully. 'I came to see you!' She lowered herself into a nearby chair.

By appearance Amelie and Miss Summerfield could be sisters, both blonde haired and blue-eyed. Genna was a bit taller and her figure more lithesome, but they looked more like each other than Miss Summerfield looked like her sisters. Amelie and Tess had accompanied her and Lady Tinmore to some society entertainments last Season, but Amelie still felt as though she hardly knew her.

'How are you?' Miss Summerfield gave her a significant look.

She *knew*. Tess said she'd written to her sisters. Must Amelie talk about it to this young woman? She was nearly a stranger. 'I am well, thank you. And you?'

'Come now! None of that. You know I know my brother has got you with child. I cannot believe it of him, but there it is.' She took a breath. 'I came to let you know that I am an ally. I presumed you might need a friend at such a time.'

Once Amelie would have melted with gratitude at such an invitation for friendship, but her trust was hard-won now. Even Tess could not be entirely trusted.

She proceeded cautiously. 'That is very kind of you, Miss Summerfield.'

The young woman smiled. 'Oh, call me Genna. We are so connected now through brothers and sisters that we might as well be sisters ourselves. Shall I call you Amelie?'

'If you like.'

Throughout most of Amelie's growing up, including the very unhappy year she spent at school, others her age had stayed away from her. She was certain it was because of the stories about her mother—a commoner with family in France active in the Terror. Amelie's mother and father thought she did not know of this, but there had been other girls only too eager to inform her precisely who her French relations were and where their names had appeared in old French newspapers.

Only last spring, in her first Season, had Amelie thought she'd begun to make friends. When Fowler began courting her, she was certain she'd finally been accepted for herself.

How foolish she'd been.

The tea came and Miss Summerfield busied herself with the pouring of it. She handed Amelie a cup of tea and a biscuit. Amelie's stomach roiled at the smell of the tea at first, but the sensation passed. She was grateful. She did not desire to vomit all over Edmund's youngest sister.

What errands kept Edmund away today? she wondered. Spending time with him these last few days had made her feel almost happy.

'So.' Genna took her first sip. 'What are the wedding plans? Edmund has told us nothing about it.'

Amelie glanced up at her. 'You saw Edmund?'

Genna nodded. 'He called upon us this morning. Upon Lorene and me. Not Lord Tinmore.' She spoke that man's name with the same disdain as Tess and Marc always did. 'But he would not tell us a thing. He came only to talk about money, the money Lord Tinmore gave him that he says he will give back.' She took another sip of tea. 'In any event, he did not stay long enough to tell us *anything*. I would love to help you with the wedding, you know. I could help you choose your bride clothes.'

'Bride clothes?' Amelie had not even thought of

bride clothes. 'I am sure I have some gown that will suit.'

'Oh, no! You must have something new. A beautiful dress to be married in! Otherwise, people will think you do not care very much about marrying.'

Amelie certainly wanted to minimise the gossip that would occur. Even so, purchasing a bride dress seemed very unimportant. Even her mother, who prided herself on being *au courant* in fashion, had not mentioned a dress. Who would know, after all? It was not likely anyone outside the family would attend the wedding.

'Does not Tess have a maid who designs gowns?' Genna asked. 'Why not let her make you a bride dress?'

'Nancy is now apprenticed to my mother's modiste, Madame LeClaire,' Amelie said.

'Well, we should go there and have them make you a pretty dress!' Genna clapped her hands together. 'Shall we go tomorrow morning?'

Edmund would be checking on the special licence then, he'd told her, but she did not want to provide even that much information to Genna.

Amelie remembered Tess's wedding, how Tess and Marc had gazed at each other, how beautiful Tess had appeared in the gown Nancy made for her. Amelie could not hope to receive a loving glance from Edmund, but she could at least try to look her best.

'We can go to Madame LeClaire's tomorrow,' Amelie said.

'Excellent!' Genna jumped to her feet and gave Amelie a quick hug. 'I am so delighted! I think someone in my family must treat you well, since my brother certainly did not.'

'It was not your brother's doing,' Amelie said.

Genna's eyes grew wide. 'Do you mean he is not the father?'

'No. No.' She meant only to defend him. *She* was to blame. 'Edmund is the father, but it is not his fault about all this. It is mine.'

Genna gave her the same look of scepticism that Tess had given her when she attempted to accept the blame for what had happened between her and Edmund. 'I am certain Edmund knew precisely what he was doing.'

Amelie sighed.

Something seemed to catch Genna's eye and she rose to look out the window. 'Oh, no.'

'What is it?'

'What is he doing here?' Genna asked, but spoke to herself.

'Who?' Amelie asked.

'Lord Tinmore.'

Chapter Eight

Edmund opened the sealed note that had been delivered to him early the next morning.

An invitation.

To dine at the home of Lord and Lady Northdon, Amelie's parents.

He blew out a breath. What had precipitated this?

He supposed he owed them a visit to apprise them of the status of the special licence, although he would have told Amelie today when he saw her.

He would attend, of course, even though Amelie's was the only company he did not dread.

He'd send a message accepting the invitation and then go to his bank to arrange his repayment to Tinmore.

He wrote out his response and walked down to the hall to find a servant to arrange for its delivery.

'Another message arrived for you,' the man said.

Edmund opened it.

It was from Amelie, saying she would not be at

home if he planned to call. Instead she would be at the dressmakers with his sister Genna.

With Genna?

That evening Edmund started out early because waiting in his hotel room seemed a waste of time. He strolled down Bond Street, gazing in the shop windows and stopped in front of Trelegon & Co., Jewellers.

Why not?

He entered the shop.

'May I be of assistance, sir?' the clerk asked.

'I am in need of a gift,' Edmund said. 'And a wedding ring.'

He left the shop twenty minutes later, now late for the dinner on Grosvenor Street. At least the package in his pocket made the delay worth it.

He was admitted to the Northdon town house and announced by the butler, who had been attending the hall. He entered the drawing room, ready to make his apology for being late.

Instead he stopped in his tracks.

He'd not been told there would be guests.

Lord Tinmore, Lorene and Genna were there, seated with Lord and Lady Northdon, Glenville, Tess and Amelie.

'Well this is a surprise,' he said without enthusiasm. He turned his gaze on Amelie, who was the only one in the room who did not look as if a snake had just slithered into the gathering.

'How are you, Amelie?' he asked.

'I am well, Edmund.'

But she was paler than the last time he'd seen her, when they'd walked through Bullock's Egyptian Hall, gazing at the curiosities Captain Cook brought back from the South Seas and the displays of African beasts.

Lord Tinmore waved his hand as if ordering Edmund to approach him. 'I am certain you will agree that a family meeting was in order,'

Edmund stood his ground. 'I do not agree at all, but I see that is what has been manipulated.'

Tinmore was behind this. Lord Northdon would certainly not have desired a *family meeting*.

Amelie rose from her chair and walked over to a table with a wine decanter and glasses. 'Shall I pour you some claret?'

'Please,' he responded.

'What is the news of the special licence?' Lord Northdon demanded as if Edmund had wilfully withheld that information.

Edmund answered as civilly as he could muster. 'I checked at Doctors' Commons today, but there has been no word from my home parish as yet.'

'And you simply left it at that?' Tinmore sniffed.

'A gentleman must be a man of action if he is worth any salt at all.'

Amelie deserved to hear about the licence, and, Edmund supposed, her parents had a right to know, but it was none of Lord Tinmore's affair.

Edmund took a sip of his claret before facing Tinmore. 'I am not quite certain where to locate the insult in your words, sir. Are you accusing me of not being a gentleman? Or of not being a man of action? Or, perhaps, you merely wish to make the point that I am not worth my salt.'

'Impertinent puppy,' Lord Tinmore grumbled.

Edmund ignored him and spoke to Amelie as if only she were in the room. 'I hired a man to go to my old parish to see about the delay.'

A tense silence came over the room. Edmund did not care if his resentment of Tinmore was the cause. Except on Amelie's behalf. She did not deserve this *family meeting*.

Luckily the butler came to announce dinner.

Amelie expelled a relieved breath when Matheson announced dinner. How much ruder could these people be to Edmund? Her own family and his?

No one had even greeted him.

Her mother and Lord Tinmore led the procession to the dining room.

What a disagreeable man Lord Tinmore was. He

offered his arm to her mother without even looking at her. He'd not spoken more than two words to her. Her father escorted Lady Tinmore and Marc, Tess.

Edmund glanced at both Amelie and Genna and offered them each an arm. 'Ladies?'

As they walked to the dining room, Genna spoke to Edmund in a low voice. 'Don't antagonise Tinmore. Let him think he's ordering you around but then do whatever you like.'

'Is that what you do, Genna?' Edmund responded.

'Yes. It is,' she admitted.

Amelie disagreed. She'd thought it rather admirable that Edmund had stood up to such a formidable man.

In the dining room, her mother had deviated slightly from the standard tradition of seating everyone by precedence. She'd placed Lord Tinmore at her father's right and Lady Tinmore at his left. Unfortunately Amelie was seated on the other side of Lord Tinmore. Edmund sat across from her between Lady Tinmore and Tess. Genna and Marc were on the same side of the table as Amelie.

The deadly silence was broken by Lady Tinmore admiring the table setting. This led to a general discussion by the ladies of what was the latest fashion in dinner service.

When the soup was served, Lord Tinmore took a loud sip that seemed to echo though the room. He conversed with her father exclusively, except for an occasional remark to his wife. Edmund attended to his food and nothing else.

Amelie could not help looking at him. She could make the excuse that he was seated across from her, so she had little choice but to look at him, but to her he seemed the only important person in the room. Though he did not show any discomfort for it, she thought it shabby that he was not included in the conversation.

Of course, she was not talking either.

Genna finally turned to her. 'What did you think of Nancy's idea for a bride dress?'

The two young women had spent the morning with fashion prints and fabric swatches. Tess's former maid, now dressmaker, had taken over the design of the dress.

'It was lovely, but I fear it would take too much time,' Amelie replied.

'Did Madame LeClaire approve of the design?' Amelie's mother asked.

Madame LeClaire made all of Amelie's mother's gowns. In some ways she was the closest thing to a friend her mother possessed. They'd known each other as young girls in France.

'She was impressed,' Genna answered. 'Nancy is so very talented. She designed the dresses Lorene and I are wearing tonight.'

Marc asked questions about the apprenticeship agreement between Nancy and Madame LeClaire. More women were coming to Madame LeClaire's for Nancy's designs.

'Has the business grown?' he asked.

'Madame is thinking of expanding to the house next door. They've hired new seamstresses and they are running out of space,' Genna replied.

Lord Tinmore raised his voice. 'What is all this talk about dresses?'

Tess replied, 'Amelie and Genna visited Lady Northdon's modiste. We were discussing her business.'

Tinmore's brows rose, and his tone turned indignant. 'You were discussing *trade*?'

Amelie shot a glance to her mother, who had been the daughter of a tradesman, a linen draper, one of the trades that supplied dressmakers. Her mother's lips thinned, but she sat up straighter and lifted her chin. Amelie glanced to her father next. His eyes flashed with anger.

Lady Tinmore tried to smooth over the moment. 'Tess's maid recently became a partner to Lady Northdon's modiste.'

Tinmore swung back to his wife. 'Talking about servants? Not proper dinner conversation, my dear.'

The room fell silent as the tension banked.

Edmund took a sip of wine and set down his glass.

'Well, it is a family party,' he said, ever so casually. 'Why should the family not discuss what interests them? Besides, to ladies, dressmaking is not simply a trade; it is a collection of other people whose lives they care about. Servants. Dressmakers. Seamstresses.'

Amelie gaped at him. It struck her. *Struck her.* Like a lightning bolt from the sky, like an arrow piercing her heart.

Edmund was unlike any man she'd ever known. He was strong. And kind. And stepped up to whatever situation was placed before him.

No other man at the table confronted Lord Tinmore when he'd spoken so cruelly. Only Edmund. Edmund had defended all of the women at the table. Especially Amelie's mother. Tinmore's insult had been intended to hurt her, Amelie was convinced.

Her heart beat faster. It was hard to breathe. Even harder to look at him now.

But harder to look away.

Lord Tinmore sputtered. 'You dare to instruct the rest of us?'

Edmund looked from one sister to another and smiled. 'I come by my expertise honestly…by having grown up with three very excellent teachers!'

He was glorious!

Amelie glanced around the table. Did they not all think Edmund was magnificent? Their expressions looked strained.

Finally her brother spoke. 'Shall we drop this topic of conversation?'

Lady Tinmore turned to Amelie's mother. 'These potatoes are delicious. They are cooked with rosemary, are they not? You have such a fine cook.'

Amelie's mother was not so ready to pretend those words had not been spoken. She answered in a tight voice, 'Thank you.'

Amelie stared at Edmund, who had returned to his food. He glanced up and caught her looking at him but cast his gaze back to his plate.

Amelie's father quickly signalled for the final course, the dessert. At least dessert gave them all more food to discuss. Tinmore surveyed the room and then again confined his conversation to her father, as if secure that everyone else was conversing properly. Her father's response to Tinmore, though, had turned more dutiful than cordial.

When dessert was finished, Tinmore tapped his knife against his wine glass. The crystal rang like a bell. Everyone glanced at him in surprise.

What now? Amelie thought.

Tinmore raised his voice. 'Before the ladies retire

to the drawing room, we should discuss the wedding that has been foisted upon us.'

'No!' Edmund spoke slowly and emphatically. 'We will not discuss the wedding.'

Tinmore was undaunted. 'We must discuss how to limit the inevitable scandal. I want none of this shabby affair to reflect negatively on my wife.'

Lady Tinmore blanched. 'My lord!'

Amelie cleared her throat and made her voice strong. 'You have no right to call it a shabby affair!'

'Yes,' her father added in a milder, more tentative tone. 'We have the matter in hand. No need to discuss it.'

Tinmore leaned back. 'Well, as long as you give me your assurance that my wife's name will be kept out of the gossip...'

How could anyone assure him of what other people might do?

He nodded officiously. 'The ladies may retire, then.'

The others exchanged glances. Tinmore was a guest, not the host or hostess of this party. Amelie and the others looked to her father. All except Edmund.

Her father nodded.

The ladies rose to leave the room. As they were walking out the door, Amelie turned to see Edmund stand, as well.

'I must take my leave,' he said.

'You will do nothing of the sort!' Tinmore said.

Edmund glanced towards Amelie's father. 'I will call upon you tomorrow, sir, if that is agreeable.'

Her father nodded.

The dining room was across the hall from the drawing room, but the other ladies, who'd heard Edmund, hung about in the hall. Amelie stood just outside the dining room door.

Edmund walked out, one of the footmen behind him. The footman closed the dining-room door and waited to attend him.

Edmund spoke to him. 'Would you bring my hat and gloves, please?'

The footman bowed and went to do his bidding.

Lady Tinmore came up to Edmund. 'Why are you being so difficult?'

'Me, difficult? Your husband was insulting, rude and meddling, and I was not inclined to stand for it.' Edmund responded. 'Tinmore is nothing to me. I paid back his money. He has no say in what I do.'

What money? Amelie wondered.

He turned to her mother. 'I would like a few moments alone with Amelie, ma'am.'

Her mother nodded.

'We can go to the library,' Amelie said, her heart beating faster. She would be alone with him.

It was behind the drawing room and still had a lamp burning and a fire lit.

Edmund remained near the doorway. 'I should not remain very long.'

Amelie stood near him, near enough to inhale his scent, which had now become familiar to her. 'You wished to speak with me?' What she wanted to say was that he was magnificent! That she was so very grateful to him for defending her mother. That she was proud to be marrying such a man.

But she said none of that.

He reached into his pocket and pulled out a small velvet box. 'I've been remiss. You should have a gift. A betrothal gift. Forgive me for not thinking of it sooner.'

He handed her the box. She opened it and found a gold ring with a lovely sapphire surrounded by tiny pearls. Her hand shook. 'It is lovely, Edmund.'

He took the ring from the box and put it on her finger. 'Good. It fits. I was assured by the jeweller that it could be made the proper size if it did not.'

She lifted her eyes to his. 'Thank you.'

His gaze softened. 'I should leave. I will call upon your father tomorrow.'

'My father?' It seemed he'd been avoiding her father all week. Of course, she could not blame him. Her father was being impossibly churlish.

'Your father has a right to speak about the wedding with me.' His voice turned hard. 'Tinmore does not.'

Now. Now she could tell him how thrilled she'd been by his defiance of that detestable man.

'I will walk out with you,' she said instead.

When they reached the hall, the footman gave Edmund his things. Edmund turned to Amelie and took her hand. 'Goodnight,' he said, squeezing her fingers.

Before she could think of how to say goodbye to him, he'd walked out the door.

Edmund hurried away from Grosvenor Street and the unpleasantness he'd just endured. Curse Tinmore. And curse his father for losing his fortune and leaving his sisters in such a desperate condition. Lorene was correct. Edmund could not have helped them, not when he was still in the army, but now he could. He was determined to make his fortune by any means offered him.

Except he never, ever considered that he'd make his fortune by marrying a wealthy viscount's daughter.

He did not want Lord Northdon's money. He'd stand on his own. It was all he'd ever wanted. To make his way in the world, no matter his disreputable birth. He thought he'd achieve his fortune in

Brussels or some other part of the world, but he could manage it in London.

He made his way to Covent Garden, a place he felt more at home than Mayfair. He found his way to Rose Street and walked in to the Coopers Arms tavern.

The Coopers Arms was dark, crowded and noisy, filled with workmen, clerks, soldiers in uniform and the occasional gentleman. Plenty of brightly dressed women adorned the place, no doubt women of the town hoping to lure a man above the stairs. The clinking of glass, the smell of hops and gin and sweat enveloped him as he made his way through the room, looking for a table where he could drink in private.

'Summerfield!' A red-coated officer called his name.

Edmund looked closer. 'Upton?' Upton had served with him at Waterloo. In fact, it had been Upton who'd told him Tess had been in Brussels.

'Come! Sit with me!' Upton was at a small table alone.

Edmund joined him. 'What the devil are you doing in London? Is not the regiment still in Paris?'

Upton signalled the tavern maid to come to the table. 'They are. I had to come home.'

The maid approached. Upton lifted his tankard. 'More ale.' He turned to Edmund. 'You?'

'Ale,' he told the woman.

Upton continued. 'M'father died.'

'I am sorry to hear it,' Edmund said.

Upton sounded as if he'd had plenty of ale already. 'M'brother is such a loose screw, m'mother wants me to stay. Must sell out. Do not want to.' He peered at Edmund. 'Where is your uniform?'

'I sold out.' Edmund said. 'Without the war, the army offers no opportunities.'

'You sold out?'

'I did.'

'I'll be damned.' Upton waved a finger, which finally pointed to Edmund's leg. 'How's the injury?'

'Healed.'

'Good.' Upton drained his tankard.

Edmund had been drinking with Upton and others that last night in Brussels. Perhaps he'd consumed too much ale that night. What if he hadn't...?

The maid brought the ale, and Edmund drank thirstily. It tasted better than the wine at Lord Northdon's dinner.

Upton raised his tankard. 'Here's to the 28th!'

Edmund tapped his tankard against Upton's. 'To the 28th.'

'What'll you do now?' Upton asked. 'Now that our days of glory are at an end?'

Edmund leaned closer to his friend. 'I'm going to be married.'

'Married?' Upton's voice rose. 'Noooo. Not you. What of all that talk about seeking your fortune?'

Edmund stared into his drink. 'I'll still find my fortune.'

'I thought you would stay in the army or go to India or something,' Upton said.

Edmund shrugged and took another sip.

'Who are you marrying, then?' Upton asked.

There was no reason not to say. 'Miss Glenville, Lord Northdon's daughter.'

'Northdon?' Upton's brow creased in thought. 'Oh, I know Northdon. Married to the Jacobin commoner.'

It was an unkind way to refer to Lady Northdon.

'Met his son in Brussels.' Upton's eyes widened, as though something had struck his mind. 'Hey. Your sister is married to him. Told you about her. Where she was.' He poured a great deal of the contents of his tankard into his mouth, then gaped at Edmund. 'Do not say you are marrying that beauty! That golden-haired angel?'

'Miss Glenville. Yes.' He did not know what else to say about her.

'I'll be damned. That beauty?' Upton shook his head. 'I'll wager she has money, too. Big dowry. How the devil did you manage that?'

Yes, he should be thought lucky. Beauty and

wealth were to be desired in a wife, were they not? But what about Amelie?

He certainly was nothing a woman desired in a husband.

The next morning, before calling upon Lord Northdon, the man Edmund hired to travel to his home parish found him at his hotel.

The man handed him a packet. 'Here it is.'

Edmund was stunned. 'You've only had two days.'

'I was lucky with the mail coaches,' the man said.

Lucky? He must have spent most of the two days in coaches.

He pointed to the packet. 'It is all there, the vicar said. He also sent his best wishes.'

The vicar at Yardney had always been kind to him. In a pitying manner.

Edmund lifted his hand. 'Wait a moment.' He went into the bedchamber and came out with an extra guinea. He placed it in the man's palm. 'You did well. I am grateful.'

The man grinned. 'Thank you, sir. If you ever need another service—'

'I will seek you out,' Edmund said. 'And I will recommend you.'

After the man left, Edmund brought the packet directly to Doctors' Commons and the office of the

Archbishop. He handed it to the clerk, who pursed his lips as he unsealed it.

'That is the information you require, is it not?' Edmund demanded.

The man lifted his chin so that he looked at Edmund through spectacles worn low on his nose. 'It appears to be so.'

'The Archbishop is here today, is he not?'

'He is,' the clerk admitted.

Edmund folded his arms across his chest. 'Then I will wait here until you hand me the special licence.'

Not an hour went by before the clerk placed the required document in Edmund's hands.

Edmund walked from the Archbishop's office to Grosvenor Street to call upon Amelie's father. He was escorted to the library, where Lord Northdon and his son appeared to be waiting for him with their typical expressions of displeasure.

'Good morning.' Edmund bowed.

He'd be polite even if they would not.

Lord Northdon nodded to him. 'First let me tell you that I found Lord Tinmore's manners most offensive last evening.'

That might have been the most civil statement Amelie's father had ever spoken to him.

He went on. 'Had I known he would act in such

a reprehensible way, I would not have agreed to the dinner.'

'Had I known Tinmore had engineered the encounter, I would have declined your invitation,' Edmund said. 'Even at the risk of offending you, sir.'

Glenville spoke up. 'I have no fondness for the man.'

'Yes, he is most unpleasant,' Lord Northdon agreed. 'But I must work with him in Lords, so I must watch my tongue.'

'I have no such restraints.' Edmund paused a moment before continuing. 'But be clear about this. Tinmore is no relation of mine. He is married to my sister, but that does not make him my relation.' Edmund would change that if he could. 'Tinmore has no part—no say—in my marriage to Amelie or in anything I do.'

He thought Glenville gave him an approving look. It was fleeting, however.

'That is another thing.' Lord Northdon went on without any apparent acknowledgement of Edmund's words. 'Why is the special licence taking so long? I think we might all agree that the sooner you marry the better.' Northdon glanced away. 'Not that I wish for this marriage. Tinmore suggested we send Amelie away for a year and foster the child out to someone, but she would not hear of it.'

Tinmore thought he could decide what was to be done with the baby? That was the outside of enough.

Edmund glared at Lord Northdon. 'The baby is mine and will have my name.'

'Well, that is what Amelie wishes, so it must be.' Lord Northdon sighed.

'It is for the best that Amelie and Edmund marry, Papa,' Glenville said. 'You know that.'

Support from Amelie's brother?

'Enough discussion.' Edmund pulled the paper from his pocket. 'I have the licence. The wedding can take place today, if a clergyman can be found to perform it.'

'We know someone who might officiate.' Glenville looked relieved. 'The clergyman who married Tess and me.'

Edmund nodded. 'I want the wedding to be as Amelie wishes.'

'It will be,' Glenville said. 'I will make certain you are informed of all the details.'

'There should be nothing required of you except to show up,' Northdon said, his tone dismissive.

'What of the marriage-settlement papers, sir?' Edmund asked.

Northdon's face turned red with anger. 'Yes. I comprehend you would be very interested in the marriage settlement.'

'I am,' Edmund said, trying not to display his own anger. 'I want them drawn up so Amelie retains control of her dowry, not I.'

Northdon's mouth opened in surprise. 'What?'

'I can support Amelie and our child,' Edmund said. 'I know what people will say of my marrying her, but I want you to know I am not marrying her for her money. I want Amelie to know that, as well.'

'I do not believe you,' Northdon said.

'Have the papers drawn up the way I wish, and I will sign them.'

There was nothing more to say. Edmund turned and strode from the room.

Chapter Nine

Two days later, Amelie woke feeling sicker than ever. She thought the morning sickness was easing, but it seemed to have returned threefold. And on her wedding day, as well. At least beginning her day by vomiting saved her from any fanciful illusions. She was marrying for one reason only. She was pregnant and there was no other choice.

Amelie had once had romantic dreams of a wedding day. Not grand romantic dreams. She'd never expected anything more than the small family wedding Marc and Tess had, but she'd dreamed about the beauty of the words spoken in the ceremony. She'd dreamed about happiness, her family's happiness about her marriage, the happiness she would feel in her heart and see in the eyes of her groom.

Instead, her family acted as if this were her funeral, and she could not even keep toast and tea in her stomach.

What would she see in Edmund's eyes? She feared that would be the worst of all.

Sally was little help in the preparations. Amelie worried about her, but Sally evaded her concern.

Nancy, Tess's former maid, now dressmaker, came to help with the gown and Amelie's hair.

'I am so sorry we could not complete the gown we planned,' Nancy said.

'It does not matter,' Amelie said.

This dress was one Nancy altered from a very plain pale blue silk Amelie had in her wardrobe. Nancy had quickly embellished the gown with an overdress of white net and with white lace at the sleeves and the hem.

'I am pleased with this dress,' Amelie told her.

At least the dress was light as air, making it easy for her to move. This day also saw a return of her fatigue. Moving was an effort, when all her body wished to do was sleep.

There was a knock on the door and Tess entered. 'How are you faring?'

Tess tried to be cheerful, but her eyes looked strained. Tess blamed herself for Amelie's situation, because Tess had introduced her brother to her. Amelie could not convince Tess that the real blame was solely Amelie's.

She could not convince anyone of that. Except herself.

'We are doing splendidly,' Nancy answered in seeming good cheer, although how she could miss the morose mood in the house was beyond Amelie.

A moment later, Amelie's mother walked in. 'All is in order downstairs,' she reported, although Amelie had not given those preparations a thought.

'Is my brother here yet?' Tess asked worriedly.

'Not yet.' Her mother pressed her lips together.

Amelie stared down at her sapphire ring. The blue gem caught sunlight from the window and glowed with blue light.

Edmund would come, she knew. Edmund was honourable that way.

Edmund made his way up Bond Street, as busy as usual with people entering and leaving shops, hurrying to appointments or simply sauntering leisurely on the pavement. This was no ordinary day for him, though, his wedding day.

This would be the day he and Amelie would forge their own life together separate from her parents, her brother and his sisters.

A family of his own.

He'd endure the Northdons' animosity towards him for a family of his own. He'd even put up with his sisters' disappointment in him. He and Amelie—and the baby—had a chance for happiness.

He arrived at the Northdon town house and was

admitted by the footman he now could address by name. 'Good morning, Staines.'

'Good morning, sir,' Staines replied, his expression neutral.

What did Staines know about him? Edmund wondered. Surely the servants knew that Amelie's family was not happy about this marriage. He'd bet they knew all about his birth. For Amelie's sake, he hoped they did not know about her pregnancy. He hoped she'd be spared that scandal.

Tess walked down the stairs as he entered the hall.

'There you are!' Her face was pinched. 'I was beginning to worry.'

He was still in her black books, obviously. 'Did you think I would not show up?'

She gave him a frank look. 'I wondered.'

There was another knock on the door.

'Am I late?' It was Genna. 'I rushed all the way here.'

Edmund had not expected her. 'You were invited, then?'

Genna grinned. 'I would have come even if I had not been invited.'

Edmund kissed her on the cheek.

'Do not worry.' Genna handed her shawl and gloves to Staines. 'Lord Tinmore will not attend. That means Lorene won't come, though.'

'I am sorry about Lorene. Not about Tinmore.' Lord Tinmore was the last person he wished to witness his marriage.

Tess crossed the hall and gave her sister a hug. 'How pretty you look.'

Genna opened her arms and displayed her dress. 'It is one of Nancy's designs.'

'Come,' Tess said. 'We should go to the drawing room.'

Edmund was glad to walk into that room with his sisters. They might still be angry at him, but they supported him.

As they crossed the threshold, Tess called out, 'Edmund is here.'

The room had been rearranged for the ceremony, furniture moved out of the way to provide a sort of aisle leading to where the clergyman stood and where, presumably, he was to stand. Glenville and Lord Northdon were conversing with the clergyman.

Glenville approached Edmund and extended his hand. 'Good morning, Edmund.'

At least Glenville was being cordial.

Edmund accepted the handshake. 'Glenville.'

Glenville turned to Genna. 'Good to see you, Genna.'

She returned a wan smile. 'I would not wish to be anywhere else.'

He glanced back at the clergyman. 'I'll introduce you, Edmund.'

Glenville presented him to Reverend Cane. 'Reverend Cane performed the ceremony for Tess and me.'

'And I am happy to be here again.' Reverend Cane smiled. He had a kind face and looked Edmund directly in the eye.

'Thank you for being available.' Edmund glanced at Lord Northdon, who stood next to the reverend. 'Good morning, sir,'

'Morning.' Northdon looked at Edmund as if he were the wolf at the sheep's door.

Edmund wished he could convince Northdon he intended to be a good husband to Amelie. He hoped she would not regret marrying him.

Lady Northdon entered the room. Her worried look disappeared when she caught sight of Edmund, but she certainly did not break into a smile. 'Good. You are here. Amelie is ready.' She turned to Tess. '*Chérie*, would you tell Staines to ask the servants to come in and let Amelie know we may proceed?'

'Of course.' Tess hurried out of the room.

Lady Northdon greeted Genna and chatted with her.

A few minutes later the servants filed in and stood against the walls. It seemed to Edmund that no one expected a joyous occasion.

And then the door opened and Amelie appeared.

Edmund was reminded of that night in Brussels when she had appeared ethereal, an angel in the midst of chaos. She was even more beautiful today, with a gown that seemed to shimmer around her. Her hair was loosely dressed with a crown of fresh flowers. She resembled a mythical woodland creature.

Even better, she walked tall, head held high.

Well done, Amelie, he thought.

Where were the flowers?

When the door to the drawing room opened, Amelie saw how few there were. Her mother had filled the room with flowers when Marc and Tess were married. Today there were but two big vases on two of the tables.

The gloomy mood of the room threatened to suffocate her. She took a deep breath and looked up.

Edmund gazed at her, not with the frown visible on the faces of her family and his sisters, not with the carefully neutral expressions of the servants, but with an admiring gleam.

It was enough.

She straightened her spine and walked towards him, keeping her eyes on only him.

When she came to stand beside him, he reached over and took her hand. His skin was warm and comforting, and she knew then that she was not alone. She did not know what their future held, but at this moment they were together.

Reverend Cane smiled at her and looked from her to Edmund and back again. 'Ready?' he mouthed.

She and Edmund nodded.

'Dearly beloved,' he began. 'We are gathered together here in the sight of God, and in the face of this congregation, to join together this Man and this Woman in holy Matrimony….'

That one reckless act now bound them together. That and the baby growing inside her, the baby created that night. With Edmund's hand holding hers, though, she could not regret any of it.

Reverend Cane continued. He spoke the words as if it were only Amelie and Edmund in the room, as if the words had been created just for them and not over decades and decades of nuptials.

He turned to Edmund. 'Wilt thou have this Woman to thy wedded Wife, to live together after God's ordinance in the holy estate of Matrimony? Wilt thou love her, comfort her, honour and keep her in sickness and in health; and, forsaking all other, keep thee only unto her, so long as ye both shall live?'

Edmund looked into Amelie's eyes. 'I will.'

Of course he would say yes. He was honourable and kind.

The reverend directed his gaze at Amelie. It would be her turn to decide.

'Wilt thou have this Man to thy wedded Husband, to live together after God's ordinance in the holy estate of Matrimony? Wilt thou obey him and serve him, love, honour and keep him in sickness and in health; and, forsaking all other, keep thee only unto him, so long as ye both shall live?'

She answered, 'I will.'

A wave of nausea swept over her, and she lost the words that Edmund repeated when making his vows. She heard nothing past, 'I, Edward, take thee, Amelie...'

She fought through the sensation, knowing her vows came next, and she was able to repeat them in a clear but trembling voice.

When she had finished, Edmund reached into his pocket and handed the reverend a ring. Reverend Cane gave it back to him, having him say, 'With this ring I thee wed, and with all my worldly goods I thee endow...'

Edmund placed the ring on her finger. It was a gold band with a circle of blue sapphires all around it. She glanced up at him. It was beautiful. Something special. A worldly good that he'd taken some trouble to purchase for her.

Reverend Cane said more prayers and then placed

their right hands together. 'Those that God hath joined together, let no man put asunder.'

At the end, the clergyman lowered his voice and spoke with more intensity. 'I pronounce that they be Man and Wife together.'

He finished with the blessing in the same manner, as if he were instructing them that they would be able to manage a marriage together.

And then it was over.

She was married. Her reputation would be rescued. With any luck, no one would guess that the baby was conceived before this date.

She glanced up at Edmund. He took her hand again and smiled at her.

After the ceremony, there was cake and punch for the servants, just as there had been at Marc and Tess's wedding. There were congratulations from servants Amelie had known her entire life. She introduced the servants to Edmund. He spoke to each one of them in a personal way, not annoyed like some people become when they must interact with their inferiors. Another thing about him that pleased her. Many of these people were very dear to her.

Still, there was a restraint that had not been in this room when the previous wedding took place. The servants, no doubt, had caught the mood from her parents.

Her maid, Sally, was the last to come shake her hand. 'Best wishes, miss.' Sally almost choked on the words, and her eyes filled with tears.

'Thank you, Sally.' Amelie almost burst into tears herself, although she did not know why either of them should be weeping. 'Allow me to present you to my husband, Mr Summerfield.'

Sally looked at him quizzically. 'How do, sir.' She curtsied.

Did she remember him from Brussels?

Edmund offered Sally his hand to shake. 'You've made Miss Glenville look very beautiful today.'

He thought her beautiful? Amelie turned warm inside.

'Wasn't me, sir. T'was Nancy.' Sally walked away.

'You met Nancy,' Amelie reminded him. 'She made my gown. She used to be Tess's maid.'

'I remember,' he said, standing very close to her. He smiled. 'But I forgot to call you Mrs Summerfield.'

She felt her face flush at his nearness. 'I forgot, too.'

The servants left the room and returned to their duties. Marc, Tess and Genna walked up to them.

'It was a lovely ceremony,' Tess said. Surely Tess noticed that there had only been a perfunctory attempt at making the room look like a celebration.

'Let me see your ring,' Genna asked.

Amelie lifted her hand, and the sapphires glittered on her finger.

'I've never seen such a wedding band!' Genna exclaimed. 'Well done, Edmund. Did Tess help you pick it out?'

'Not at all.' Tess gazed at the ring and then at Edmund. 'It matches the other ring you gave her.'

Genna asked to see the other ring, which Amelie wore on the other hand. 'I didn't know you gave Amelie a ring.'

'It was a betrothal present,' Amelie said.

Marc sidled over to Amelie and kissed her on the cheek. 'You make a beautiful bride.'

'Maman has said nothing.' She spoke so only he could hear. 'You know how she scrutinises what everyone is wearing. I think she might have preferred I dress in black bombazine.'

'She wished for something very different for you,' he said.

She lifted her chin. 'I think Edmund has done all that is admirable.'

'Not all.' Marc frowned, and she knew he referred to their encounter in Brussels. 'But I own he has behaved well since.'

Their butler announced that the breakfast was served, and they all went to the dining room. Much effort was made for all to appear as it should be— happy—but Amelie assumed that was for the benefit of Reverend Cane. When it came time for the reverend to leave, Genna said she would go as well and the goodbyes were said in the hall.

Genna gave Amelie a brief hug. 'I am happy to have another sister,' she said. She presented her cheek for Edmund to kiss. 'Behave yourself, Edmund, or answer to me.'

If Edmund resented this, he gave no indication. He kissed her cheek and said, 'You have nothing to fear, Genna.'

Reverend Cane came up to Amelie and Edmund and took both their hands in his. 'I wish you both joy.' He leaned towards them with a conspiratorial air. 'And, remember, joy is something you make yourselves. I've no doubt the two of you are very capable of it.'

When the guests had left, Edmund turned to Amelie. 'There has been no discussion of where this wedding night should take place.'

Amelie had certainly not thought that far. Apparently her family had not seen fit to discuss the matter with Edmund either.

Amelie's parents and Tess and Marc stared at him as if surprised he was still there.

He seemed to ignore them. 'I have a choice for you,' he said to Amelie. 'We may stay here, if that was your and your parents' intention. I have also engaged a hotel room at the Clarendon Hotel for us and one for your maid, if you would like her to come.'

'Of course you may stay here, Summerfield,' her father snapped. 'Where else would you stay?'

Her mother looked distressed. 'We assumed you would stay with us.'

Amelie was out of patience with them. They'd barely been civil to Edmund and they'd treated this occasion as if it were her funeral instead of her wedding.

'I choose the hotel,' she said.

Amelie hurried up to her bedchamber to find Sally and have her pack a bag.

'You may also come to the hotel, Sally,' she told the girl. 'Mr Summerfield has procured a room for you, as well. Would you like to come?'

'If you wish it,' she said without enthusiasm, as she folded a nightdress and a dress to wear the next day.

'It will be a little adventure for you.' Amelie tried to cheer her up. 'Or, at least, a nice respite alone.' Amelie was less sure of what the night would mean to her.

Her mother knocked on her door and entered the room. 'How *stupide* of us not to plan for this night.'

She and Amelie's father had barely planned for

the wedding ceremony, but Amelie did not say that. 'It is of no consequence, Maman.'

'We have so little room,' her mother went on. 'There is only a small bedchamber on the floor with Marc and Tess's rooms. That is not ideal.'

Maybe Edmund would stay in her room. 'I will explain the situation to him, Maman.'

Her mother sighed. 'Perhaps you should come to the country with your father and me. Your papa needs to return to the estate.'

'We shall see, Maman.' She did not have the heart to tell her mother they would stay in London.

Amelie sat at her dressing table and unpinned the garland of flowers she wore in her hair. The blooms were drooping, but she was trying not to let her spirits droop, as well. Her mother's unhappiness and Sally's glumness threatened her own mood.

After packing her bag, Sally helped her change out of her wedding dress.

'You've become so thin,' her mother said when she was only in her corset and shift.

'I've had the nausea, you know,' Amelie said.

Her mother inclined her head to Sally, a warning not to speak aloud about the scandalous family secret.

'I am better now,' she said, although that morning had been one of her worst.

Sally helped her into a blue sprigged-muslin day dress while her mother watched.

Her mother went into her wardrobe and chose a shawl and bonnet. 'These will look *très jolie* with that dress.'

Once dressed, Amelie sent Sally to pack her own bag. She was alone with her mother. 'Do not worry about me, Maman. I will be safe for one night in a hotel.'

Her mother glanced away. 'You were not safe from him in the hotel in Brussels.'

'He did not attack me, Maman,' Amelie said. 'And he has done all that was right about it since. Edmund has not hesitated. Not once.'

Her mother nodded. 'I was so certain you would marry that nice young man, Captain Fowler.'

She shuddered. No matter what, she was glad she had not married Fowler. 'That does not bear thinking of.'

Her mother crossed the room and put an arm around her. 'I only wanted your happiness, *ma fille*. I believed you would make the respectable marriage. Not like your father and me.'

Amelie turned and embraced her mother. 'Papa was always lucky to have married you, Maman.'

'We did not always feel it to be so,' her mother admitted.

For most of Amelie's life, her parents had quarrelled or had simply not spoken to each other, but they'd reconciled in Brussels, their love coming together as hers fell apart.

Amelie put on a brave smile. 'Perhaps some day we will say I was lucky to have married Edmund.'

Her mother's expression turned sceptical.

Chapter Ten

Edmund and Amelie did not speak much in the coach he'd arranged to carry them to the hotel. Amelie's maid rode with them, but that was not the only reason, Edmund suspected. Did either of them know what to say to each other? He certainly did not know what to say to her.

Instead he spoke to the maid. 'You will have a dinner prepared by a French chef, Sally. You will like that.'

'Yes, sir,' she said without enthusiasm.

He glanced at Amelie, who raised her brows and shook her head.

Edmund held Amelie's gaze. 'We will have the dinner in our room.'

She seemed to force a smile. 'That will be pleasant.'

Deuce take it. Now he had two women he could not please, not even with French cooks and fine hotels.

He glanced out the carriage window and wondered how it would be to escape. Jump out and run down the road. He could probably manage to be back in Brussels within days and from there could easily disappear.

He glanced back at Amelie. Abandon her? Abandon his family? He would never do that.

Although he worried about how it would be for her if her family and his continued their resentment and anger at him. How could they not? He remained cognisant of what she would be required to give up for him. They would be even more on the fringes of society than her family had been. In fact, they would be completely outside of it. Their child would have his name but would never belong in the world her family planned for her.

The carriage drew up to the hotel's entrance, and soon they were settled into their room. Sally unpacked Amelie's bag and left for her own room.

Edmund arranged for refreshment so they had something to converse about. Was the wine to her liking? Did she enjoy the cheese and blackberry tarts?

She dutifully nibbled at the food and agreed that the wine was perfect and the cheese and tarts the best she'd ever tasted.

Edmund was exploding inside. They could not go on like this. There had been more ease between them in Brussels when they did not know each other at all.

He faced her from across a small table in the sitting room adjacent to the bedchamber. 'We should speak plainly to each other, Amelie.'

She looked up at him uncertainly. 'Speak plainly? About…?'

'About how we are to go about,' he said. 'About how we are going to manage.'

She met his gaze. 'I do not know how to answer you.'

His frustration grew. 'Well, for one thing, where will we live until we find rooms to let?'

She glanced away. 'Am I foolish for admitting that I have not thought of this? I could only think of marrying as quickly as we could.'

'Let us talk about this now,' he persisted.

She shrugged. 'I suppose we could stay with my parents. I am certain they will return to Northdon House soon, and then there will be more room.'

In his mind's eye he saw the caged lion in the King's menagerie at the Tower, pacing back and forth behind bars, its eyes flashing. That's how it would feel if he were forced to stay in the same house with her father even for a few days.

His feelings must have shown on his face, because she glanced away. 'I realise it would be difficult for you to stay with my parents, though.'

He set his jaw. 'It would not be for long.'

She reached across the table and touched his hand. 'What alternative is there?'

Her touch aroused him. What was he to do with that sensation? What was he to do about the physical side of marriage? Would she wish to make love? After all, making love had created this undesired situation for her. At the moment she was grateful to him, but how long would it be before she resented him as much as her parents did?

He pulled his hand away. 'This hotel?' Why even speak it?

She stared at her hand before wrapping her arms across her chest. 'If you wish it,' she said stiffly.

'Just say what you want!'

She flinched and looked wounded.

'I spoke too sharply. Forgive me.' He instantly softened his tone. 'I want you to be honest with me. Do you wish to stay in your parents' town house or do you wish to stay in the hotel?'

Amelie met his gaze. 'You would prefer the hotel, would you not? My parents treat you so shabbily.'

'I am quite used to shabby treatment, Amelie,' he said. 'I asked what you want.'

She averted her face. 'I want to please you, Edmund. I realise you are merely being kind. We may stay in the hotel.'

'I am not merely being kind,' he responded. 'Your needs are more important than mine.'

'Why? Was not marrying me the ultimate kindness, Edmund? Even though I have trapped you—'

He shook his head. 'Do not keep saying you trapped me.'

She was feeling obstinate. 'It is true, though.'

'I made a choice,' he said. 'You chose marriage, as well.'

But it was a choice he could not have wanted. He'd made it because of the baby, and she'd accepted for the same reason—that and it prevented more scandal befalling her family. Why could he not simply acknowledge the truth—that she was responsible?

She stood and paced in front of him. 'I wish we were visiting the Tower or a museum. It was easier to talk, then.'

He looked uncertain. 'We could visit the Tower if you wish.'

'No!' she cried. 'I do not want to visit the Tower.'

'What do you want, Amelie?' he persisted. 'I am waiting for you to tell me.'

She took a breath.

Could she dare tell him?

She mustered her courage. 'I—I want a marriage like Marc and Tess's. And my parents'. I know I cannot have that, because you do not love me. How could you? But maybe if we came to know each other better, we—maybe we would like each other.'

His mouth slowly stretched into a smile. 'I already like you, Amelie.'

Her face flushed and she stopped pacing. 'But you do not know me, not after a few outings and—and—' And one scandalous night.

His eyes shone with humour. 'Are you saying you have some dark secret? If so, this might be the time to tell me.'

She liked that he was teasing her. It reminded her of Brussels when he had cajoled her into confiding in him.

Brussels.

Did he not remember? Brussels had revealed her dark secret, the one he alone knew. Did he know she possessed it still?

Ever since their hands touched, thoughts of that night, of lovemaking, were rushing through her brain. If he knew how easily wanton thoughts possessed her, would he rise from his chair and stride out the door? Would he abandon her as she'd been abandoned on the streets of Brussels?

She stopped herself.

It had not been Edmund who'd abandoned her. Edmund rescued her. He stayed by her side. He made love to her.

She sat again and finished her glass of wine.

He poured her another. 'So is there a dark secret?'

If he wanted honesty, she would dare to give it to him. 'I want a marriage where we—we share the same bed.'

His eyes darkened. 'That is the secret?'

Her heart beat faster. 'Does it offend you?'

His features softened. 'Offend me?' He took her hand in his. 'I would very much enjoy sharing your bed, Amelie. I remember Brussels with great delight.'

Her skin tingled. 'You—you do not think me wicked to say that I *want* it?'

His hand tightened around hers. 'Not wicked. What we did in Brussels was not wicked. It was wrong. Wrong because we did not consider the consequences.'

She lowered her lashes. 'I considered the consequences, but I thought a woman could not get with child the first time.'

He scowled. 'Who told you that?'

Her face grew hot. 'I overheard the maids talking.'

His brows lifted. 'They were wrong.'

She laughed. 'I have since surmised that.' Her mood quickly sobered. 'I should have known better.'

He glanced away. 'I knew better. I knew the risks and I ignored them.'

She tightened her fingers around his hand. 'Hush, Edmund. No one else will listen to me, but you and I must agree that I was responsible. I was the one who wanted the lovemaking.'

He stroked her hand again. 'I wanted it, too.'

The sensations inside her grew, like a wild vine winding into every part of her.

'I want it now.' She looked at him expectantly. 'Do you?'

'Of course I do.' His brow furrowed. 'If it is safe for you and the baby.'

'It is safe.' She spoke with surety, but she really had no idea if it was safe. She merely knew she wanted it to be.

He released her hand and poured more wine for each of them. She drank hers quickly, handing her glass to him for more. He poured again, but already her head began to swim and a languor came over her limbs. At least the nausea had stopped. It had eased after she'd spoken her wedding vows.

The hands of the clock on the mantel were nearing six o'clock. A long time before bedtime. 'When must we eat dinner?'

'Eight o'clock. It will be brought up to us.'

Two hours.

'Can one make love in the afternoon?' She blinked. 'Or is that too wanton?'

He grinned. 'It is our wedding day, Amelie. Let

us be as wanton as we like. Shall I call your maid for you?'

She recoiled in horror. 'No! No. I can manage without her.' Otherwise Sally would guess precisely what she would be doing. Perhaps Edmund would not censure her profligate nature, but her maid might.

'Very well.' He rose from his chair and came to her side. 'We have managed before, have we not?' He extended his hand.

She took his hand and let him help her stand. The edges of her vision blurred, softening the reds, blues and greens in the room into a pleasant sort of rainbow. He led her to the bedchamber, and her legs gave the illusion of floating. Once inside the room he closed the door, and the space immediately became more intimate. She turned her back to him and waited while he unlaced her dress. She pulled off her sleeves, and the garment slipped to the floor. He unlaced her corset, and she stepped out of both pieces of clothing and turned to Edmund dressed only in her shift.

He gazed at her as he kicked off his shoes, removed his coat and unbuttoned his waistcoat. She reached up and started pulling pins from her hair, combing it with her fingers until it fell upon her shoulders.

His gaze had feasted on her nakedness in Brussels, and she flushed with anticipation at seeing the admiration in his eyes again. She removed her stockings and her shift and stood before him. His gaze swept over her before capturing her own. He, dressed now only in his shirt and trousers, stepped closer to her, put his hand behind her head and drew her into a kiss.

His mouth was warm and sent flames darting through her. A moan came from the back of her throat. She wrapped her arms around his neck and pressed herself against him as their lips parted and his moist tongue, tasting of wine, touched hers.

She longed to feel his skin against hers. Still kissing him, she reached down and unbuttoned the fall of his trousers. A sharp shard of need pierced her. She felt his arousal and her need intensified.

She'd yearned for a repeat of the delights of his lovemaking in Brussels, but what she was feeling now, merely at the beginning, was unexpectedly intense. She needed him inside her so the intensity could be appeased.

She reached under his shirt and moved her hands over his firm chest. Her fingers felt the scars she'd glimpsed before. He pulled off his shirt and backed away from her to remove his trousers and stockings. She forced herself to wait for him to make the next move, although her need screamed for him to hurry. His naked body, illuminated by the waning sun shining through the window curtains, seemed beautiful to her, even though scarred. On his leg one long jagged scar remained pink.

His Waterloo injury. She'd forgotten he'd been injured. He seemed so vital. So strong. She knelt and traced her finger down the long jagged scar. She glanced up at him, wanting to say something—to tell him she was sorry he'd had to suffer it, to say how glad she was he'd not lost his leg—but that seemed a selfish thought.

He seized her hand and pulled her up. 'It is an ugly scar, but the wound is healed.'

Surely it would not be so pink if it had completely healed. Did it still pain him?

'My scars repulse you.' Pain flickered through his eyes.

'No!' She threw her arms around him. 'No. Do not think it.' She wanted to recapture that moment of closeness between them. 'I merely wondered how it happened.'

'I will tell you.' He reached for her. 'But not now.'

His touch ignited her need. 'After?'

'Perhaps.' He lifted her in his arms as if she were a mere feather and carried her to the bed. The bedcovers had already been folded back for sleeping.

Or for making love.

She lay on her back and eagerly awaited him

rising over her. His legs straddled hers, and he leaned down to kiss her once more. She put her arms around him and arched her back to him as his hand caressed her breasts and made need shoot through her like a sabre thrust. She could not wait. She opened her legs and tried to press him to her. He groaned and gently pushed himself inside her.

Her need would have been happier if he'd thrust himself inside her, but she tried to hold back her sense of urgency and follow his lead. He stroked slowly, carefully, but she was beyond care. She wanted him to rush her to her climax, to the release she knew she would feel.

But he set a slow, easy pace, and she writhed in passion beneath him, until, more suddenly than she expected, her release came in wave after wave of pleasure, pleasure so acute it was almost painful.

His thrusts accelerated and soon he, too, reached his climax, spilling his seed inside her, the seed that had created a child that night in Brussels.

He relaxed next to her and held her close, as he had in Brussels. The familiarity of it was a comfort. Would it always feel so comfortable? Would they be able to make a marriage out of this?

She hoped so.

'That was lovely, Edmund,' she murmured as she snuggled next to him. 'Might we do that again?'

* * *

Edmund gladly complied with her request to make love a second time. They could build on this pleasure they gave each other, this physical connection that now bound them with the baby inside her. He might never deserve her, but perhaps he could make her happy. He would certainly try.

He entered her intent on again giving her delight, of showing her that all would be well. They would make a good life together.

Need, not rational thought, drove him. Her desire pushed him harder. This coupling was not gentle, not worshipful, but rough and wild and dictated by a carnality neither one of them seemed able to control.

She cried out in her release, and a moment later he groaned with the spilling of his seed. They shuddered together, suspended in time and in the moment. No thought, no censure, no self-blame. Only pleasure in each other.

Afterwards they did not speak. He held her against him and felt truly calm for the first time since seeing her in London. He sensed her ease as well. He simply relished the comfort of her next to him and let time float by. There was hope for them, for the family they were creating.

The clock struck eight.

Blast. 'They will be delivering dinner soon.' He rose on one elbow. 'I must dress. You stay here if you like.'

She sat. 'I will get up.'

He donned his shirt and trousers in time for the knock on the door. He closed the bedchamber door and walked out to their sitting room. Opening the door, he instructed the two servants to place the trays on the table.

'Wait a moment.' He went to the writing table and jotted a quick note to Amelie's maid that they would not need her until morning. He folded it and handed it to one of the men. 'Would you deliver this to the maid's room two doors down?'

'Very good, sir.' The servant bowed.

Edmund tipped them both and closed the door behind them.

Amelie stood in the bedchamber doorway, covered by a silk wrapper. 'I am famished.'

They shared a leisurely dinner, talking together. He told her about growing up with Tess and his sisters, how they escaped from their governess's lessons and explored the far reaches of their father's property, about swimming in the cool pool formed by the stream that ran through the property, climbing trees in the woods, racing each other to the folly.

She shared a lonelier childhood but said the only person lonelier had been her mother, with whom she had spent many hours, listening to her tales of her childhood in France or learning needlework from her mother's instruction.

He did not talk of the bad times. Of losing his mother when he was nine. Of watching her die giving birth and of being quickly whisked away from the only house he'd known to the mansion of a father who, until that time, had barely noticed him. His growing up at Summerfield House had been privileged, but no one, not even the servants, governesses or tutors ever let him forget he was the illegitimate son.

He did tell Amelie about Lady Summerfield, who, even though she had been his father's wife and ought to have despised him, had been the one person besides his sisters who'd treated him as if he mattered. Years after she abandoned the family, he began a correspondence with her and lived with her before the Waterloo battle and recuperated there afterwards.

When he and Amelie returned to bed, they made love again, this time more leisurely, like two people who had all the time in the world to be together.

She fell asleep almost immediately afterwards. He gazed at her lying next to him, looking much like he imagined she must have looked as a little girl. The wonder of it, he would be sharing her bed for the rest of their lives.

With that thought, he drifted contentedly off to sleep.

A pain, horrible and intense, woke Amelie. She cried out.

Edmund woke. 'What is it?'

She sat up. 'Something is wrong. In here.' She pressed her belly. Another pain hit, and she cried out again and hugged her knees.

He bounded out of bed and began dressing. 'I'll get help. Send for a doctor.'

'No. No doctor,' she pleaded. 'I want to go home. Take me home, Edmund. I want my mother!' Another pain in her belly, worse than any she'd ever had during her courses, shook her. 'M-my mother will know what to do.'

He continued to pull on his clothes. 'Are you certain? A carriage ride might not be good—'

She cut him off. 'I do not care. I want to go home.'

'Yes. Right away.' He headed for the door, still putting on his coat. 'I'll send Sally to you.'

He rushed out and she was alone.

Something was wrong with the baby! Something terrible. She knew it.

Another pain hit and she hugged her legs tighter.

When it passed she got herself out of the bed and put on her shift.

The door opened and Sally rushed in. 'Miss! What is wrong?'

'It hurts! I am afraid I'll lose it.' She shook.

'Lose what, miss?' Sally asked.

'My baby,' Amelie whispered. 'My baby.'

'Baby?' The girl's eyes grew wide.

Amelie had forgotten that she'd kept the baby a secret from Sally, who had never questioned why she threw up most mornings.

Sally recovered quickly. 'Mr Summerfield is getting a carriage. Let me get you dressed.'

Sally helped her step into her corset, which she laced very loosely. Next she helped her into her dress.

'I am bleeding, too,' Amelie said, more to herself than to Sally.

Sally laced her into her dress and wrapped her in a shawl.

Edmund rushed in as Sally was packing the clothes she'd so recently unpacked. 'Leave the bags, Sally. We'll get them later. There should be a coach downstairs by the time we get there.'

He picked up Amelie and carried her down the stairs and out the door to a waiting hackney coach.

Chapter Eleven

They soon reached Grosvenor Street and Edmund jumped out of the coach to sound the knocker. Someone should be awake. If not, he'd bang at the door until they roused.

Matheson, the butler, dressed in a banyan, opened the door.

'What is this?' he cried, then saw it was Edmund.

'Quick,' Edmund said. 'Miss Glenville is ill.' He forgot she was Mrs Summerfield now.

'What should I do?' Matheson asked.

'Pay the coachman.' He handed Matheson a purse of coins. 'I'll carry her inside.'

With Sally's help, he gathered Amelie into his arms again and carried her through the door.

The butler and Sally were right behind him.

'Wake Lady Northdon,' Edmund ordered. 'And my sister. Tell them Amelie is here and needs them.'

'I'll find Mrs Glenville,' Sally said, bounding up the stairs.

By the time he'd carried Amelie to her bedchamber, Lady Northdon rushed in behind him. 'What has happened?'

Edmund laid her on the bed.

'I'm having pains, Maman,' Amelie cried. 'In my belly. And I am bleeding.'

'Mon Dieu!' Her mother exclaimed. 'We must send for the physician.'

'I'll attend to it,' Matheson said.

'An *accoucheur*,' Edmund clarified.

The butler's brows rose.

'Rapidement, s'il vous plait!' Amelie's mother lapsed into French.

Matheson hurried off.

Lord Northdon appeared at the doorway. 'My God.' He swung to Edmund. 'What did you do?'

'Papa! It is not because of Edmund!' Amelie cried. 'It is the baby!'

Edmund was not so certain. They'd made love three times. Had that caused the harm?

Her brother and Tess rushed down the stairs to Amelie's room. 'Sally said something is wrong with Amelie's baby.'

Lord Northdon inclined his head to Edmund. 'He's done something. I am certain of it.'

Glenville took his father by the arm. 'Control yourself, Papa. Can you not see how distraught Edmund is? Accusations are not going to help. Let us stay out of the way.'

'Oui,' his mother said. 'We must get her undressed. Tess, come help.' She turned to Edmund. 'You go, too. We will take care of her.'

'I am staying,' Edmund said.

'Come with us,' Glenville said.

'Yes,' Tess agreed. 'Go with Marc and his father. We will keep you informed.'

'I am staying,' he said.

'This is no place for a man,' Tess said.

'It is my place,' he countered.

'Amelie will not wish you to stay,' Lady Northdon insisted.

'He—can—stay,' Amelie managed, talking through another pain.

Sally dared to speak up, although she usually did not when Lord or Lady Northdon was around. 'Mrs Bayliss might be able to help her. She knows of such things. Shall I wake her, ma'am?'

'Oui! Oui! Bring Mrs Bayliss,' Lady Northdon said.

Sally heard Mrs Bayliss, the housekeeper, say she used to accompany her mother, a midwife, on her calls. She'd seen dozens of births before she was even fifteen years old, she'd said. One of the other maids also told Sally that midwives knew how to get rid of babies before anyone knew of their existence, but Sally could not bring herself to ask Mrs Bayliss about that.

She hurried below stairs, where Mrs Bayliss and Mr Matheson had their rooms.

She knocked on Mrs Bayliss's door. 'Wake up, Mrs Bayliss! Lady Northdon needs you!'

She heard the housekeeper moving in the room. 'I am coming.' She opened the door, dressed in her nightdress and a wrap. 'For goodness' sake! What is it, Sally? Why does her ladyship need me at this hour?'

Sally took a gulp of air. 'It is Miss Glenville— Mrs Summerfield, I mean—she—she is having a baby, only it is too soon to have the baby!'

Mrs Bayliss gaped. 'She is what?'

'She is having a baby!' Sally repeated. 'Please come and help her.'

'Where is she? Did she not leave with her husband?'

'He brought her back,' Sally explained. 'Oh, please, just go to her.'

The housekeeper retied the sash of her wrapper. 'Yes. Yes. Indeed.' As they rushed to the stairs, she added, 'Fetch some towels and linens, Sally. Lots of them.'

* * *

'Merci, merci!' cried Lady Northdon when Mrs Bayliss appeared.

Thank goodness, thought Edmund, because none of them had a clue what to do to help Amelie.

'Let me see her.' The housekeeper went straight to Amelie's bed. 'What are you feeling, miss?'

'Pain,' answered Amelie. 'In my belly. And my back. It feels wrong! Something is wrong!'

'Let me touch you.' Mrs Bayliss put her hand on Amelie's abdomen. 'You are not far along?'

'A little over three months.' A day before Waterloo.

Sally came in, carrying several towels. She handed them to Mrs Bayliss and helped her place them under Amelie.

Afterwards Mrs Bayliss told Sally to bring some tea for Amelie. Sally nodded and left the room.

'What is wrong with her?' Tess asked.

'A miscarriage, likely,' Mrs Bayliss said quietly.

'What is to be done?' Tess wrung her hands.

Mrs Bayliss patted Tess's hands. 'Nothing but waiting and hoping, dear.'

The women stood around Amelie's bed, but Edmund waited in a corner of the room, fighting memories of another room, another woman surrounded in just such a way.

His mother. Dying. Her baby born dead.

Not again, he prayed as time ticked by.

Sally brought the tea, but sipping it made Amelie throw it up again.

Edmund had seen men pierced through with bayonets. Shot in the chest from musket fire. He'd seen cannon balls take off a man's head, but, somehow, watching Amelie seize up with pain, over and over, seemed more difficult to endure.

'The pain. It is worse.' she moaned.

She sat up and clutched her abdomen, keening in agony, a sound that only brought back his mother's cries from so many years ago. Amelie lay back down again, gripping her mother's hand, her arm trembling.

'Oh, dear. There it is,' said Mrs Bayliss, her voice sorrowful.

'Non. Je prie, non.' Her mother's voice was anguished.

Amelie half sat up again. When she collapsed back on the bed, she did not stir.

Edmund stopped breathing. 'Is she—?'

'She's lost the baby, sir.' Mrs Bayliss quickly pulled the towels from beneath Amelie and folded them into a bundle.

Amelie rose onto her elbows. 'I've lost the baby?'

The baby! But not Amelie. She was alive.

Her voice became more strident. 'I've lost the

baby?' She reached for the bundle, which the house-keeper pulled away.

'There is nothing for you to see, miss,' Mrs Bayliss said. She gestured for Sally to follow her. They left the room.

'Maman!' Amelie cried.

Her mother sat on the bed and hugged her daughter, comforting her as if she were a small child.

Tess also put an arm around Amelie, murmuring to her that she would be all right.

She was alive, Edmund said a prayer of thanksgiving for that. But nothing was right. There was no baby. Nothing to connect them together.

No family.

He walked out of the room and leaned against the wall.

From an open door to another bedchamber, he heard Lord Northdon's voice. 'Why the devil could she not have lost the baby yesterday? Now it is too late.'

Was the man glad the baby was gone? Edmund could not bear it. He thought of the little girl in Hyde Park. Now he'd never smell the sweet scent of his own baby. He'd never feel his own baby's chubby arms around his neck. Lord Northdon thought this a good thing?

He closed his eyes and let his grief turn to anger.

He stepped into the doorway. Lord Northdon and Glenville turned to him.

'It is unfortunate that your daughter's miscarriage did not come at a more acceptable time for you, sir.' Edmund bowed and walked away before he could no longer resist the temptation to put his fist into Lord Northdon's face. He continued down the stairs to the hall and stepped out into the chilly night air.

Why had this happened this night? Edmund could think of only one reason. He'd made love to her. Lord Northdon was correct on one score. Edmund was to blame.

A carriage entered the street and stopped in front of the town house. Matheson stepped out, followed by the doctor.

The butler only gave him a fleeting glance before leading the doctor into the house and taking the physician's greatcoat and hat.

'Come with me,' Matheson said to the doctor. 'I will take you to Lady Northdon and her daughter.'

Edmund went below stairs in search of Mrs Bayliss to let her know the *accoucheur* had arrived.

He found her in the kitchen with one of the maids.

'Carry on, Kitty,' Mrs Bayliss said. 'Add one cup for the doctor and I will be down shortly to bring the tea upstairs.' She glanced at Edmund. 'I expect you'd rather have brandy.'

'You have the right of it,' he said.

She touched his arm, a look of sympathy on her face. 'These things happen sometimes, sir.' She dried her hands on the apron she'd donned and bustled off to Amelie's room.

Edmund walked slower. When he reached the floor where Amelie's bedchamber was located, her father, the doctor and Mrs Bayliss were all deep in conversation.

'You are confident she expelled all the tissue?' he heard the doctor ask.

'Oh, yes, sir,' Mrs Bayliss assured him. 'I've seen many of these untimely deliveries. I know what to expect.'

'I'll just look in on her, then,' the doctor said.

'This way.' Mrs Bayliss knocked on the door and opened it. 'The *accoucheur*, Dr Croft.'

Edmund followed the man in to the room. The *accoucheur* turned to him with haughty eyebrows raised. 'You cannot march in here, sir. Who are you?'

Edmund glared at him. 'The lady's husband.'

Lady Northdon and Tess were still at Amelie's bedside. Amelie appeared to take no notice of the doctor's entrance. Or Edmund's.

'This is Dr Croft to see you, Amelie,' her mother said gently. 'He will want to examine you.'

Dr Croft examined Amelie without her seeming to care.

'All looks well,' he said. 'But contact me immediately if she develops a fever.'

While the doctor spoke to Lady Northdon and Tess, Edmund kept his eyes on Amelie, who now lay on clean linens and wore a clean nightdress. Her gaze drifted over to him and paused for a moment before she turned her head away.

'Let us go to the drawing room to talk about this,' Lady Northdon said. 'Will you bring refreshment, Mrs Bayliss?'

'Yes, m'lady,' the housekeeper said.

Lady Northdon looked at Tess. 'You will stay with her?' She did not address Edmund.

'Of course I will.' Tess rearranged Amelie's bedcovers. She kissed her on the head. 'Close your eyes and try to sleep, Amelie.'

As soon as the room had cleared, Tess glanced over at Edmund. 'How unforeseen,' she commented.

He nodded. 'My father-in-law reckons it happened a day too late.'

'Did he say that?' She sounded surprised.

He wondered if Tess felt the same. He wondered if she blamed him, too.

There was merit in what Lord Northdon had said, after all. But if it had happened one day earlier and Amelie then had refused to marry him, Edmund would feel no relief.

A knock sounded on the door and Tess answered it. Tess took a small tray from whoever it was and carried it over to Edmund. 'I gather you ordered this?'

A decanter of brandy and two glasses. He said a silent thank you to Mrs Bayliss.

'You should sit, Edmund,' Tess said.

There was a chair right next to him. He lowered himself in it and poured the brandy into a glass. 'May I offer you some?' He lifted the glass to her.

She took it from his hand and drank the whole. 'Thank you.' She peered down at him as he poured more brandy into the glass. 'How are you faring, Edmund?'

'Me?' He lifted his face to hers. 'This did not happen to me. It happened to Amelie.'

She returned a sceptical look. 'Still it must affect you.'

It was eviscerating him, but he could not speak of it.

She walked back to Amelie and sat in a chair beside the bed. Edmund drank his brandy in his dark corner.

When the glass was empty again, he spoke. 'Would you do me a service, Tess?'

'If I am able,' she responded.

'Leave Amelie to me.'

She whirled around and looked about to protest.

'I will sit with her. I promise to alert you or her mother if she has any difficulty at all, but I want to be the one to sit with her.'

'Oh, Edmund.' Tess sighed. 'Do you think that is wise? I am perfectly happy to sit by her side all night, if need be.'

'I am her husband,' he said more firmly. 'I need to be with her.'

She smiled at him—a little sadly. 'Yes, of course! I am unused to this change. It has not yet been a whole day.'

He returned her gaze. 'And yet so much has happened...'

Amelie opened her eyes to daylight. It took her a moment to realise she was in her room and a moment longer to remember what had happened. She squeezed her eyes shut again and rolled over, curling up in the bed and trying not to feel the emptiness inside.

Now that there was no baby.

She heard a rustling and opened her eyes again, resting her head on one arm.

In a chair near her bed sat Edmund, legs stretched out before him, his coat and waistcoat open, his shirt half out of his trousers. His face was shadowed with a dark beard but seemed pinched with worry. He shifted in the chair again, then stilled. Watching the rhythmic rise and fall of his chest and listening to the soft hum of his breathing was comforting.

Had he been at her side all night? He certainly looked as if he'd spent the night in a chair, but why had her mother not found him a bed?

She remembered that her mother and Tess had stood at her side during her awful ordeal. She also remembered Edmund standing in the corner, refusing to leave.

Blinking against tears that threatened to sting her eyes, she gazed at him. Much easier to think of him than the pain and the loss.

Had it been her fault? She'd wanted the lovemaking. Had that caused her baby to die?

He shifted again, startling her.

Did he blame her? She'd told him there was no harm in making love, but she did not really know.

He suddenly took a deep breath, and his eyes opened into narrow slits. They widened and he sat up straight in the chair. 'Amelie. How are you feeling?'

How was she feeling?

Numb. Best she stay numb. To feel anything seemed too risky.

'I am better,' she finally said.

He leaned towards her, 'What can I do for you? Do you need anything?'

She shook her head. 'Would my mother not give you a bed?'

'I did not ask for one.'

She remembered the commotion she'd caused. How he carried her inside and set the house into an uproar. 'I've caused everyone so much trouble.'

He pushed his chair closer to her. 'Not so very much.'

'I lost the baby.' Her voice cracked. 'I am so sorry.'

'It happened,' he said carefully. 'We simply go on from here.'

But how? she thought.

'We could not have foreseen this, Amelie.'

'Yes, but...' She could not finish her thought. It had been the wedding that had caused it. Or rather, her desire for the marital bed. Did he comprehend? It would not have happened if they had not married—if they'd not made love.

She moved in the bed and became aware she was bleeding still. It frightened her. She did not know how to tell Edmund about it, either. Such a womanly thing. But urgent.

She sat up. 'Could I trouble you to send Sally to me?'

'Right away.' He stood and put his clothing in order.

He still looked exhausted, though.

'And then you must get some rest,' she said. 'I am in no distress.' She hoped.

His expression turned puzzled. 'I am rested enough.'

'I really do not need you to stay here, Edmund.' She needed him to leave, actually.

His brows knitted again as they had in sleep. 'If you would rather I not be here, I will attend to other matters. I will collect our bags from the hotel.'

'You could send Staines for the bags. You need not go yourself.' She wanted him to rest—and for Sally to come and change the linens folded beneath her. 'My mother will have a bed fixed for you.'

'No need. I am well able to return to the hotel. I have other matters to see to today, as well.' He walked to the door. 'I'll send for Sally. Rest, Amelie.'

He walked out of the room without a second glance.

Amelie sat up and hugged her knees. She'd forgotten to tell him something important. She'd forgotten to thank him for not leaving her alone.

She lay back down in the bed and let her misery envelop her.

Chapter Twelve

Edmund found a servant to summon Sally. He also left word that he had gone out. He returned to the Clarendon Hotel and arranged to have Amelie's and Sally's luggage sent back to them. He carried his bag to the Stephen's Hotel, where he still had his rooms.

He stripped off his coat and waistcoat, kicked off his shoes and flopped down on the bed. He was in no condition to stay at the Northdon town house and risk encountering Lord Northdon, not with his emotions in such a volatile state. Best he rest here.

He did not need to witness everyone else holding him to blame. No one knew that better than he did. Besides, no one desired his presence there. Everyone wished the marriage had been scheduled for today rather than yesterday. Even Amelie seemed impatient to be rid of him this morning.

He'd battled being unwanted his whole life. Certainly his mother's life would have been happier—

and longer—had he not been born. His father had only wanted a legitimate heir, not a bastard son. No schoolmaster, tutor, governess or servant wanted to deal with him. His superiors in the army had preferred junior officers with proper family connections.

Still, his sisters and Lady Summerfield accepted him, even though his sisters were now angry at him. What would Lady Summerfield say if she knew what had happened, why he'd had to marry Amelie? The selfish risk he'd taken with the baby's life? How he'd lost it all?

She'd probably tell him to buck up and stop feeling sorry for himself. Lady Summerfield always chose to be happy.

He'd thought happiness had been in his grasp, too, but now there was no baby and he was not at all certain Amelie wanted him.

He rubbed his face. He'd had to live with things he'd done on the battlefield; he supposed he'd have to learn to live with this, as well.

The baby he'd almost held. The family they'd almost created.

He slept until nearly the dinner hour. Dragging himself out of bed, he dressed in a clean shirt and brushed his coat until it looked presentable again. He'd look the proper gentleman and act the proper gentleman. Let no one push him too far, though. His emotions, while under control, were very raw.

He kept his room at the Stephen, though. Lord and Lady Northdon had never offered him a room at the town house.

He walked outside into a grey, drizzling evening that perfectly matched his mood. When he reached the house and sounded the knocker, he wondered what would happen if he asked for a key so he could come and go as he pleased.

Staines answered the door. 'Evening, sir.'

As he handed Staines his coat and hat, he asked, 'Anything I should know about, Staines?'

Lines appeared on the footman's forehead. 'It is quieter, sir. No more harm to Miss Glenville— I mean Mrs Summerfield—that I know of. She's been resting, I hear.'

'Good. I am glad.' Very glad. 'I'll go up and see her.'

Staines's brows rose. 'Should I announce your arrival?'

Edmund smiled. 'No one knows quite what to do with me, do they? I do not know myself. Do tell the family I am here, though. They will want to know.'

Staines's mouth twitched, and his eyes indicated some empathy.

Edmund climbed the stairs to Amelie's room. He

knocked softly, not wishing to wake her if she was sleeping.

The door was opened by Tess. Instead of letting him in, she stepped out in the hall.

'Where have you been?' she said in a scolding tone.

He glared at her. 'I am not likely to tell you when you talk to me that way. How is Amelie? She is not worse, is she?'

'No.' She looked chastened. 'She's slept most of the day, and she is weak, but no worse, the poor dear.' Her disapproving look returned. 'She asked about you, but no one knew what to tell her.'

'I told her I was going out. I did not know when I would return.' His voice turned acerbic. 'I doubt anyone else here desired my presence.'

'Edmund, you must understand,' Tess cried. 'You seduced their daughter!'

'It is not only that, Tess, and you know it.' He looked her in the eye. 'Tell me. How might they have reacted if it had been Captain Fowler instead of me?' There would have been celebration, he'd stake his life on it.

Tess's face showed that she saw his point.

He shrugged. 'All that matters now is that Amelie gets well.' He reached for the latch on the door. 'I want to see her.'

'She is sleeping. The doctor told us to give her laudanum.'

'Laudanum?' he asked. 'Is she in pain?'

Tess shook her head. 'It is just to help her sleep. Just for today, he said.'

He nodded. 'I will not awaken her. But I want to see her.'

He lifted the latch and slipped quietly into the room.

The curtains were drawn and only one lamp was lit. He could see her on the bed, but only as a shadow.

The shadow stirred. 'Who is there?'

He stepped closer. 'It is Edmund.'

'Edmund.' She sat up against the pillows. 'You came back.'

He walked to the side of her bed. 'Of course I came back. I only left to do some errands.' And to sleep.

'I thought you would never come back.' Her voice slurred. 'I thought you ran away to Belgium.'

He wiped a stray hair from her forehead. 'Why would you think that?'

'Oh…' She blinked as if keeping her eyes open was difficult. 'Because of the baby.'

Had she wanted him to leave? He could not tell.

'No, I am here, as I said I would be.' He rested his hand on her bed.

She placed her hand over it, and her lids fluttered closed. 'Your hand feels very nice.'

'How are you faring, Amelie?' he asked.

'Oh…' Her eyes opened again briefly. 'I am so very sad. But the bleeding stopped so that makes me grateful.

'Bleeding?' His voice rose in anxiety.

She nodded. 'Mrs Bayliss said it is all right to bleed. I much prefer her to the doctor.' She added, 'Sally helped me, though.'

'I am glad.' She was not making much sense. Perhaps he could contrive to speak to Mrs Bayliss, discover whether bleeding was serious or not.

She started drifting off to sleep.

'I'll leave you now. Sleep well,' he murmured.

Her eyes flew open. 'Do not leave! Do not go to Brussels.'

He clasped her hand. 'I am not leaving. For Brussels or anywhere else.'

'Not leaving…' She started drifting off again.

'I will look in on you tomorrow,' he said.

She nodded, but her eyes were closed and he was uncertain if she knew what he was saying.

He left the room and found Tess waiting in the hall.

'Lord and Lady Northdon know you are here,' she said. 'They told me they would be pleased for you to stay to dinner.'

Pleased? He doubted it. 'Do they mean it, Tess, or am I expected to refuse?'

'Of course they mean it!' she said a little too forcefully. 'I am going to stay with Amelie, but you go on. They will probably be gathering in the drawing room by now.'

Tess would not be present? Luck would have it that way, wouldn't it? Tess was the closest thing he had to a right flank.

'I'll head down.' He started for the stairs but stopped and turned back to her. 'Oh, Tess?'

'Yes?' She was about to enter Amelie's room.

'Thank you for helping to care for Amelie.'

Her brows rose. 'Oh, my goodness. You really care for her, don't you?'

He gave her a direct look. 'I do indeed.'

When he reached the hall, Staines said, 'They are waiting for you in the drawing room, sir.'

He made a wry smile. 'Thank you.'

He crossed the hall to the drawing-room door, hesitated a moment and straightened his spine, promising himself to remain civil and gentlemanly, no matter what.

He entered the room.

Lord and Lady Northdon were seated together on the sofa, their heads close together in conversation. Glenville had his back to the door and looked to be pouring a glass of wine.

'Good evening,' Edmund said.

They all glanced his way. Wariness in Glenville's expression. Anxiety in Lady Northdon's. Lord Northdon looked upon him with raw antipathy.

Lord Northdon spoke first. 'Where have you been all day?'

Glenville crossed the room, shook his hand and handed him a glass of wine. 'Good evening, Edmund.' He was trying to be cordial, at least.

Edmund was grateful.

Edmund turned to Lady Northdon and bowed. 'I hope you were able to get some rest, *madame*.'

'*Oui*, a little,' she said.

Glenville gestured for him to sit, and he took a chair not too close to Amelie's parents. He took a sip of wine.

'Sir,' he said to Lord Northdon. 'I did not immediately answer your question. I returned to my hotel and slept most of the day.'

'Your hotel?' Lady Northdon exclaimed.

'I kept my room there.' He did not explain he'd kept it because they'd never invited him into this house. 'It is best I stay there until Amelie recovers. Less trouble for you.'

'We can make up a room for you,' Lady North-don said.

'Your offer is appreciated, *madame*, but it might be better if I am not underfoot.'

'Humph!' Lord Northdon shot him a contemptuous glance. 'You simply abandon my daughter after all she has been through? All you caused?'

Edmund bristled and fought to hold his tongue. And his fists.

'Papa,' Glenville broke in. 'You need to give Edmund a chance. We all do.'

Maybe Edmund did have one more ally besides Tess.

He leaned towards Lord Northdon. 'I sat with your daughter all last night, sir, and I just went up to see her before this. I will not abandon her.' She could send him away, but he'd never abandon her.

Lord Northdon averted his head and drank his glass of wine.

Edmund understood to a point. Lord Northdon wanted to know him only as the bastard son of a baronet who'd defiled his daughter, not the man he was. Too many people in Edmund's life had been like that.

He shrugged inwardly. He could only control his own behaviour, not how others reacted to him.

'Amelie seemed comfortable,' he said, seeking a normal conversation. 'Although she was not entirely making sense. That was the laudanum, though, I'm certain.'

'Hmmph.' Lord Northdon took a sip of his wine. 'You are certain. Are you an expert on laudanum now?'

Edmund faced him. 'Not an expert, but I had some experience with laudanum when I was injured in Spain.'

'You were injured in Spain?' Glenville asked.

'At Albuhera,' he responded.

Lord Northdon finished his wine and turned away.

The butler came then to announce dinner.

Dinner was a strained affair, but Edmund tried to make pleasant conversation with people who wished he had never existed.

No one mentioned the baby.

After dinner Edmund excused himself to return to Amelie's room, but before going there, he used the servants' stairs to go below in search of Mrs Bayliss.

She was in the servants' hall, talking to two of the maids.

'Mrs Bayliss,' he called to her from the doorway. 'Might I have a word with you?'

'Mr Summerfield, sir.' She stood and walked towards him. 'Of course. What may I do for you?'

He liked this housekeeper. She was both efficient and kind. 'I had a question. Miss Glenville—Mrs Summerfield, I mean—said she'd had bleeding. Is that something serious?'

The cook patted his hand. 'Not at all. It is like her monthly, you know. Nothing to worry over. Merely her body coming back to normal.'

'I thank you, ma'am.' He hesitated before speaking again. 'May I ask how you come by this knowledge? It seems considerable.'

'My mother was a midwife, sir, and I went with her many a time soon as I was old enough to follow her directions. I would have followed in her footsteps, but she died young and I went into service instead.'

Another person whose plans in life had been abruptly altered. 'I am very grateful you were here when we needed you.'

She blushed. 'Thank you, sir.'

He started to leave but turned back to her. 'Ma'am, I wonder if you might beg a favour from the servants. Ask them not to speak of these events? I wish to protect my wife's reputation and that of the family. They have all suffered enough from gossip.'

'We have already agreed upon it, sir,' she told him, her expression firm. 'We are devoted to the family.'

He extended his hand to her, and she placed hers

in his. 'If ever I can be of assistance to any of you, let me know.'

She curtsied. 'Thank you, sir.'

He walked back to the stairs, acknowledging the curious stares of the kitchen maids and other servants he passed.

When he reached Amelie's room, he knocked and waited for Tess to come out.

'She's still sleeping,' Tess said.

'Has she eaten?' he asked.

Tess frowned. 'Nothing to speak of. We were able to convince her to take some broth, but that is all.'

She had to eat.

'Have you eaten?' he thought to ask.

'No,' Tess responded. 'I feared I would wake her.'

He waved a hand. 'Go. Have dinner. I will sit with her.'

'Are you staying here tonight?' she asked.

'In the room with Amelie, you mean?' He had not planned to. 'Yes. I'll stay with her.' He wanted to, he realised.

'You do not have to stay in her room, you know,' Tess said. 'We can have a bedchamber ready for you.'

They'd obviously not gone to that trouble yet. 'No need. All my belongings are at Stephen's Hotel. I'll return there in the morning.'

'You will not move in here?' she asked, clearly disapproving.

He gave her a direct look. 'Tess. I have yet to be invited to stay.'

'Of course you are welcome to stay!' she protested.

'I am not welcome,' he said. 'I dare say they wish I had left the day before yesterday.'

She put her hands on her hips and leaned forward. 'You must stop this, Edmund. For better or for worse, you are connected to this family, and you must learn to get along with them.'

He bent his head and nodded. 'I will try. I am trying.'

She touched his arm. 'Good! We should all try to make something good of this, right?'

He shrugged. 'If something good can come from losing a child.'

'It is awful, I know.' She gripped his arm and shook it. 'Marc and I had to overcome a great deal to make something good of our marriage. You can, too.'

He was puzzled. 'What did you and Marc have to overcome?'

She released him. 'Some day I will tell you. Not now. I am famished, and I intend to take your direction and find something to eat.'

She walked away, and he opened Amelie's door

and entered the room, where curtains were drawn and only one lamp was lit.

She stirred and he halted, watching her, but she did not wake. He lowered himself into the chair and drew a hand through his hair.

How could they make something good of this? It seemed impossible.

Chapter Thirteen

When Amelie woke the next morning, it was like swimming through a dark, murky sea into the light. Even her room was bright with sunlight. She remembered strange dreams and a feeling like floating in water, bobbing along like a fish caught in a current too strong to swim against. Her head ached and she felt a little dizzy, but at least the objects in the room remained still and did not alter their appearance.

Was she alone? Any time she woke before, when the room was dark, someone was sitting with her. Or at least she thought she'd been awake. She rolled over to see.

Edmund was with her. Sleeping on the chair as he had done the night before. She'd thought he'd left her! That is what her muddled mind and frantic dreams had told her. Yet here he was.

She checked herself. Her bleeding was not so alarming now. Mrs Bayliss said it was normal, and even the *accoucheur* told her to expect bleeding for a week or so. She need not stay in bed. She longed to be out of it, longed to be anywhere but this room, this bed, with the memories of what had happened here.

No reason why she could not rise now, put on a wrapper and sit by the window. She glanced over at Edmund, still sleeping, and moved as quietly as she could. Her legs seemed weak, and her head spun as she tried to stand. Steadying herself on the bed, she reached the trunk upon which her wrapper was folded. She sat on the trunk to put it on and then slowly rose and moved as if she were Madame Saqui, the Vauxhall Gardens tightrope walker.

She was surprisingly weak for just being in bed a day. Perhaps that was what happens when… No, she did not want to think of why she felt this way. She only wished to look outside at the street and reassure herself that carriages still rolled by, that trees and grass still grew. Her world seemed so changed, why not all of it?

She stood at the glass and discovered the same street, the same row of houses as always. A cat crossed the road and that small thing felt even more reassuring.

'Amelie?'

She turned. Edmund had risen from the chair, his hair mussed and his face again in need of a shave.

He walked over to her. 'Are you feeling better?'

She nodded. 'Merely a little weak.'

'Hungry?' he asked.

Food seemed so utterly unimportant, but his mention of it made her stomach growl. 'Yes. I suppose I am.'

He buttoned his waistcoat. 'I will have some food sent up to you. Shall I summon Sally, as well?

Her heart started to race. 'Are you leaving?'

'I should,' he said. 'But I will be back. I'll come in the afternoon and look in on you.'

She could only stare at him. He smiled, but whether it was in reassurance or apology, she could not tell. Perhaps it was pity.

He walked out the door, and she was helpless to stop him.

There was nothing in his leaving to make her bereft, she told herself, yet her throat tightened and tears pricked her eyes. She willed them away. Why should he stay? His reason to stay existed no more.

She should be happy he had stayed with her these past two nights. She'd rather he'd lain next to her.

There she went again, thinking shameless thoughts. Such thoughts had led to—to all that had happened.

Why had he spent the night in her room? She could not figure it. He stayed and he left. He seemed kind, but it felt as though a wall stood between them.

A wall erected because—because of what she had lost.

There was a knock on her door, and Sally peeked her head in. 'Mr Summerfield said you might want me, miss—ma'am, I mean.'

Amelie smiled at the girl. 'Good morning, Sally. Yes. I think I would like to get dressed, but before you help me, would you tell Cook that I will not need a plate of food sent up to my room? I would like to eat in the dining room.'

She did not wish to sit alone with her memories in this room.

Amelie held on to the banister but managed the stairs fairly well. The more she walked, the steadier she felt. Staines was in the hallway, and he opened the door to the dining room for her.

Marc and Tess were seated at the table.

'Amelie!' Tess cried.

Marc jumped to his feet to assist her to a chair. 'What are you doing out of bed?' he asked. 'Where is Edmund?'

'Edmund left.' She did not like the frowns that appeared on both their faces. 'He had several errands.'

'You must be feeling better.' Tess forced a smile. 'But are you certain you should be up and about?'

Amelie stared past them. 'I could not stay in that room.'

'Well, now you are here,' her brother broke in. 'Shall I fix a plate for you?'

'Thank you.' She was not certain she could balance a plate of food and walk at the same time. 'Some toasted bread and jam would be lovely.'

He cut pieces of bread and put them in the toasting rack and set it near the fire.

Tess poured her a cup of tea. 'Tell us how you are feeling.'

Unhappy, confused, aching. *Grieving.*

'Almost back to my old self,' she said instead. 'I do feel a little weak, though. Almost as though I had too much wine to drink.'

Tess handed her the cup of tea. 'The doctor gave you laudanum to help you sleep yesterday.'

Marc turned her toast. 'Do not exert yourself today,' he said.

'I promise,' she responded. 'But I would love to sit in the library, unless Papa needs it to work.'

Marc brought her the toast, a dish of butter and one of raspberry jam. 'I do not know his plans.' He paused and glanced at Tess again. 'I must go out, but Tess may be able to keep you company.'

She actually preferred to be alone. 'That would be lovely, but unnecessary. I do not need anyone with me all the time. I am sufficiently recovered.'

The only person she wished to have as company

was Edmund. Until she saw him, talked to him, she did not even know what tomorrow would bring.

After Edmund returned to the hotel and shaved and changed clothes, he sat down to read his correspondence.

Anything to distract him.

A letter from Count von Osten detailed some possible investment opportunities Edmund could explore. He ought to look into it today. He needed to stay occupied.

He should write to the Count and Lady Summerfield. Inform them of his marriage, but then he would have to tell them about—the other. He was not ready to write those words.

He rose from his chair and picked up his hat and gloves. In the hall he told the servant where he was going, just in case he was needed. In case anything happened to Amelie.

He walked briskly to Threadneedle Street and the office of his stockbroker. When he finished with the man, though, his malaise returned. He wandered through the Exchange, watching its vendors energetically sell their varied wares.

Perhaps he should buy Amelie a gift?

What a paltry idea. As if a mere gift could compensate.

'Summerfield!' a voice behind him shouted. 'I would speak with you now.'

He turned.

A few feet away, Lord Tinmore leaned on his cane, a footman in attendance. Other gentlemen in the area stared curiously. If he cut the man, likely the tongues of the *ton* would start to wag. Better he not add to the inevitable gossip.

He strode over to Tinmore. 'Sir?'

Tinmore's eyes glinted with triumph. At having one of his orders followed, probably.

'What is your business here?' Tinmore demanded.

Could this man be any more insufferable? Edmund leaned down to him and spoke in as mild a tone as he could muster. 'I will not answer that question, sir.' He bowed. 'I hope you are well, sir. How is my sister, your wife?'

'Hmmph,' the man uttered. 'She is in excellent health, of course. If you must know, I kept her from that patched-up affair of a wedding of yours.'

As Genna had told him. 'It saddened me not to have her there.'

Tinmore grimaced. 'I would not have her distressed.'

'It was not a distressing event.' Edmund did not need this. His temper was worn thin as it was.

'And now the whole reason for it is gone. Ha! How is that?' Tinmore's expression turned smug.

Edmund felt the blood drain from his face. Tess! Could she not keep her mouth shut? He closed his eyes and fought for control. When he opened them again, he glared directly into Tinmore's face. 'You have crossed a line, sir. Our conversation is finished.'

He turned away.

'It would be a shame for that whole mucked-up story to leak out, would it not?' Tinmore called after him.

Edmund swung back. 'What is your meaning?'

Triumph returned to Tinmore's eyes. 'I am greatly desirous that my wife and her unmarried sister have as little contact with you as possible. I would not be so unkind as to forbid it of them, but...' He grinned, revealing yellowing teeth.

'You damned blackguard,' Edmund said just loud enough for Tinmore to hear. 'You are blackmailing me.'

'That is it.' Tinmore's smile merely widened. 'I want you gone. Leave or somehow the whole story of your sordid mess will become known to everyone.'

Tinmore hobbled away, signalling his footman to come with him.

That cursed reprobate! Threatening to expose Amelie's secret. Edmund stood frozen with rage.

'What did he want?'

Was he to have no peace this day? Edmund swung around. It was Glenville who'd spoken.

Edmund evaded Glenville's question. 'To be as unpleasant as possible.'

Glenville frowned. 'He threatened you, didn't he?'

Edmund's brows rose. 'Why should he threaten me?'

'Because he's a damned autocrat who enjoys manipulating people.' Glenville snapped.

Edmund regarded him closely. 'And how do you know this?'

His brother-in-law's eyes flashed with anger. 'He once threatened me.'

Indeed? 'Well, he is still up to the same old tricks.'

Glenville did not press him to say more. 'Where are you bound now?' was all he asked.

Edmund's eyes narrowed. 'Why?'

'Because I would like to talk to you,' Glenville responded mildly.

'You came looking for me,' Edmund realised.

'Yes,' Glenville admitted. 'The servant at the hotel said you would be at the Exchange.'

His anxiety rose. 'Amelie! Is she ill again?'

'No. No.' Glenville made a placating gesture. 'She is much improved, as a matter of fact.'

Edmund's shoulders relaxed.

'I merely desired to talk with you away from the house,' Glenville explained.

Away from his parents? Tess? Or from Amelie?

'Very well.' Edmund was eager to be done with it.

They found a nearby tavern and sat in a secluded booth. The tavern maid brought them two tankards of ale.

Glenville took a sip of his. 'One thing I miss about Brussels is the beer, but this will do for now.'

Edmund was in no mood for friendly chitchat. 'What did you want to speak to me about?'

'I want to apologise for my parents. And for myself. We have not made any of this easy for you.' Glenville sounded sincere.

'I understand it,' Edmund said.

'You are welcome to stay at the town house,' he went on. 'My mother and father are remiss at not making that clear to you.'

He appreciated the gesture, but Glenville was mistaken. He'd be tolerated, perhaps, but not welcome. 'It is better I remain at the hotel, at least until Amelie is recovered and we can leave.'

'Leave?' Glenville's brows rose. 'Where will you go?'

'I am not certain,' Edmund responded. 'But after this encounter with Tinmore, we'll not stay in London.' And risk having what Amelie would wish kept secret become the latest on dit in town.

* * *

Amelie curled up in one of the comfortable chairs in the library, using her shawl to help keep her warm. She really did not have the energy or concentration to read or do needlework, so she merely watched the glow of the coals in the fireplace.

Staines came to the doorway. 'Miss Summerfield to see you, ma'am.'

Ma'am. She could not get used to being ma'am instead of miss, but, then, there was not much around that would remind her she was married. She glanced down at her hands. Her rings. Her lovely rings.

'Ma'am?' Staines asked again.

'Yes.' She tried to focus her mind. 'Show her in.'

Genna breezed in. 'Amelie! How are you?' She came over to her and bussed her on the cheek. 'How terrible for you.'

She knew? 'Tess told you what happened?'

'Of course she did,' Genna said.

Amelie slumped in her chair. Why had Tess spoken so soon?

'I am very well now,' Amelie said. 'No one need be concerned about me.'

'Well, I am.' Genna lifted her chin. 'What an ordeal and the night after your wedding.'

She wished Genna would go away. 'It is over.'

'Did you regret it had not happened before the

wedding?' Genna's voice was without malice and entirely sympathetic.

Still, the question jarred Amelie. It also jarred her that she did not know the answer. 'Have you asked your brother that question?'

'Goodness, no!' Genna laughed. 'He'd chew my head off if I did and would never answer me. I am half-surprised that you have not told me to go to the devil, but, then, you are much too nice.'

Was that a compliment or an insult? Amelie was unsure.

'It is what everyone is thinking, you know,' Genna went on. 'How much better it would have been and all that.'

Amelie bristled. 'Is that what you think?'

Genna sobered. 'I think all of this must be very hard for you, Amelie, and I wish my brother would have thought of what might happen before he indulged in an indiscretion.'

Edmund was not to blame for any of it. Not even the loss—

'I indulged in the indiscretion, too,' Amelie said.

Genna considered this. 'Yes, I suppose you did. How easy it must have been to be carried away by emotion that night of all nights. I confess I have never felt such emotion towards a man. They all seem like fortune hunters to me. Not that the fortune Tinmore has settled on me is all that great.

It does seem the most important thing to them, though.'

It had been for Fowler. 'At least that did not matter to Tess and Marc. They are a love match.' It certainly hadn't mattered to her parents either.

'Tess and Marc?' Genna sounded surprised. 'I admit they seem to be devoted to each other now, but—' She peered at Amelie. 'Do you not know the circumstances of their marriage?'

'They met in Lincolnshire,' she said lamely.

'Yes,' Genna agreed. 'They met in a storm. He rescued her and they took refuge in a cabin overnight. Tinmore found out about it and forced them to marry or he threatened to cause a big scandal.' She glanced away. 'If I had been Tess, I would have called his bluff, though. Or let the scandal happen.'

Marc and Tess had been forced to marry? That explained why Marc had left her after the wedding. Why had no one ever told her? 'It worked out for them, though. They seem besotted now.'

'Amazing, isn't it?' Genna said. 'But they are the exception, do you not think? What other married persons do you know who truly care about each other?'

Her mother and father, although throughout most of her life they'd been at loggerheads with each other. Somehow they had reconciled in Brussels.

The clock on the mantel chimed, and Genna

stood. 'I must go. Heaven forbid I arrive home after Tinmore and need to explain where I've been!'

Amelie started to rise, but Genna gestured for her to remain sitting.

She walked over to Amelie's chair and clasped her hand. 'You continue to recover, do you hear? I will see myself out.'

Like a whirlwind zipping through a meadow, she was gone.

Amelie's mind was spinning with what Genna had left in her wake. The idea that Edmund might wish she'd had the miscarriage a day earlier. That Marc and Tess had been forced to marry. That she could trust no one to tell her the truth.

Chapter Fourteen

Edmund and Glenville talked of other things on the walk back to Mayfair. Glenville asked about his investments. Edmund told him, even though he suspected his sister's husband worried that he'd lose everything the way their father had.

When they reached Bond Street, Glenville asked, 'Will you come home with me?'

'I'll come after I change for dinner.' He'd promised Amelie he would return.

'Good,' Glenville said.

They reached the entrance of Stephen's Hotel.

Glenville extended his hand. 'I'll leave you here, then.'

Edmund accepted the handshake.

'I am glad I had an opportunity to talk with you,' Glenville said.

Edmund was still not certain of this man. Was he friend or foe?

'I will see you shortly,' he said.

* * *

Edmund arrived at the Northdon town house within an hour. Again he sounded the knocker like the outsider the family felt him to be.

Staines opened the door and greeted him with less surprise than the day before.

He handed Staines his hat and gloves. 'Is Mrs Summerfield in her room?'

'The library, sir,' Staines responded.

'Ah,' Edmund remarked. 'She must be feeling better.'

'I believe so, sir,' Staines said.

Edmund went to the library and knocked on the door before entering. He could not see her, and the light was low in the room. 'Amelie?'

She peeked out from a large chair facing the fireplace. 'I am here, Edmund.'

He crossed the room to her.

'Please have a seat.' She, too, spoke as if he were a visitor.

He longed to touch her, to enfold her in his arms and tell her how sorry he was, but her reserve held him back. Instead he lowered himself into a chair flanking hers. 'I am pleased to see you up.'

'I do not like staying in my bedchamber.' She shuddered. 'My mother or Tess comes in to check on me. They seem to believe I cannot be left alone too long.'

'Likely they worry about you.' He worried about her. Her sadness enveloped her like a shroud.

'Your sister Genna called,' she went on, although her conversation seemed forced. 'Out of curiosity, I suspect. Or because Lord Tinmore would not want her to come.'

Either sounded like Genna. 'Tess would have told her what—what happened.'

'Yes.' She glanced away. 'Genna asked me if I had wished it had happened the day before instead.'

'Genna asked you that?' He blew out a breath. 'Damned impertinence!'

Amelie lifted one shoulder. 'She merely said what everyone is thinking.'

Was Amelie wishing that, too, wishing she had waited one more day before marrying? That assumed the baby would be lost anyway and not because he'd made love to her.

'It suits no purpose to think about what might have been.' Of the baby who never quite was.

The door opened and Amelie's mother entered. 'How are you? I have brought tea.' She saw Edmund and stopped. '*Pardon.* I did not know you were here.'

Edmund rose and bowed. 'Good afternoon, *madame.* I hope you are well.' He stepped over to her. 'Let me take the tray off your hands.' He placed the tray on a nearby table.

'*Merci,*' she said, glancing away.

'Maman,' Amelie said. 'Why have you not arranged for Edmund to stay? Surely a room could be provided for him.'

'*Bien sûr*, he may stay. He stays the night in your room, no?' she snapped.

He broke in. 'Until you are fully recovered, it may be best for me to keep my room at Stephen's Hotel.'

'Is that what you want?' Amelie asked him.

What did *wanting* have to do with it? Nothing happened as he wanted.

Lady Northdon answered for him. 'I think it is best.' She gave Amelie a significant look. 'Your father. *Tu comprends?*'

'I agree,' Edmund said. 'Your father will be more comfortable if I am not underfoot.'

Lady Northdon nodded approvingly. '*Là*, I will leave you to your conversation. Amelie, you can pour the tea, no?'

'I will pour, Maman.'

'And do not dress for dinner, *ma chère*. It is only family.' She leaned down to give Amelie a kiss on the cheek and hurried out the door.

Amelie carefully rose from her chair and moved unsteadily to the tea table. 'How do you take your tea, Edmund?

'A little milk.' Lawd. They did not even know how the other took tea.

He reached for the cup so she would not have to hand it to him. She balanced her own with difficulty as she walked back to her chair.

'You are still weak,' he said.

She shrugged. 'A little.'

He sat. 'You should stay in this house until you are completely well.'

'And then?' There was no expression in her voice.

'Then we should leave London.'

She looked puzzled. 'But we decided—'

He did not have the heart to tell her of Tinmore's threat. It was too cruel and she was too vulnerable.

He searched for what to say. 'Until the gossipers forget all about us.'

Her blue eyes turned sad. 'But the reason for the gossip is gone now.'

He felt the pang of that loss, too, like a rapier thrust into his heart.

'Still…' What could he say?

She eyed him suspiciously. 'There is something you are not telling me.'

He glanced away.

Edmund was hiding things from her, too. She turned away from him, wishing he would leave.

Fearing he would leave and never return.

Finally he made a frustrated sound. 'Forgive me.

You should know this. I fear it will hurt you, but you should know this.'

Was he leaving, then?

His eyes were pained. 'Tinmore sought me out today. He threatened to reveal everything. About our marriage. About the—the baby—'

She turned back to him. 'Why would he do such a thing?'

'Because he wants me far away from my sister. His wife.'

She shook her head. 'No, it is because you stood up to him.'

He made a disparaging laugh. 'And all I accomplished was to hurt you.'

Did he think a little gossip hurt? She might have once agreed, but now she knew what real pain felt like.

He gazed at her again. 'I do not wish to trap you with me, if you do not wish it. I could go away. You could stay with your parents. Go with them to the country.'

She gaped at him. 'Do you wish to leave me?'

He left his chair and knelt at hers. He touched her hand, but it only reminded her of how the feel of his skin against hers had once ignited her senses. Everything seemed dead inside now.

'I know our—our loss changes things,' he said.

'We are married, though. I will not leave you unless that is what you desire.'

She pulled her hand away and curled up in the chair, covering herself with her shawl. 'Then let us go far away. Together. Where we know nobody.'

She closed her eyes, needing to be alone. His was the only company she could bear, but, at the moment, she could not even stand to be with herself.

She heard him rise.

'When it is time for dinner, shall I come for you, Amelie?'

She nodded.

As soon as she heard the door close behind her, she instantly regretted not asking him to stay with her. Where would he go? To the drawing room where her father would snap at him and her mother look upon him with disappointment?

Getting away. Going far away. The idea grew inside her. New scenery. Unfamiliar walls in some strange house. People who never knew her before. It all sounded lovely.

A place without reminders.

When Edmund came for her and escorted her to dinner, they did not speak. At the dinner table he sat across the table next to Tess. It was easier to look at him than the rest of them. Her father still seemed ready to explode at any moment. Her mother's lovely face was etched with worry. Tess's was all sympathy.

Why could they not at least pretend everything was normal?

Amelie had no appetite. She stirred the soup with her spoon.

'You must eat, *chérie*,' her mother chided.

She did not want to cause more worry. 'Yes, Maman.'

She made herself lift the spoon to her mouth but tasted nothing.

At least her mother's worry lines eased a bit.

Maybe that was the trick. Maybe if she pretended everything was as it should be, her family would follow suit.

'The soup is very nice.' She forced a smile and put another spoonful in her mouth.

Her mother, father and Tess smiled back. Her brother, seated next to her, gave her a playful tap on the arm.

When the main course was served, she made herself eat a little of everything.

'I believe I was hungry,' she said to murmurs of approval.

Yes, pretending would work.

'I think my health will return in a day or so,' she said.

Her mother frowned. 'Do not rush so, *chérie*.'

She girded herself. 'Edmund and I will wish to leave as soon as possible.'

'Leave!' her mother, father, and Tess all cried in unison.

'Non,' her mother said. 'There is no hurry. You must rest. '

'Give yourself time,' Tess added.

Her father glared at Edmund. 'What is this about leaving?'

Edmund put down his knife and fork. 'We talked today about living away from here for a while.'

'Then you must come to the country with us,' her mother said. 'There is plenty of room at Northdon House.'

'Not Northdon House, Maman,' Amelie said. 'Some place new that I never saw before.'

Her father turned to Edmund. 'This is your idea, no doubt.'

'It is,' Edmund agreed.

'It is not a bad idea,' Marc said. 'By the time they return, no one will pay them any mind. We'll all be spared the sort of mean-spirited gossip we've suffered in the past.'

'I will miss you,' Tess said. 'I'll miss you both.'

Amelie took a breath. This was going well. She could almost believe she cared about where she lived or what she did.

She looked at Edmund. 'I was thinking we should

go to the Lake District. Wordsworth says it is beautiful there.' They had all read the poet's *Guide to the Lakes*.

He gazed at her, his expression soft and...hopeful. 'Would you truly like to go to the Lake District, Amelie?'

Could he tell she was pretending?

'Yes,' she replied as emphatically as her pretence would allow. 'It will be a lovely adventure, and everyone says the air is like a tonic.'

He smiled at her, a tentative smile. 'Then that is where we shall go.'

Marc slammed a hand down on the table. 'Middlerock!'

'Middlerock?' Her father's brows knitted.

Marc addressed Edmund. 'Middlerock is one of Father's properties. A sheep farm in Cumberland.' He turned to his father. 'You have not travelled there for years. Would it not be advantageous for Edmund to see how it is faring?'

Her father frowned. 'True, I have not travelled there for years, but my man of business keeps tabs on it.'

'Do you not say it is wise to make an appearance at your properties?' Marc persisted. 'Have I not heard you say you should visit Middlerock?'

'Cumberland is so far away,' her mother murmured.

'It is very remote.' Her father seized on that idea. 'And it is a bit rustic for Amelie. More like a hunting lodge than a comfortable house.'

'I would like rustic.' Amelie made herself sound enthusiastic. 'I want a complete change of scenery.'

Her father's stern expression wavered.

'You must be comfortable with this, sir,' Edmund told him.

'Bah!' Her father waved a hand. 'What do you know of sheep farming?'

Edmund cocked his head. 'We had sheep on my father's estate. I was often my father's companion when he visited the estate manager and the farm workers. I learned a great deal about running a farm.'

'Please, Papa,' Amelie said.

Her father loved her, she knew. He had difficulty denying her anything. Her pretending was working rather well. She almost believed she wanted this.

'One thing, though,' Edmund said. 'You must give me complete authority to act on your behalf. I will not go there unless I can be useful to you.'

Her father reached for his wine glass and drank its contents. He shot a glance at Amelie before staring down at his plate. 'Very well. I'll give you permission to act in my stead.'

'Fully?' Edmund asked.

'Well, I would not like it if you sold the place

or lost it in a card game or something,' her father snapped.

The corners of Edmund's mouth twitched as if he were suppressing a smile. 'I give my word I will do neither of those things.'

'We can go to my solicitor tomorrow and draw up the papers.' Her father's shoulders slumped.

'Mon Dieu,' her mother muttered.

Amelie's hand trembled. She was suddenly weak with fatigue. It took too much effort to keep up her façade.

She stood. 'Forgive me. I am very tired. I must retire.'

Her mother rose as well and darted to her side. *'Ma chère pauvre*! I will take you to your room *tout de suite!'*

Amelie drew away from her. 'Edmund will take me, Maman.'

Edmund was already on his feet. He walked around the table to her. 'Can you walk, Amelie?' he asked her gently.

She nodded.

He wrapped his arm around her, and she leaned against him. His scent, his warmth enveloped her. She wished she'd let her mother help her upstairs. Her mother would not make her think of what it had been like to lie with him.

And what happened as a result.

When they reached the stairs, she took hold of the banister. 'I can manage.'

He remained next to her, though, and he offered her his arm when they started down the corridor to her room.

'Are you in any pain?' he asked her.

She shook her head. Not the physical kind anyway. 'I am tired. I did too much.'

'Promise you will rest tomorrow?' His voice was filled with concern.

She planned to pretend to be all better if she could. 'I will.'

As they neared the door she shrank back. 'I hate this room.'

He hugged her next to him, but she pulled away. His kindness was hard to bear when he should be furious with her.

'I—I feel I pushed you into this idea of the Lake District,' she said. 'I should have spoken to you privately.'

'It is an excellent idea, Amelie,' he said. 'If you desire it, it is where we will go.'

She leaned against the wall. 'Are you certain?'

He stood close but did not touch her. 'It meets our needs. If that changes we will go elsewhere.'

'What I need, I cannot have.' She gazed up at him, her sadness nearly choking her.

He nodded.

She pushed away from the wall and braced herself before reaching for the door handle. She turned back to him. 'Goodnight, Edmund.'

'Goodnight,' he murmured.

She opened the door and quickly entered.

Edmund stared at the closed door for a few moments before turning back towards the stairs. He still did not move. Instead he pressed his forehead against the wall where Amelie had leaned and fancied he could still feel her warmth.

It was a good idea to take her away, away from wagging tongues, away from families, away from the memories.

This farm, though, sounded like the furthest thing from the power and energy of Brussels or the excitement of foreign lands that Edmund had once wanted. But he wanted to please Amelie, to make up to her what he'd caused them to lose. If a sheep farm in Cumberland pleased her, then that was where he wanted to go.

If they could be alone, away from all this, perhaps they might find a way to reconcile themselves to this forced marriage, even though the reason for marrying was lost.

He pushed away from the wall and walked down the corridor to the stairs. He descended slowly, reluctant to rejoin her parents, who so clearly did not welcome him into their home.

Amelie only woke a few times during the night to toss and turn with memories and grief. When morning came, she felt stronger.

Perhaps it would not take as much effort to pretend to be recovered as it had the evening before.

Sally came into the room, carrying fresh linens and looking pale and unhappy. 'You are awake, ma'am.'

What was troubling the girl? Whatever it was, Amelie's grief so consumed her she had nothing of herself to give to her unhappy maid.

'Will you wish to dress this morning?' Sally asked.

Amelie sat up in the bed. 'Yes, please. I am going to try to have a normal day.' As if she could ever have a normal day again.

Sally helped her out of her nightdress and set out her clothing while Amelie washed herself. She helped Amelie into her dress before she sat down to the dressing table and began to brush the tangles out of her hair.

'They say below stairs that you will be leaving soon,' Sally said.

The servants knew already. They knew everything now.

'That is so,' Amelie responded. 'Mr Summerfield and I will be moving to the Lake District.'

In the mirror she saw Sally's face contort in distress. The girl turned her face away, but when she again resumed brushing Amelie's hair, tears rolled down her cheeks.

It made it almost impossible for Amelie to keep her tears at bay. 'Do not worry. I will tell Maman to keep you on. You will not be without employment.'

'I am not so certain.' Sally's words came haltingly.

Amelie turned around to face her. 'Tell me what troubles you.'

Sally shook her head. 'I cannot tell you after all that's happened to you!'

Tears stung Amelie's eyes. 'Of course you can tell me. I am nearly all better.'

'I am in such a fix.' Sally dropped the brush and sobbed.

Amelie left the chair and guided Sally over to sit with her on the bed. She held Sally's hands. 'What is this fix?'

Sally blinked her tears away. 'Do you know the soldier you saw me with before Waterloo? Calvin Jones?'

The poor young man who was killed in the battle. 'Of course, I remember.'

'Do you remember he was to marry me as soon as he could get leave?' Sally's voice trembled.

'Yes.'

'I—I—that night—it did not seem so bad—you must know—but what can I do now—?' she sputtered.

Amelie trembled. She knew what Sally was about to say. 'Tell me.'

Sally faced Amelie, her eyes red from crying. 'I am going to have a baby.'

A baby.

The words caused an ache deep in Amelie's belly. It felt as if a dozen swords were slashing her. She couldn't breathe. She closed her eyes, pushed the pain away as hard as she could.

She put her arms around Sally, who began to sob against her chest.

'There. There.' Amelie comforted the girl. 'We will make this right. I will help you.'

'I—I thought I should get rid of it, but I didn't know how,' Sally wailed.

Amelie hugged her tighter. 'No, you mustn't try to get rid of it. Never think that.'

Sally leaned against Amelie's heart. 'I don't want to take my baby to the Foundling Hospital!'

'Not that either. We will fix this. I promise.'

Sally pulled away to stare at her. 'Truthfully?'

Amelie's heart pounded. 'You will come with me to the Lake District. I will not leave you.'

She could not save her own baby, but she would save Sally's.

Chapter Fifteen

Four days later they were on the road to the Lake District, beginning a journey that would take at least three days to complete. Lord Northdon provided the carriage so that the trip would be as comfortable as possible for Amelie. Lord and Lady Northdon rode with them the first day to their country house, where they spent the first night.

Lady Northdon had arranged separate bedchambers for them, and Edmund was rarely alone with Amelie more than a few minutes at a time. When they continued the journey, the bulk of which covered the Great North Road, it was no more private. Amelie's maid rode with them and spent the night in Amelie's bedchamber.

Edmund could not ascertain how Amelie felt about anything on the journey. She seemed more concerned with her maid's comfort than her own, and everything on the journey was acceptable to her. The food at the inns, the rooms for the night, the times they rose, the times they retired. Agree-able as she was, she seemed to keep herself at a distance from him.

He could not blame her, though. Before that fate-ful night in Brussels, she had been the cosseted daughter of an aristocrat. Now she was the wife of a reckless bastard who was taking her far away to live on a sheep farm.

On the last day they turned off the main road onto smaller and smaller ones that wound over and around hills covered in green grass and dotted with sheep. Majestic mountains rose in the distance, tinged with the reds and yellows of autumn. The air seemed crisper and cleaner than it even had been in the countryside near Northdon House. The lakes they glimpsed shimmered with water as blue as—

As blue as Amelie's eyes.

'This country is unlike what you are used to, is it not?' he asked.

'It is lovely,' she said politely.

Was she seeing it? Or merely staring into space? Her maid seemed to be taking it in.

Compared to the wilder hills and mountains of Spain, this land seemed comfortably tidy. He'd rel-ish long walks on hills like these.

Would Amelie?

They passed through the tiny village of Middlerock, where the people on the street stopped to stare at their carriage. The farm could not be far.

About a mile from the village the carriage passed through a wrought-iron gate and made its way along a woodland drive. A white stucco house, gleaming in the afternoon sun, came into view. It was definitely small compared to the very grand Northdon House, and it looked as if it had been constructed without any notion of symmetry. Additions grew like appendages off each side of the house, one side earning three distinct sections, the other side merely one.

'There it is. What do you think of it?' Edmund asked Amelie.

An expression of dismay flitted across her face, but she quickly schooled her features. 'It should do.'

The house had five bedrooms, Lord Northdon told him. Edmund wished it had only one. Perhaps he would not feel so distant from her if he could hold her in his arms all night.

The carriage reached the unimposing entrance, a single door under a small portico with only two thin and unembellished columns. It came to a full stop before the door opened and four people emerged. Two older women, an older man and another woman of uncertain age. All were plainly dressed, and the women wore white caps.

'Our servants, I believe,' he said to Amelie.

She peered out the window. 'Oh, I did not think,' she murmured. 'I must run the house.'

'Does that worry you?' He'd take it over if she did not feel up to the task.

She darted a glance at him as if surprised he'd heard her. 'No,' she said in that annoyingly bland tone. 'I'll manage.'

The older man met the carriage as it stopped. He pulled down the steps and opened the door. One of the coachmen jumped down from the box and held the horses' heads.

Edmund disembarked first so he could help Amelie and Sally out of the carriage.

He leaned down to Amelie's ear. 'Shall we greet our servants?'

He turned to the older man who'd attended the carriage. 'I am Mr Summerfield,' Edmund said. 'And this is my wife, Mrs Summerfield, Lord Northdon's daughter. You were expecting us, I believe.'

'We were, sir,' the older man said. 'I am Lloyd, your butler.' He stepped back to where the women were waiting. 'This is Mrs Wood, the housekeeper. Mrs Stagg, the cook. And Jobson, the maid.'

It seemed too thin a staff to run a household, Edmund thought.

Amelie smiled at the servants. 'A pleasure to meet you.' She turned to Sally, who had gathered their belongings from the carriage. 'Let me present my lady's maid, Sally—Mrs Brown, I mean.'

Edmund's brows rose. How had Sally become *Mrs Brown*?

'You will help her settle in?' Amelie asked.

The housekeeper nodded. 'We'll see to it.' She opened the door and led them inside.

They entered a small hall with a slate floor and a rather handsome arched-mahogany staircase and banister.

Mrs Wood pointed to the right. 'That is the drawing room. The dining room is on the other side of the hall. Both have been prepared for you. We do not have the whole house in order yet, I fear. The bedchambers are ready, however.'

'Show us to our bedchambers first,' Edmund told her.

'And then perhaps you would like some tea?'

He glanced to see if Amelie would answer, but she seemed to preoccupy herself with gazing at the wainscotted wall.

'Tea would be most welcome,' he said.

They climbed the mahogany stairs to the first floor, where two adjoining bedchambers had been made ready for them. The rooms were adequately, if not finely, furnished.

Amelie and Sally disappeared into one bedchamber. Edmund thanked the housekeeper and entered the other.

After a few minutes, Lloyd and the coachman carried in Edmund's trunk. After they left, Edmund changed his shirt and brushed the dirt of the road off his coat and trousers. He tested the bed. Comfortable enough, but would be much more so if shared with Amelie.

He waited, giving Amelie a sufficient amount of time to change her clothes, remembering when he'd helped her with the task and wishing they had that measure of closeness now.

What must he do now to help her recover? To make amends?

He walked to the connecting door. His hand remained suspended in the air before he finally knocked.

'Come in,' he heard her say.

He opened the door but stayed in the doorway.

Her gaze rose from where she sat on the bed. 'Sally has gone to see her room.'

He tried a smile. '*Mrs Brown*, you mean?'

She averted her face. 'I will explain that to you later. Not now, if you please.'

'Whenever you wish,' he said mildly. He glanced around the room, which was as serviceably furnished as his own. 'Will this room do, Amelie?'

She looked at it as if seeing it for the first time. 'Yes. It is fine.'

It was so difficult to talk with her.

'I've endured much worse,' he said for something to say. 'Like a leaking tent on a cold and rainy night in the Pyrenees. But you are used to finer things.'

Her expression turned fleetingly sad. 'I do not need finer things.'

The word *need* hung in the air. She meant that she needed her baby, he supposed. The loss seemed so much more important than physical discomfort, he could agree.

He stepped into the room. 'Shall we see about the tea?'

Mrs Wood brought a tea tray with biscuits as soon as they entered the drawing room. Amelie poured the tea and handed Edmund a cup.

Poor man! she thought, so concerned with her comfort and trying so hard to make things right for her. Her efforts at responding in kind fell short.

The long, idle hours in the carriage had been a horror for her. Too much time to think and so difficult to pretend she was well when tears were ever ready to fall.

She did not want this—to be weak and weeping. She wanted to be strong. To convince Edmund—and herself—that she was recovered.

She took a sip of tea and a bite of biscuit and discovered her appetite had returned. She could taste the flavours and feel the hunger for more. She finished the biscuit, took another and glanced around the room.

She liked this house, she decided. It was rustic and sparsely furnished and reminded her of nothing she knew.

The drawing room had tolerably comfortable chairs and sofas, tables, lamps, a fireplace. A carpet on the floor. Everything had been dusted, polished and brushed clean.

She thought of something positive she could say to Edmund, who leaned against the mantel drinking his tea.

'They did a fine job cleaning this room, did they not?' It occurred to her she must tell the housekeeper so.

He looked surprised she'd spoken. 'It is clean.' There was the tiniest bit of sarcasm in his voice.

It almost made her smile.

'I wonder if the room once had more adornment,' she went on.

'Perhaps we will be able to discover if it had,' he responded encouragingly.

Her sadness crept back. What did it matter whether there were porcelain figurines or vases of flowers or colourful paintings on the walls?

The clock chimed the quarter-hour.

Edmund gestured to it. 'At least there is a clock.'

It was the plainest clock she'd ever seen. A plain white face with black numerals encased in an oak box.

'Is the time correct, I wonder?' she asked. If so they had hours to go before it would be time for dinner, after which she could beg fatigue and retire to her room.

He reached in his pocket and pulled out his timepiece. 'Three twenty. Close enough.'

What was she to do with so much time?

Edmund adjusted the hands of the clock and turned away from the mantel to place his cup on the tea tray. 'Shall we explore the house?'

It was an excellent idea, a good distraction, a way to pass the time. Plus she needed to walk after days of being cramped in the carriage.

Across the hall where Mrs Wood had indicated, they found the dining room and behind it a corridor which they guessed led to the kitchen. The back of the house revealed a library, tucked behind the drawing room, and another sitting room, this one bright with a wall composed almost entirely of windows. It was perfect for a breakfast room, Amelie thought.

They entered the library and examined the books

on its shelves, the titles mostly referring to agriculture and sheep farming.

'I suppose I shall have to read some of these,' Edmund said. 'Something to look forward to.'

If there were novels tucked between such titles, Amelie did not discover them.

Off the sitting room was a surprise—a conservatory, empty of plants, but with large glass doors leading to the back garden and walls completely made of windows.

'Someone once must have cared for this house,' Amelie said. 'To build this.'

'We can grow things here,' he said encouragingly.

She tried to imagine the room filled with greenery, fragrant with flowers, filled with life. It was now a desolate, abandoned place, too much like the interior of herself, the place she was trying to keep hidden.

She wished she could respond to his efforts to cheer her. He alone knew her secrets. He alone knew she was the cause of...everything. It once had drawn her closer to him; now she'd effectively destroyed his every ambition. How could running a sheep farm compare to travelling the world and seeking a fortune?

Edmund opened a door. 'Let us go outside.'

He opened the door, and they stepped out on a

terrace that had weeds growing between its flag-stones.

'Oh, my!' she exclaimed, forgetting her misery.

In front of her was a great expanse of green lawn with a view of mountains turning blue in the late afternoon light, moors wild with heather, lush forest and a peek of pastures dotted white with sheep.

'It is beautiful,' she whispered.

Off to the right were the farm buildings built of ancient stone and slate roofs. A man wearing a flat wool cap stood near the buildings, elbows akimbo. Spying them, he began to approach. When he came close enough, Edmund walked forward to meet him.

'You must be Summerfield,' the man said, offering his hand. 'I am Reid, the farm steward.'

Edmund accepted the handshake and acknowledged the introduction. He turned to Amelie. 'Let me present you to my wife, Mrs Summerfield, Lord Northdon's daughter.'

'Ma'am.' He tipped his hat.

She nodded. 'This land is beautiful, Mr Reid. How lucky you are to wake to this every day.'

His brows knitted for a moment. 'It is sometimes cruel, as well,' he commented. He turned to Edmund. 'I meant to give you time to settle in before calling.'

'Kind of you,' Edmund responded. 'I am eager to speak with you. When might it be convenient?'

Reid looked wary. 'I keep early hours. Up at dawn. I'm out in the pastures shortly after.'

'I am used to early hours,' Edmund replied.

Reid's expression turned sceptical.

Amelie spoke up, 'My husband was an officer in the army, sir. That is why he is used to early hours.' Reid should know Edmund was more than the husband of Lord Northdon's daughter.

Reid looked no more interested. 'I see.'

The conservatory door opened, and Sally hurried out, coming up to them out of breath. 'Mrs Wood sent me to find you.' She noticed Mr Reid and stepped back.

Reid gazed at Sally in return, and his countenance softened.

Sally pulled her gaze back to Amelie. 'Mrs Wood said I was to ask if you would mind keeping country hours here and having dinner in half an hour.'

'Of course. We will be happy to.' Amelie turned to Mr Reid. 'Sally, this is Mr Reid, the steward.'

'Miss.' He tipped his hat to Sally.

'*Mrs Brown*, I should say,' Amelie corrected. 'Mrs Brown is a widow. She is my lady's maid.'

'Ma'am,' he corrected.

Sally blushed but did not speak to him.

Edmund broke in. 'I will meet you at the farm building at six in the morning. Will that do?'

'I will look for you.' Reid nodded to both Amelie and Sally. 'Good evening to you.'

'Good evening, Mr Reid,' Amelie said.

After their dinner, which consisted of mutton stew, bread, cheese and stilted conversation, Amelie could not feign exhaustion and retire for the night. It was too early. Instead she and Edmund returned to the drawing room.

Austere as the room was, a wood fire crackling in the fireplace gave it a welcoming warmth. The hissing and popping of the burning wood took Amelie back to the last year's yule log. A lifetime ago, it seemed. Before she'd met Fowler, before she travelled to Brussels, before the scandalous night she spent with Edmund, before the baby...

Tears stung her eyes, but she blinked them away. She glanced over to see if Edmund had noticed, but he was bent forward, rubbing his injured leg.

'Does your leg pain you?' she asked.

He looked up at her. 'A bit tonight. I think the carriage ride did it no favours.'

She'd been too self-absorbed to think of *his* comfort during the journey.

He straightened again. 'It has been a long day.'

Every day seemed long to Amelie. This evening

seemed long, too, as they continued to strain for things to talk about. Amelie knew what preoccupied her, but what was Edmund thinking? How could he not be wishing he'd never met her?

'Mr Reid seemed taken with Sally,' he remarked.

'Sally is a pretty young woman,' Amelie's voice had a churlish tone, she feared.

'She is,' Edmund agreed.

They lapsed into silence again, until she remembered she owed him an explanation.

This would not be easy. 'I promised I would explain about calling Sally Mrs Brown.'

He merely raised his brows and waited for her to continue.

She took a breath. 'That night in Brussels.' She did not have to explain what night she meant. 'Do you remember that we encountered Sally in the *parc*?'

'With her soldier. I remember.' His voice was deep and smooth, and she seemed to feel it as well as hear.

'He died in the battle,' she said.

His expression turned bleak, and he averted his gaze. Remembering that day, she supposed.

She went on quickly. 'Sally is going to have his baby.' Like us, she wanted to say. Only what might have been.

'A baby,' he repeated, his voice low.

'No one knows her here, so we are calling her a widow. She is, really, in many ways, because he was going to marry her.' At least Amelie hoped Sally had not been deceived the way she had been. If so, better she never know. 'She will not be disgraced this way.'

'I see.' He frowned. 'But what of when we return to London?'

'I shall worry about that later.' They could concoct another story, if necessary. 'Her baby will have every chance in life. I am resolved in that.' To make up for her own lost child. 'I will see to it.'

He turned silent, staring into the fire.

She bit her lip. 'You do not approve?'

He glanced back at her. 'I approve. I very much approve.'

She released a relieved breath. 'You will allow our deception?'

'It is not for me to allow or forbid it, Amelie. I support it, though, and am willing to help.' He reached over and touched her hand. 'This is good of you, Amelie.'

His touch warmed her, just as it had done on their wedding day. She pulled her hand away. 'I—I believe I shall go upstairs and retire for the night. I—I am much fatigued.'

He nodded, but his eyes were pained. 'I will go, too. Since I am to rise before dawn.'

Edmund carried a candle to light their way as they walked up the winding staircase to their rooms. Amelie did not take his arm out of fear that desire would ignite if she touched him. How awful that would be, showing she wanted him only days after—

He walked her to the door of her bedchamber, their little candle making a cocoon of light around them. In the darkness the house seemed eerie and strange, full of shadows and creaking floorboards.

He put his hand on the latch of her door. 'Do I say good-night to you here, Amelie?'

She could not look at him. 'I—I am very weary.'

He turned the latch and opened the door. 'Sleep well,' he murmured.

She darted a glance to him. She wanted to tell him to knock on the connecting door after Sally readied her for bed, but she couldn't.

'Goodnight,' she said, a little too shrill.

She hurried into the room and shut the door behind her.

Sally was in the room waiting for her.

'I—I believe I'll go to bed early,' she told her.

'Very good, ma'am.'

Sally helped her change into her nightdress, after which she sat at a small dressing table while Sally pulled the pins from her hair and brushed out the tangles.

'How has this day been for you?' Amelie asked her.

'The others have been kind to me,' Sally answered. 'They've been very busy but helpful.'

'Did you get enough to eat?'

'Oh, yes, ma'am,' Sally assured her. 'As much stew as I could want.'

Amelie was glad to hear it. Sally must eat well and stay healthy for the baby's sake.

'And your room,' she asked. 'Is it comfortable?'

'It is very comfortable, ma'am.' She plaited Amelie's hair. 'It is on the second floor. A small room next to the stairway. Very plain, but all I need. Even a chair and table. I have never had a room of my own before.'

'I am glad you like it.' Amelie was determined that Sally have every possible comfort.

Sally tied the plait with a ribbon and Amelie stood.

'Will it be all right if I stay up a little?' Sally asked. 'I am not sleepy.'

'Of course,' Amelie resisted asking the source of her sleeplessness. Sally would not like it, and it would cause too many questions among the other servants if Amelie hovered over her the way she wanted to.

'You have my permission to make use of the library, although it looked thin of anything that might appeal to you.'

'I might look for a book,' Sally said.

When she left, Amelie blew out the one remaining candle. She climbed into bed and curled up under the covers and tried not to think.

Sally went to her room on the second floor. Not only did she have a room of her own, she also was the only one on this floor. The other servants had rooms on the same wing as the kitchen. This room even had a window that looked out on the garden in the back.

She pulled the chair up to the window and sat gazing at the garden, bathed in moonlight. It was such a lovely night, like the ones in Brussels when she had slipped out of the hotel to meet Calvin.

Poor Calvin. She'd known him since they were children in Hampstead. Even then they'd meet at night, sneaking out to explore the Heath. Her happiest times had been at night, with Calvin. She missed the nights; she missed Calvin, terribly.

Her solitary room suddenly no longer seemed spacious. It seemed suffocating. She grabbed her shawl and lit a candle and walked as quietly as she could down the stairs and to the conservatory, where she knew she could easily reach the outside without anyone knowing. She carefully opened the door and made certain it would not lock behind her.

Leaving the candle in the conservatory, she

stepped out onto the lawn and gazed at the wild expanse in front of her. The mountains surrounded her, black shapes against the cloudy grey sky. She'd never seen mountains before. She wished Calvin were here to see them with her.

Would he mind that his baby would be born in this wild place? Miss Glenville—Mrs Summerfield, she meant—said she'd be protected from scandal here where no one knew her, but what would happen to her and her baby later? What would Mr Summerfield do? Mr Summerfield knew she wasn't a Mrs. Sally remembered him from Brussels. He'd been with Miss Glenville that night, not Captain Fowler, the man Miss Glenville had been betrothed to. It had taken a while for Sally to remember him.

Mr Summerfield was a kind man, though, Sally thought. And an honourable one. He had married Miss Glenville to give their baby his name.

Sally had always assumed any baby she had would have Calvin's name. This baby would not have a father's name, merely her family name, but, for his whole life, she would have to lie to him, making up a marriage that never happened and a father who wasn't Calvin.

'Hoo doo, ma'am?' A man's voice made her jump.

She swung around. It was the man she had met earlier, the steward. 'Mr Reid. You startled me!'

'Is anything amiss?' he asked.

She was embarrassed to be caught like this. 'Nothing. I—I felt like some fresh air, is all.'

He stood beside her and gazed out over the mountains. 'I like coming out here on nights like this, as though there was naught but me and the mountains.'

She smiled sheepishly. 'I have spoiled it for you, then.'

His gaze was warm. 'Nae. It is nice to meet someone who appreciates the night.'

His accent was unlike any she'd heard. She had to concentrate to understand him.

'It is peaceful,' she said, even though the night had not brought her peace.

'You've not been here long, but what do you think of it?' He glanced out at the mountains.

'I've never seen the like,' she said. 'It is all hills and trees.'

'And where are you from?' he asked.

'London.' she asked. 'It is mostly buildings and streets except for the park.'

'I've never seen the like of that.' He gazed at her again.

His was a nice face. Tan from the sun but pleasant to look at. Not tall and thin, like Calvin, but shorter and thicker as if there was much power packed inside him.

She suddenly felt bashful. 'I—I should go inside.'

'Mebby we will meet out here again some night,' he said.

'Perhaps.'

'Goodnight, then, lass.' He tipped his hat.

'Goodnight.' She turned around and ran back in the house.

Chapter Sixteen

Edmund woke to a cry.

Amelie's voice came through the connecting door. 'No! No! No!'

He bounded out of bed and donned the banyan he'd pulled out of his trunk before going to bed.

'No!' she cried again. 'My baby.'

He opened the connecting door and ran to her side. She thrashed in the bed.

'Amelie,' he called, holding her still.

Her eyes opened but did not focus. 'I lost the baby, Edmund.'

She was still asleep, he realised.

She reached for him. 'I lost the baby. I cannot find her anywhere.'

If she woke, she would remember the dream and suffer the loss all over again. If she slept there was a chance she would forget the nightmare.

He climbed onto the bed, and she clung to him. 'Find my baby, Edmund!'

'Sleep, Amelie. I'll find the baby. Sleep.' His throat turned raw. This was too much like that awful night. Her crying out in her bed. Her distress.

Their loss.

'Very tired,' she murmured.

'Yes. Sleep.' He laid her back against the pillows and leaned down to kiss her forehead.

Her unfocused eyes opened again. 'Do not leave me.'

Of course he did not want to leave her. Every night he'd spent apart from her had been difficult, especially when she was a mere door, a mere wall, away. Edmund was used to being alone, even among officers in his regiment, schoolmates, sometimes even among the people at Summerfield House. With Amelie, though, so distant, emotionally if not physically, he felt acute loneliness. He hadn't felt such loneliness since—

Since watching his mother die.

He crawled into bed with her and spooned her against him. She relaxed and slipped deeper into sleep. It took longer for Edmund.

When he woke, Amelie was still next to him, soft and warm and tempting him to let Mr Reid and the farm go to the devil so he could hold her longer.

But he was uncertain if she would like finding him next to her. He waited a moment, savouring the scent of her and the soft sounds of her breathing, before carefully moving away from her the way he'd done on that night in Brussels when he'd thought he was merely leaving her with a pleasant memory, a memory that had helped sustain him during the battle and when he lay injured.

Too much had happened since that time.

His bare feet hit the floor, and his skin felt the room's chill. The fire had nearly died. He padded quietly over to the fireplace and put on two more logs so the room would be warm when she woke. Out the window the mountains were haloed in a faint glow.

Dawn was near.

He grabbed his banyan and walked silently to the connecting door and quietly lifted the latch.

She stirred behind him and he froze.

He turned to see if he'd woken her, but she became still again. Her hair had come loose of its plait and tumbled over her shoulders. Her face was relaxed, as untroubled as a child's. He caught his breath at the sight. If only he could keep her untroubled for all her days.

He opened the door and slipped out of the room.

He'd left his trunk in disarray from searching for his banyan the night before and now he disturbed its contents even more, looking for clean drawers and a shirt.

He pulled on his drawers first, then shaved quickly and put on his shirt and a pair of buckskin pantaloons.

The connecting door opened.

He swerved around.

Amelie stood in the doorway. 'I heard you moving about.'

He buttoned his pantaloons. 'I did not mean to disturb you.' He ransacked the trunk again, looking for a coat and waistcoat fit for touring a farm.

She walked over to him. 'You did not disturb me. I just woke up. I slept well, though.'

Except for her nightmare, but, as he'd hoped, she didn't seem to remember it.

She peered into his trunk, which was a rumpled mess. 'Shall I have Sally unpack for you?'

'If she has time.' He put on his stockings and boots.

She handed him his hat and gloves.

'I have no idea when I will be back.' He pulled on his gloves.

'Do not concern yourself over me,' she said. 'I will find something to do. See about making some of the other rooms ready, perhaps.'

'Do not tire yourself, Amelie.' He was certain she was not as recovered as she pretended.

Her eyes turned sad. 'I must keep busy.'

He understood. Keeping busy was his only means of relief from his thoughts. His regrets.

He smiled at her. 'I suspect I will be busy if I make the meeting with Reid in time. Wish me luck.' He opened the door. 'I shall need it.'

She gazed at him earnestly. 'I wish you a wonderful day.'

His heart pounded at her words as he hurried down the stairs and out the front door.

He walked around the house and towards the farm buildings. One long building off to the side he'd guess to be the stables. He trusted Lord Northdon's coachmen had been given good beds and would be provided with a hearty breakfast before they started back to Hertfordshire.

When he reached the place Reid had designated to meet, Reid was not there. The sky was turning lighter by the minute. Edmund pulled out his time-piece. Five minutes past six. Had Reid not waited for him? He paced back and forth in the yard, both to keep warm and to wake himself up.

Finally Reid emerged from the far end of the last building. He did not walk faster even though he saw Edmund.

'You are here,' Reid said.

'As I said I would be,' Edmund responded.

'Not much happening today,' the man went on. 'The sheep are grazing.'

The night before, Reid had made it sound as if he would be consumed with work. Was he putting Edmund through some kind of test? If so, he had passed the punctuality part.

Edmund ought to be the one to test Reid, to see if Reid did his job properly.

'Show me the farm,' Edmund said firmly. 'I need to see everything. No more delays.'

Reid nodded. 'Let us begin with the buildings. I'll show you each of them.' He opened the big wooden door to the building they were standing near.

After Edmund left, Amelie stood at the window and watched him cross the lawn to the farm buildings. He looked so impressive, walking briskly, the tails of his coat surging behind him.

She felt better this morning. Not exactly cheerful, but not despondent either. For the first time since her miscarriage she had woken to something besides her morose thoughts. She'd woken to the sounds of Edmund moving about in his room. It had comforted her.

She refused to be idle today. She needed to be busy, so busy she couldn't think. Making the house more comfortable and pleasant was something she could do.

Starting with this room.

She gathered the clothing he'd left strewn around. Picked up his drawers—what an intimate thing, picking up his drawers! A proper wifely task. She remembered him removing them, both in Brussels and—and on their wedding night.

But she should not think of either of those nights.

She set his drawers aside and the shirt he wore the previous day. Both would need to be laundered. She hung the coat he wore on the back of a chair and folded his trousers. Kneeling next to Edmund's trunk, she refolded the clothes he'd tossed around in his rush to get dressed. She held a shirt up to her nose. It had been laundered, but she could still smell his scent on the fabric.

Why did he not have a valet? She must ask him some time.

At the bottom of the trunk she spied a packet of letters tied up with a string. She picked it up.

The writing on the outside was in a feminine hand. Amelie had a sick feeling deep in her stomach. Was there another woman he truly loved? How would she know? Had a woman been the reason he wanted to return to Brussels?

She dropped the packet of letters.

They could just as easily be from his sisters. Or from Tess's mother. He'd lived with Tess's mother in Brussels before the battle, he'd said.

If Amelie untied the string and read the letters she'd know for certain.

No. She would not snoop where she was not wanted. If he had a woman he loved somewhere, she would just have to wait until he told her.

Because he would tell her. Unlike everyone else Amelie knew, Edmund always told her the truth.

She put the letters back exactly as she'd found them and refolded all the clothing in his trunk before going back to her bedchamber. The fire in her fireplace was reduced to a few glowing embers. She put on another log and stood warming her hands when flames began to curl over it.

There was water enough in the ewer to wash herself. It was something she could do while waiting for Sally to come and help her dress. She stripped out of her nightdress and washed herself, shivering as she did so. Her bleeding had stopped, that reminder of what had happened. Mrs Bayliss had told her to wait until after her courses before having relations with her husband again.

But she did not want to think about that.

She donned a shift and covered herself with a wrapper and sat in a chair right by the fire, wondering what Edmund was doing. He wanted to be of some use to her father, she knew. She must do her part, as well. Manage the household.

There was a light knock on the door, and Sally crept in.

Amelie swivelled around in her chair. 'I am up, Sally.'

Sally looked alarmed. 'Sorry, ma'am. I thought you would still be asleep.'

'I woke up.' She did not explain that she had woken up and heard her husband in the next room and had had a sudden desire to see him.

'Would you like me to help you dress?' Sally asked.

Amelie smiled. 'First I would like you to tell me how you are feeling.'

'Ohhh.' The maid drew out the word. 'I suppose I am feeling well enough.'

'And how did you sleep?'

Sally looked abashed. 'It felt strange to be up on that floor all alone.'

'I can imagine.' Amelie had not wanted to be alone either. She stood and walked over to the girl. 'You must tell me if you feel unwell or fatigued. I will not have you work yourself too hard.'

'Yes, ma'am.' Sally sounded as solemn as ever.

'And here I am going to ask you to do more than your duties.'

'What is it, ma'am?'

Amelie suddenly felt guilty for it. 'I wonder if you

would unpack Mr Summerfield's trunk for him and put the clothes in the wardrobe in his room.'

'Oh, that will not be hard, ma'am. I will do that.' She spoke with more energy.

'Thank you,' Amelie said with feeling. 'I think today I want my plainest dress. And I wish I had thought to have some caps made. I plan to see all of this house, and I have a feeling dust will be everywhere.'

'Would you like one of my caps, ma'am?' Sally offered.

'How kind of you.' She was sincerely touched. 'I will consider it, but first I'll see how it is without wearing one.'

A clock somewhere in the house struck eight as Amelie descended the stairs. She went directly to the dining room, but it was as she and Edmund had left it after the dessert dishes were removed. Amelie had said nothing to the servants about breakfast, and she ought to have done so.

She walked through the dining room to the door she and Edmund had presumed led to the kitchen. As she walked through the corridor she heard voices and headed towards them.

'The thing is, why did Lord Northdon send them here?' It was Mrs Wood's voice. 'Why now?'

'I am worried about what Mrs Summerfield will

expect,' another voice said—Jobson, perhaps. 'I can't do all the cleaning of this whole house. It is too much.'

'And I need help in the kitchen.' That must have been Mrs Stagg.

They were all seated around a kitchen table. Mugs of tea or coffee or chicory sat in front of them as well as slices of bread and cheese.

'Good morning.' Amelie tried for a cheerful tone.

They all scrambled to their feet.

Her whole life she'd watched her mother deal with servants. Her mother did the job so well that their houses had always been harmonious—even when matters between her mother and father had not been.

She stepped into a room that must be the servants' hall. 'I could not help but overhear your conversation. Please do not worry about our being here. We know we create more work for you and that you will need more help. Perhaps you can advise me on exactly how much help you require.'

The three women stared at her wide-eyed.

She smiled. 'I came in search of breakfast. And to speak to you, Mrs Wood. Please meet with me after I eat. Simple fare will suffice, Mrs Stagg.' She gestured to the contents of the table. 'Bread and cheese. Some jam, if there is any. And tea. That will do nicely for me this morning.'

They continued to stare.

'Thank you.' She turned around and left.

It was near the dinner hour when Edmund finally returned to the house. He walked in the front door and found the hall deserted as it had been that morning. He checked the drawing room just to see if Amelie was there, but it was empty, as well. Something seemed changed about the place, though.

It smelled better.

Maybe that was because he was no longer riding through fields dotted with cattle dung or holding pens filled with sheep. He climbed the stairs, his legs weary, his injured leg aching. He'd spent the day on his feet or on horseback, and his leg was making a justifiable complaint.

When he reached the first floor he called for her. 'Amelie?'

Her bedchamber door opened. 'You are back! I did not know whether to worry or not.'

She almost took his breath away, and he was struck dumb for a few moments. She was dressed in a gown of pale pink silk that shimmered when she moved. Her hair was pulled up to the top of her head and tied with a pink ribbon, but her curls were loose about her head.

He finally found his voice. 'You look fresh.' Not merely fresh. As lovely as a rose in bloom.

She twirled around. 'Do I? Sally dressed me for dinner and made me presentable. Believe me, I was not presentable before.'

Very presentable, he thought. He, on the other hand, was covered with dirt from the fields, the road and the pens of sheep. He looked down at himself. 'I need to clean myself.'

Her smile wavered. 'Of course. I will not trouble you.'

No! He had not meant to upset her. 'You do not trouble me, Amelie. I am eager to hear of your day, but I must get this dirt off first. '

'Knock on my door when you are finished, if you like.' Her voice had turned more subdued, though. She retreated into her bedchamber.

He opened his door and went inside.

The room had been straightened, he saw immediately. His trunk was gone. Certainly part of what Amelie had done was see that the room was put in proper order.

He hated to bring his soiled clothing in there. He stripped down and washed himself and shaved again.

He found his clothes in drawers and in the wardrobe and chose his whitest linen and his formal coat and waistcoat. When he finished dressing he knocked on the door connecting their two rooms. She opened it, but her demeanour had turned wary, like a butterfly ready to take flight.

He smiled at her. 'I suspect you had something to do with tidying my mess.'

'Yes.' She lowered her lashes. 'Well, Sally, actually. Sally unpacked for you.'

'If I do not see her, thank her for me.' He offered his arm. 'Shall we go downstairs?'

They walked down to the drawing room, where a decanter of wine waited for them.

'Wine?' He needed wine right now. 'Nothing suits me more at the moment.'

She looked pleased.

That was an even better tonic than the wine. 'Shall I pour you a glass?'

'Indeed.' She lowered herself into one of the chairs.

He poured the wine and handed her a glass, placing his weight on his bad leg. Pain shot through it and he winced.

She noticed. 'Is your leg hurting you?'

He could be stoic and deny the pain, but why shouldn't she know? 'It hurts like the devil. I was on my feet or on horseback all the day.'

'Were you? You must be exhausted.' She took a sip of the wine. 'What did you do? I hope you ate something.'

He sat in a chair near hers and stretched out his leg. 'We walked over most of the fells, I think, and rode into the village. We had a mutton pie at the inn there.'

She took another sip. 'Do not be surprised if we are eating mutton again tonight.'

'I am famished enough to eat anything.' He drank some of the wine and lifted his glass to her. 'This is quite...tolerable.'

'It is some my father left,' she said. 'There are about five bottles left, Lloyd said.'

He relaxed as the wine slid comfortingly down his throat. She seemed more at ease with him again.

She sipped from her glass. 'Tell me of your day.'

He told her of walking to the closer fells, riding to the more distant ones, seeing the flock grazing. He told of people he met—the farm workers and people in the village—and how he had the sense that they were concerned about his presence among them.

'The servants here were worried about why we came, as well,' she said.

He gave her a direct gaze. 'We need not tell them why we came.'

She turned away for a moment but took a breath and faced him again. 'So what did you think of everything?'

'The farm appears to be well-run. The workers seem well satisfied.' He finished his wine and poured himself another glass. 'I like Reid, but, of course, he doesn't yet trust me. None of them trusts me.'

She looked at him questioningly. 'Shall I show you what we did today?'

He put down his glass and stood. 'By all means.'

She led him to the sitting room next to the conservatory. Its walls had been scrubbed clean, its carpet beaten, furniture polished, curtains laundered. A great deal of work for one day.

He walked around the room. 'You did well, Amelie.'

She blushed. 'There is much I wish to do in the house. Nothing extravagant like replacing furniture, but I would like to open more of the rooms so it will be more comfortable. I'd like to put plants in the conservatory, and I would love to tidy up the garden.'

She was taking an interest—that gratified him most of all. So was he, actually. For all the exertion of the day, he'd found it stimulating. He was determined to learn everything about the running of the farm.

'I want you to do whatever you wish,' he told her. 'Make this home of ours a pleasant place for us.' It was just the two of them. He tried not to think that there might have been a third. 'I mean it, Amelie. Anything you want.'

'I must keep busy,' she murmured before looking up at him again. 'We need to hire more servants. The house is too big for Jobson to clean and Mrs Stagg needs help in the kitchen.'

'I dare say we need footmen, too,' he added. 'Lloyd seems willing enough, but how much can he do? I am persuaded I do need someone to tend to my clothes, as well.'

'And a gardener?' She looked hopeful. 'I would love to see the garden tended. Do you think my father will mind the expense?' she asked.

He tried not to bristle. 'I am not without means, Amelie. I will pay.'

'Then let us go back to the drawing room and finish our wine, and perhaps we can make a list of how many servants we need.' Her eyes sparkled.

Edmund's heart swelled. Perhaps she would recover. Perhaps they could make this marriage into a good thing for both of them.

Mr Lloyd came to announce dinner—mutton stew again, but Edmund did not care. He and Amelie talked throughout the meal of what they could do for the house and the farm.

Edmund never realised how much he enjoyed having a house that was his to live in. With Amelie. Before Amelie he'd never thought of houses.

There was no fortune to be made at this sheep farm, but the day's work had been gratifying. He looked forward, too, to the hay harvest that Reid said would commence in the next few days. And to the market days in the next few weeks. And the tupping—the breeding of the sheep.

Most of all he looked forward to making Amelie happy, to making up to her all the misery he had caused her. If he could do so, perhaps life could always be as good as it felt at this moment.

Chapter Seventeen

The next morning Amelie's courses came and with it, her grief. Just as she felt a little better, her body taunted her with the reminder that her womb was empty. The bleeding and discomfort were not extreme, but she made it her excuse to stay in bed.

Her despondency had returned, and she did not want anyone to know. She smiled valiantly for Edmund, making him think her withdrawal was merely due to her monthly cycle. She fooled Sally, as well. When alone, though, she burrowed in her bed and mourned once more for what might have been.

After the third day, though, everyone became too busy to worry about her.

It was haymaking time.

'I'll be gone all day, I'm afraid,' Edmund told her that morning. 'Reid says rain is coming and the hay will be ruined if we do not get it in. Everyone must take part. Sally can stay to tend you, but the rest of the servants will be needed to help.' His colour was high with excitement.

'I'll fare well enough.' Amelie made certain to smile. 'Do not concern yourself over me.'

A short time later Sally brought her some breakfast. 'Do you need me all day, ma'am? Because Mrs Stagg asked if I could help bring food and drink to the fields.'

Again Amelie smiled. 'I do not need you at all. Just take care you do not exert yourself.'

'I will only be walking and carrying.' She sounded eager to go.

'Then you must help.' Sally ought to have some enjoyment. 'I am not ill, after all. I am well able to take care of myself.'

By mid-morning, though, Amelie could no longer stand herself. Everyone was working, and here she was secluding herself and indulging in self-pity. She could help, too, couldn't she? There must be some task she could perform.

She already wore her most ordinary dress, one that was fit for work, but she needed more if she were to help in the fields. She left her room and made her way to the still room, where she found an apron to wear over her dress and an old pair of boots that fit her feet. In a potting shed outdoors, she found gloves for her hands, a scarf to cover her hair and a wide-brimmed hat to shade her face.

There. She was ready.

But she did not know for certain where to find the hayfields.

She walked past the farm buildings and some tidy cottages until she saw women on a hilly field raking the hay into windrows. If not for the mountains, all green and grey, to frame the scene, it looked much like Northdon Hall at haying time. She strode towards the workers, relishing the exercise after sitting and moping for so long. She filled her lungs with clear, crisp air and trudged up the hill where the women were working.

As she came close, several of the workers gaped at her as if she were some oddity from a foreign land. She searched for Edmund but could not see him.

One of the women, carrying a rake, walked over to her. 'Do you need help, ma'am?'

'No. Thank you.' Amelie extended her hand. 'I am Mrs Summerfield.'

'Aye, I guessed who you were.' She hesitated before shaking Amelie's hand. 'I am Mrs Peet. Mary Peet.'

'How do you do Mrs Peet.' Amelie shaded her

eyes and glanced around. 'Have you seen Mr Summerfield?'

The woman pointed. 'Most of the men are on the other side of the hill, cutting the hay.'

'Oh. I mustn't bother him, then.' Amelie had no reason to disturb him.

'Is there something I can do for you?' Mrs Peet asked.

'No, there is really nothing.'

The other women, who had been watching her, went back to turning the hay. All Amelie had accomplished was interrupting them. She observed them, how they moved down the windrow with their rakes, flipping the cut grass so that it would dry in the sun.

Mrs Peet curtsied. 'Best I get back to work, then.' She started to walk away.

Amelie called her back. 'Might I help?'

Mrs Peet turned and regarded her. 'You?' She lowered her head. 'Beg pardon, ma'am, but what would you do?'

'Well.' She gestured to the windrows. 'Might I help you turn the hay?'

Mrs Peet looked uncertain but finally smiled. 'Come with me. I'll show you how.'

Mrs Peet found another rake and showed Amelie how to turn the grass. The women walked down the rows, turning as they went, then they moved to the next row and worked uphill. Amelie was slow at the task, but the other women offered words of advice and encouragement as they passed. Amelie learned the names of as many of the women as she could, repeating them in her head so she would not forget.

When she reached the top of the hill, she rested a moment. Her muscles seemed to rejoice in the exercise, even though they were tired. Best of all, there was no time, no space to think. Just work. And who knew she would enjoy such labour? Was this yet another way she was different from respectable ladies?

As she started down the hill, she heard her name called.

Edmund strode towards her. 'What are you doing here?' He was stripped to his shirtsleeves and carrying a scythe.

She lifted her chin. 'I am working.'

His grey eyes sparkled in the sunlight, and his face shone with sweat. Her insides fluttered at the sight of him, even though she was ready to do battle if he ordered her to stop.

He gestured to her rake. 'I see you are working, but is it wise?'

'Everyone else is working.' She held his gaze. 'I am doing my part.'

His brows knitted. 'Do you feel up to it?'

She looked into those sparkling grey eyes. 'I am not ill, Edmund, and I want to do this. I like doing this.'

A slow smile grew on his face. 'I like the work, too, Amelie. But stop if you become fatigued.'

Her shoulders relaxed and her spirits rose. 'I will.'

He gazed at her for a moment longer before climbing to the top of the hill and disappearing over the other side.

The sun was low in the sky when Edmund came off the hill. He walked with Reid.

'Will we finish before the rains?' he asked the steward.

'Another two days like this one an' we will,' Reid answered.

Edmund had turned a corner with Reid. He'd been working side by side with the man these last few days, especially with the haymaking, and Edmund thought perhaps he had started to earn the steward's respect.

He surveyed the land around him. This was not as prosperous a farm as Summerfield had been and not at all the future he'd planned for himself, but he liked the people and he liked the work.

Ahead of him, some of the farm workers walked

back to their cottages side by side with their wives. Edmund envied them.

But he caught sight of Amelie heading back to the house. Beautiful Amelie. Who would have thought a viscount's daughter would be willing to work in the fields?

'I'll bid you good day here, Reid. I'm going to join my wife.' It felt good to say those words.

'She did a fine day's work,' Reid said.

'That she did.' Edmund hurried away.

He caught up with Amelie, and she smiled when she saw him.

Edmund fell in step with her. 'How did you fare today?'

She glanced up at him. 'I am exhausted. Every muscle hurts.' She grinned. 'But I feel good.'

He felt good, too. 'It was fine work, was it not?'

'Does your leg pain you?' she asked.

'A twinge. No more,' he replied. 'Work seems to be helping. Making it stronger.'

When they reached the house they washed, donned clean clothes and ate more of Mrs Stagg's mutton stew.

As they finished the simple meal, Edmund asked, 'Should we have tea in the drawing room?'

Amelie rested her elbow on the table and her chin

on her hand. 'To own the truth, all I want is to go to bed.'

Edmund felt the flare of desire at her words, but he knew she had no idea her words were provocative. Besides, even if she were not dog-tired, she was not ready, not when she'd spent the last couple of days withdrawn in grief. He'd been grieved, too, but work had saved him.

'An excellent idea,' he responded. 'I must rise early again tomorrow.'

She straightened in her chair. 'I am rising early, too.'

'Are you?' For her to labour one day was more than anyone expected.

'Of course I am,' she responded in a wounded tone. 'Everyone is working tomorrow, is that not correct?'

He gave her a direct look. 'I am not suggesting you not work, Amelie. I am proud of you for what you've done this day. If you wish to do more, I will be prouder still.'

She quickly averted her gaze. 'Thank you, Edmund,' she murmured.

They walked up the mahogany stairs together, and he saw her to her bedchamber door. How he wished, even fatigued as he was, he could sleep with her in his arms like when she'd cried out from her nightmare.

Instead he placed his lips on her forehead. 'Goodnight, Amelie.'

She leaned into him, and he put his arms around her.

'Sleep well,' he murmured.

When he withdrew his arms, she hurried into her room.

The next two days were filled with work, turning hay, stacking it as high as the workers' cottages and covering the stacks with canvas tarps to keep out the rain.

Amelie did not mind any of it. The work, hard as it was, healed her spirits, and she felt happy for the first time since walking into the Duchess of Richmond's ball.

What a far cry from Middlerock farm that night was!

She liked the women turning hay with her more than she'd liked those society women at the ball. She liked the men who cut the hay with their scythes. She liked working with them and accomplishing such a huge task.

She perceived their stay at this farm with fresh eyes. It no longer seemed like an exile or a withdrawal from life. It seemed like life itself, or what life ought to be.

Amelie felt ready to face the future, no matter what it threw at her.

For Amelie, it was not the end of the haymaking she celebrated; it was her new beginning. Everyone gathered in one of the farm buildings large enough to seat them all. Mrs Stagg and the farm wives prepared a feast and everyone ate together, drank ale together and sang and danced.

It was the best party Amelie had ever attended, better even than the Duchess of Richmond's ball.

She glanced at Edmund, seated at the head of the table, laughing and lifting his tankard to his lips. He looked up and their eyes caught.

Her heart leaped into her throat. Edmund's eyes warmed her more than the large stone fireplace, blazing with firewood.

He rose from his seat and made his way down the long table to where Amelie sat, stopping to acknowledge something said to him, a joke told, some cajolery or simply a handshake. He finally reached her and extended his hand.

She put hers in his, and he pulled her from her seat. 'We're to bed, I think,' he said, and the room erupted in raucous shouts. Amelie felt her face turn red.

Why not, though? she thought. Why not behave as man and wife? Why not seize the pleasure it brought them both?

Sally, who sat with Mr Reid, asked her, 'Shall I come with you?'

Amelie gestured for her to stay. 'No, enjoy yourself. I'll not need you tonight.'

'Ohhhh!' exclaimed one of the women, and laughter broke out among them again. The laughter followed Amelie and Edmund out of the building.

As they walked across the yard to the house, dark clouds swept across the moon.

'Storm clouds?' Amelie stopped to look up at the sky. 'Will it storm tonight, just as Mr Reid said?'

Edmund threaded her arm though his. 'Uncanny of him to predict the rain. I do not know if he realises how much knowledge he holds inside him.'

Their bodies bumped each other as they walked. Amelie liked feeling the strength of Edmund's arm beneath her fingers. She remembered the power of that same arm swinging the scythe in a rhythmic and graceful arc. Or its gentleness when holding her in a naked embrace.

'I don't think I've ever enjoyed days more than these,' she said. 'I shall miss haymaking.'

'You impressed the farm workers.' He smiled down at her. 'One man told me he thought offcomers were all lazy and puffed up, but that you and I proved him wrong.'

'Offcomers?'

'Someone not from here.'

They reached the conservatory door and entered the house, which was nearly pitch-black inside.

'We should have brought a candle,' she said.

Edmund took her hand. 'We'll find our way.'

She could see nothing and it was only his hand that told her he was ahead of her. They climbed the stairs, and at the top, it felt as if the darkness enveloped them and shielded them from anything but each other.

He put his arms around her and kissed her.

The feel of his lips against hers, his tongue touching hers, the heat of his body and the scent of him ignited the passion in her that she'd pushed away. He pulled the scarf from her head and dug his fingers into her curls.

When his lips left hers, she murmured, 'I am healed now, Edmund.' In both body and mind.

He took her hand and opened the door to his bedchamber. Enough moonlight streamed through the windows so she could see his face, a face that now had become so familiar and so dear.

'I have wanted you all these nights,' he said, kissing her again. 'I have missed you.'

Her body flared with sensation, a harbinger of the pleasure that was to come, made even more erotic by the darkness. The room was chilled, but the cold did not trouble her. It refreshed her and made her feel more alive.

'Shall I make a fire?' he asked between kisses that had travelled to her cheek, her neck, her ear.

'We can warm each other,' she murmured.

He stepped back and pulled off his boots and stripped off his coat, a mere shadow now that he was at a distance. She watched him, spellbound by the efficiency of his movements, his masculine grace.

He stood naked before her and extended his hand to her.

She clasped it and let him draw her near.

'Your turn,' he murmured, untying her apron and the laces of her dress.

He pulled the dress over her head, leaving her in her corset, shift and boots. She took his hand again and backed to the bed, climbing on top of it and presenting him with her booted foot. He pulled off her boots and peeled off her stockings. He climbed on the bed with her and unlaced and removed her corset. All that remained was her shift. She did not wait for him but pulled it over her head herself.

The undressing seemed like a ritual. So familiar. So much the same as that night in Brussels. And their wedding night.

So much like the first time…and the last.

A loud hum seemed to come from inside her, unsettling her, and a cloud crossed the moon. The room was plunged in darkness, leaving only the memories swirling through her mind, choking off the brightness of her mood, blocking her happiness. Cutting off the very air she needed to breathe.

Edmund touched her and she started to tremble. He rose over her and her heart pounded. She could not get air into her lungs.

'No! No!' She pushed him away.

He moved to her side and sat looking down at her. 'What is it, Amelie? What happened?'

She wanted to run, to be as far away as her legs could carry her, to somewhere she could breathe.

'I—I do not know,' she managed, still trying to gulp air. This was how she had destroyed their baby. This was how she had ruined his future. Her pleasure only brought pain. 'I cannot do this, Edmund. I cannot.'

Was she never to recover completely? Would she ever find happiness?

She tried to scramble off the bed, but he held her shoulders and sat her in front of him.

'We do not have to make love.' He spoke in a quiet, calm voice. 'But stay with me, Amelie. Sleep with me.'

It was all she could do not to fight him to free herself.

'I can't, Edmund,' she cried. 'I can't.'

He released her, and she bolted off the bed and through the connecting doorway to her own room.

* * *

Sally walked across the yard with Mr Reid. The celebration had broken up, and the workers were headed for their cottages. She could have walked back with the other servants, but she lingered, listening to Mr Reid, who told her stories of other hay harvests, one he'd witnessed when he was a mere child when his whole family had worked feverishly in the fields to bring the hay in before the rain, but the rain had come, soaking the results of their labour and nearly ruining his father's small hill farm.

Everything he said seemed interesting to her, and the way he said it, as well. His strange accent made her pay closer attention, and it seemed as though she heard more that way. Her own thoughts could not interfere.

Walking with him in the dark was different than talking in the building where the banquet was held. She'd met him outside in the dark twice since that first time. She'd told herself she just wanted some night air, but sometimes she wondered if she'd hoped he be there.

'I have enjoyed your company tonight,' he said.

They walked side by side, not touching.

'And I yours,' she admitted.

Not the way she'd enjoyed Calvin's company, though. Calvin had been as familiar as her own image in a mirror, as comfortable as well-worn shoes. Mr Reid had strange ways, strange words for things, and it was exciting to be exposed to new things.

They reached the house, a servant's door off the kitchen wing. As she reached for the door latch he stepped in front of her, blocking her way.

'Wait a moment, lass,' he said.

She drew back.

He shifted from one foot to the other before looking directly at her. 'Since we enjoy each other's company,' he began, 'I was wondering if I could—could court you.'

Her stomach dropped. 'Court me?'

'Aye, you're a widow, I know, and not very long of it.' She'd told him the lie her mistress had devised for her: that her husband had died at Waterloo. 'If it is too soon, I'll wait.'

She panicked. 'You can't—you can't—you do not know—'

'Know what?' he asked.

'You do not know me!' she cried and moved around him to the door, opened it and ran inside.

Chapter Eighteen

The next morning Edmund woke alone in his bed. Rain beat against his window.

It most perfectly matched his mood.

He could not blame Amelie her panic. Sometimes memories came back to him, too, and he had to fight to push them away again.

She'd looked so beautiful the night before, so happy. He'd wanted it to last.

'It is raining,' he said aloud. 'Raining in more ways than one.'

He dressed quickly and grabbed his caped greatcoat, the one that had seen him through the rain-filled night before Waterloo and wet marches through Spain, before walking down to the kitchen to get something to eat.

Mrs Stagg greeted him with a smile. 'I did not expect you up so early on a day like this.'

No sense spreading the gloom he felt inside. He

smiled at her. 'Mr Reid was right about the rains, was he not?'

She nodded. 'He's a wise one, he is.' She cut some bread and cheese. 'And you'll be looking for something to eat, I expect.'

'This will do.' He took a piece of bread and a wedge of cheese and started to eat. 'Do you have some oilcloth? Something I can use to carry the ledger books from Reid's office to the library?'

Her face turned solemn. 'Oilcloth for the ledger books,' she repeated without enthusiasm. 'Wait a moment.'

By the time he finished his bread and cheese, she brought him some folded cloth.

'Will this do?' she asked. 'I also brought some twine.'

'Thank you, Mrs Stagg. This will do nicely.' He took the items from her hands.

He had to keep busy or he'd go mad. As long as he was not idle, he could put one foot in front of the other.

Collecting his hat and donning his greatcoat, he opened the door and paused a moment before dashing out into the rain.

He ran the distance to the farm building where Reid had his office and knocked on the man's door.

'Come in,' he heard Reid say.

'Summerfield!' Reid jumped to his feet. 'I did not expect to see you out in the weather.'

Edmund's greatcoat dripped water on the bare wooden floor.

'I thought it a perfect day to look at the books.' He did not move, confining the puddle to where he stood.

'The books?' Reid frowned.

'The ledger books. Surely you knew I would want to examine them,' Edmund said.

Reid rubbed his face. 'I meant to show you more of the workings of the farm first. The entries might make no sense to you otherwise.'

'I've seen my father's ledgers,' Edmund assured him. 'And I will ask if there is something I do not understand.'

'Very well.'

Reid moved slowly from around his desk to a locked cabinet. He took his time opening the cabinet, where several canvas-bound ledger books were stacked one on top of the other.

'How far back do you wish to go?' Reid asked.

Was that anxiety in his voice?

'When did you start here?'

'Five years back,' Reid answered.

'Then give me six years,' Edmund said.

Reid's brows lowered, but he pulled out six ledgers. 'The ink will run if they get wet.'

Edmund lifted his hand. 'I have an oilskin to wrap them in.'

It seemed as if all Reid's wariness and suspicion of those first days had returned, and Edmund did not know why.

Edmund spread open the oilcloth onto a table, and Reid placed the books on top of it. He wrapped them carefully and tied them with twine so the cloth would not open accidentally.

He glanced over at Reid. 'I do not expect to find anything amiss, Reid. I want you to know that.'

'You won't,' Reid shot back, his tone defiant.

Edmund started for the door. 'Nothing displeases me so far. The farm is run well. You should be proud of your work.'

Reid straightened. 'I am.'

Amelie sat on her bed, gazing out the window at the rain, regretting the night before. She had no idea why she had gone into a panic with Edmund. It had suddenly seemed as if something terrible would happen if she allowed herself to indulge in that pleasure. It had come as a surprise attack.

She'd been dreadful to Edmund. One more thing guaranteed to displease him. The list was growing longer.

She heard a light tap on the door. Not Edmund. Edmund would have rapped with vigour.

'Come in,' she said.

Sally entered, her head bowed, her shoulders slumped. Amelie turned away from her own misery to attend to Sally's. Perhaps she could help Sally, and at least one of them could be happy.

'What is amiss, Sally?' Amelie asked.

'Nothing, ma'am,' the maid responded in mournful tones.

'Has someone been unkind to you?' Of everyone, Sally had had the lightest duties during the haymaking. Had the other servants complained?

'Unkind? No, ma'am.' She sounded as if she might cry. 'Not unkind. Not at all.'

Amelie patted the bed. 'Come sit with me.'

Sally joined her and Amelie put an arm around her. 'Tell me what is amiss, no matter what it is.'

Sally turned away and shifted in her seat, but finally she stared at her feet and spoke. 'It is Mr Reid—'

'Mr Reid?' She'd noticed him talking to Sally. He was not the sort to take advantage of her, was he?

Of course, how was Amelie to know a man's true character if he decided to conceal it? She had once been dreadfully fooled herself.

'He—he walked me back to the house last night…' She paused as if it were difficult to go on.

Amelie blanched. Had she been wrong about Mr Reid? She'd been wrong before. 'What did he do?'

Fat tears rolled down Sally's cheeks. 'He—he asked—he asked—to court me.'

Relief washed through Amelie. 'To court you?' If he was what he seemed to be, he was a fine man with a good position. 'Would that be so disagreeable?'

'No, not disagreeable at all!' Sally cried. 'I like him. I like him, and I feel like it is betraying Calvin, but worse, he doesn't know about the baby. No one does, although I think Mrs Wood suspects. What will he think of me?'

Soon everyone would know.

Amelie kept her voice calm. 'He will think you are a widow left with child.'

Sally turned to stare into her face. 'But that is a lie, is it not? What would he think if he knew the truth of me? He would despise me.'

'Do not tell him.'

'And lie to him all my days?' She looked horrified.

Amelie took her by the shoulders, the way Edmund had done to her the night before. 'Then tell him. If he truly has a regard for you, he will not mind.'

Amelie was not as certain of this advice as she made out to be. What would a man like Fowler do with such a confession? Not every man was like Edmund. Edmund would do the right thing.

She rose from the bed. 'Come. Help me dress. You must think about this and decide what to do.'

Sally slipped off the bed and moved slowly to the wardrobe. 'What do you wish to wear today?'

'A morning dress, I think. I doubt I shall venture outside in weather like this!'

She must find something to do, though, or her thoughts and regrets would plague her all day.

It was afternoon before Edmund saw Amelie. He'd set up a space in the library to look over the ledgers, pushing a long table nearer to the window to take advantage of the light, even though not much light shone through the grey sheen of the rain.

Amelie came in the room carrying a tea tray with sandwiches and biscuits. She looked hesitant. 'I brought you some tea.'

'Amelie!' He stood and took the tray from her hands. 'You should not be serving tea. What happened to Lloyd? Or Jobson?'

She blinked as if she'd been reproached. 'Jobson is helping Mrs Stagg in the kitchen. Mrs Wood and Lloyd are busy with other tasks.'

He had not meant it as criticism.

'I—I thank you.' He placed the tray on the table. 'Now I see the food I am famished.'

'I thought you might be hungry,' she said in a quiet voice.

He hated this reserve between them, but he did not know how to break it. 'Please sit with me and tell me how you are faring today?'

Her eyes flickered with sadness. 'I am well enough,' she said.

He gazed at her, wishing he knew how to speak of the night before, deciding it was best to wait for her to speak of it.

She gestured to the table strewn with ledger books. 'What are you doing?'

'Looking through the farm's records for the last six years.' He closed the open book he'd been examining and stacked the others.

She poured his tea and handed him the plate of food. 'What are you finding?'

He sipped his tea. 'Everything seems in order. The farm is doing well under Reid's care.'

'I am glad to hear it,' she said.

They fell silent again.

Edmund put down his teacup and offered her some of the repast. 'How have you occupied yourself this day?'

She shook her head to the food. 'I spoke with Mrs Wood about hiring more help. She knows of relatives and villagers who could use the work. I'll interview them as soon as the rain stops.'

'Good.' He ate one of the sandwiches. 'And what of this afternoon? Do you have plans?' He'd love to take a walk with her away from the house to one of the beautiful spots on the property, but the rain prevented that.

She fiddled with the cloth of an apron she wore over her dress. 'I am going to look through the attic.'

'The attic?'

She glanced at him but glanced away again. 'The house needs decoration, and Mrs Wood says many of the items that once adorned the rooms were brought up to the attic. I thought I might see if we want to use any of it.' Her voice shook a little.

'Sounds like a big task,' he said.

'I must do something,' she whispered.

He stared at her. Why must they always need to get used to each other all over again? 'Shall I help you?'

Her eyes widened. 'In the attic?'

'Yes,' he said quietly. 'We can explore it together.'

She looked wary again, but she nodded. 'I will be glad for the assistance.'

He finished his tea and picked up two of the library's lamps to take with them, handing one to her. They left for the attic, up a steep flight of stairs above the second floor.

He opened the door and entered first before turning and offering her his hand to assist her into the space, which smelled of dust and old wood. They stood and surveyed the vast expanse, their lamps revealing a jumble of wooden boxes, chests and furniture, some shrouded in dust covers.

She placed her lamp on a box and wrapped a scarf around her hair. 'I do not know where to begin.'

This was more than a day's work. 'Shall we walk through and see what we can see?'

She picked up her lamp again. 'I'll go this way.'

She turned to the right, and the implication was that he should turn left. Not the togetherness for which he'd yearned, but at least they were in the same space.

He threaded his way through some boxes and trunks, obviously put wherever there was space, with no effort at organisation. It was impossible to tell if a box was placed there yesterday or a century ago. He ran his finger across one of the trunks. Except perhaps by the thickness of the dust. He squeezed around a tall chest of drawers, behind which was a dust cover thrown over several small pieces of furniture. He placed the lamp on the chest of drawers and pulled off the dust cover.

'My God,' he exclaimed.

Before him was a baby's cradle, a rocking chair and a hobbyhorse, all arranged as if they were in a nursery instead of a dusty attic.

He felt as if he'd been punched in the chest.

He could see it! Could see the nursery. The baby

lying in the cradle on soft white linens. He could see Amelie bending over the cradle. And himself, beaming with pride.

Just as quickly that vision disappeared and was replaced by another—his mother being covered by a white sheet. The baby wrapped in white, being carried away, the way their baby had been carried away. An empty cradle. An empty rocking chair.

'My God,' he cried again. His throat constricted, and he fell to his knees, the unreleased sobs painfully constricting his chest.

Amelie was at his side. 'What is it, Edmund?'

He pointed to the nursery scene and shook his head.

'Oh!' she cried.

She knelt beside him and put her arms around him.

'The baby.' His voice came out in a rasp.

'I am so sorry, Edmund.' She clung to him. 'I am so sorry. It is my fault, all my fault.'

He pulled away. 'No, the fault is mine. I planned that wedding night. I wanted it. I was not gentle with you.'

She hugged him again. 'No, I told you it would be safe to make love, but I did not know.'

They held on to each other, while he battled to rein in his emotions. To no avail. They seemed to be spilling out all over the room.

'Edmund.' She drew away and stared at him. 'Did you want the baby?'

He nodded. 'A family. I wanted a family. The baby made it so.'

'I never knew.' She rose and pulled over two wooden chairs stored nearby. 'Come sit.'

They sat next to each other, the cradle, rocking chair and hobbyhorse a tableau in front of them. Edmund took a deep breath. How could three pieces of furniture spark such a flood of emotion?

'I thought you merely wanted to do the right thing,' she said. 'I thought you, like everyone else, wished I'd had the miscarriage a day before the wedding so we wouldn't have had to marry.' She wiped her eyes with her apron.

'I should not have made love to you in Brussels.' The release of his pent-up feelings untangled a truth for him. 'But I never regretted it. My only regret is that our baby did not live. And it tortures me to think the baby might have lived if I had not—'

'No. No. No. Not you. If *I* had not!' she broke in. 'If I had not wanted the lovemaking.' She turned her face away. 'How you can bear to be kind to me? I have ruined your life in every way possible. You have every right to wish me dead.'

He turned his chair to hers and took her hands in his. 'Never say that, Amelie! When you were in such pain, I feared I would watch you die.' He closed his eyes and saw it all again. 'I watched my mother die. They carried away her baby, too. My brother who never lived. Seeing this—' he gestured to the nursery furniture '—it brought it back.'

'You saw your mother die?' Her eyes grew wide. 'In childbirth?'

He nodded.

She left her chair and held him again. He pulled her into his lap as his grief washed through him and they trembled together.

'Mr Summerfield!' a faint voice called. 'Mr Summerfield! Where are you? Come quickly!'

He groaned. 'It sounds like Lloyd.'

Amelie moved off his lap. 'Let us forget the attic today.' She picked up his lamp. 'Go on. I'll get the lamps and close the door.'

He hurried and found Lloyd on the first floor, still calling his name.

'What is it, Lloyd?' Edmund felt raw inside, but he was back in control of himself.

He hoped.

'A leak in the pantry,' the old man told him. 'I need help moving the stores to a dry place.'

'Yes. Let us go quickly.'

Amelie extinguished one of the lamps and carried them both out of the attic, returning them to the library. She went back to her bedchamber to wash her hands of the attic's dust. It all repeated in her mind. Edmund wanted the baby. He'd wanted a family. He thought the miscarriage was his fault, but it was hers.

He did not deserve to suffer guilt when she was the one at fault. If she could only convince him.

As she washed the dust from her hands, her arms, her face, Sally entered the room.

'Oh, beg pardon, ma'am,' Sally said. 'I did not think you were in here.'

'No reason to apologise,' Amelie said.

Sally carried freshly laundered clothing, which she started putting away.

Amelie curled up on a chair by the window.

'Did Mr Lloyd find Mr Summerfield?' Sally asked. 'He needed his help.'

'Yes. He is with Mr Lloyd now. We were in the attic.' She lay her head on her knees.

'The attic?'

'To see what was up there.' Her voice cracked.

Sally closed the wardrobe. 'Beg pardon, ma'am. Is something wrong? You look so sad.'

She could not help herself. 'Oh, Sally! We—we talked about losing the baby. About how guilty we feel about it!'

'Guilty?' Sally sounded surprised. 'Why would you feel guilty?'

'If—if I had been more careful—' She would not say more. 'That is why I insist you be careful.'

Sally looked puzzled. 'I do not understand. Mrs Bayliss told me the baby was not growing right. She said the baby had no chance of being born.'

Amelie straightened in the chair. 'What?'

'Mrs Bayliss said it happens sometimes. I asked her, because I was afraid it would happen to my baby. She said sometimes the baby does not grow right from the start and the mother's body lets it go, but if I passed three months, I could be pretty sure my baby was growing right.'

Amelie rose from the chair and faced Sally. 'My baby did not grow right?'

Sally nodded. 'Mrs Bailey said it could never have lived.'

Amelie released a pent-up breath. 'It was not our fault?'

'She said there was nothing anyone could do about it. It just happens sometimes. No one knows why.'

Amelie rushed to the door. 'I have to find Edmund!'

She hurried out of the room and down the stairs to the kitchen, where Mrs Stagg was stirring something in a large bowl.

'Mrs Summerfield!' the cook said in surprise.

Amelie needed to speak to Edmund right away. 'Where is my husband?'

Mrs Stagg pointed to a hallway and Amelie entered it. She heard voices and followed the sound. Mrs Wood emerged from the doorway of one room and soon Edmund and Lloyd appeared.

'Edmund!' Amelie cried.

All three looked at her.

'I must talk with you.' Amelie tried to temper her emotions. 'Come talk with me now.'

Edmund blanched. 'What has happened?'

'Nothing has happened,' she assured him. 'I need to speak with you, that is all.'

'Beg pardon, Mr Summerfield,' Mrs Wood broke in. 'We need to move quickly. The damp.'

Amelie took a step back. 'I can wait.'

Mrs Wood rubbed her hands. 'If you've a mind to help us, it will go faster.'

'Oh!' She moved towards them. 'Of course.'

She and Mrs Wood carried the small items while Edmund and Lloyd tackled large barrels or canvas bags. Amelie's heart pounded.

When all the foodstuffs were secure in a dry room, Amelie seized Edmund's arm and hurried him away.

As soon as they were out of earshot of the servants, he stopped her. 'What is it, Amelie? What has happened?'

Those were almost the exact words he'd spoken after she'd panicked during their lovemaking. 'Let us go to your room.'

No one would interrupt them there. She took his hand and quickly climbed the stairs.

Once inside his room, she turned to him.

His face was grim. 'We are here. Tell me now.'

Her words came out in a rush. 'It was not our fault. Not yours and not mine. Sally told me. Mrs Bayliss said our baby was not growing right and could not have lived no matter what.'

He stared at her.

She took his hand. 'There was nothing we could have done. Don't you see? Nothing we did caused it.'

His voice turned low. 'Say it again. More slowly.'

She took a breath. 'Mrs Bayliss told Sally that the miscarriage happened because our baby was not growing right and could not have lived, no matter what. She said it happens sometimes and no one knows why.'

'We did not cause it?' he asked cautiously.

She shook her head.

He put his arms around her and held her tight.

'It was not your fault,' she murmured. 'It was not my fault.' She rested her head against his chest and felt his heart beat fast.

He held her shoulders and gently moved her

away from him. He gazed down at her, his grey eyes filled with relief. 'I feel scraped raw. But this is good news. You must never reproach yourself again, Amelie.'

She touched his cheek. 'You must not either. You have done everything right.'

He glanced away, but she turned his head back to look at her. He was close, so very close. She rose on her tiptoes and reached for his lips. He dipped his head down and closed the distance.

His lips ignited the passion that had panicked her the night before. It would not do so again, she had no fear. Her carnal desire had not destroyed her baby. She was a married woman and free to couple with her husband.

He murmured against her lips, 'We have made love in the afternoon before, Amelie. Shall we do so again?'

A mere hour ago she would have berated herself for wanting the pleasures of the flesh so much she could not wait for night, but that had been when she thought she'd hurt her baby. Now what harm could it do?

She nodded.

This time the ritual of undressing seemed a veneration. She gloried in seeing him naked and felt humbled by the look on his face when he gazed at her. He lifted her onto the bed as if she were some precious idol. When he lay next to her, she ran her fingers over his finely sculptured muscles, reverently fingering his scars and wanting to weep for all he'd endured in battle. She touched the male part of him, now as hard as his muscles.

He groaned and laid her on her back while he rose above her. 'I cannot wait.'

She nodded. 'I cannot wait either.'

Still, he entered her slowly and gently, and the sensation intensified the acute passion already wafting through her. They were joined to each other, made one flesh. She understood those words now, understood that this was the marriage. They'd been one flesh since Brussels. He said he never regretted it. She didn't either, and she did not regret now that they were together in this rustic place and had worked in the fields like ordinary people.

As he moved inside her, her thoughts blew away like leaves in the wind. But he remained. Nothing existed but Edmund, moving inside her, intensifying her need. Promising pleasure.

She clung to him, digging her fingers into his buttocks, pressing him against her, as he moved faster and faster, rushing her towards what she now needed more than air to breathe.

He burst inside her, and she felt his seed spilling into her. A hairsbreadth of a moment later her own climax came, a glorious paroxysm of joy pulsating within her and wafting through her entire body.

His muscles relaxed first, then hers became like jelly. He slid onto the bed beside her, holding her close. 'I feared we would never have this again.'

It had been her fear, too. 'I thought what—what happened was a punishment for my wanting this so much.'

A part of her wondered again if that made her different from other women in her circles. Perhaps it made her different from even the women she'd worked beside these last few days.

'I like it very much, too,' he said, his voice rough and arousing.

What did it matter? If Edmund liked it and she liked it, what did it matter?

'We have the whole afternoon, do we not?' She ran her fingers through his lovely dark brown hair. 'We must occupy ourselves in some way.'

He rose over her again. 'That we must.'

Chapter Nineteen

Edmund did not mind the two more rainy days that kept them inside and free to enjoy the togetherness of their days and nights. They returned to the attic and found several items to bring down to the rooms below. They discovered paintings for the walls, portraits of unknown men and women, presumably one-time tenants of the house, landscapes, mostly scenes from the Lake District, and still-life paintings with grapes and cheeses and dead fowl.

The days were an idyll, each moment together helping them become used to each other and comfortable in each other's presence.

Their nights were a delight.

When the rains were done, though, Edmund worked with Reid on the farm. One day when they were off to the sheep market in Keswick, Edmund suggested Amelie and Sally come along to shop and to see the town that Thomas Gray had described as 'the Vale of Elysium in all its verdure', where famous poets such as Coleridge and Wordsworth had lived.

The streets of the town were filled with well-dressed ladies and gentlemen who'd come to see the Vale of Elysium. After Wordsworth's *Guide to the Lakes* was published the area became a fashionable place to visit. The war had also contributed. When Napoleon had been amassing his empire, travel to the Continent had been impossible.

Keswick was also a market town where farmers came to do the business of buying and selling livestock. Today sheep were up at auction, and Reid had chosen which ewes and tups he wished to sell and knew the ones he wanted to buy. The farmers showed their sheep in turn, and the others examined the sheep's feet, teeth, their wool and ears. Edmund shadowed Reid, listening and learning.

He learned the qualities Reid looked for to improve their stock and which rams and ewes they'd bred were prized by others. He also gained new respect for the steward.

When they were done, they met Amelie and Sally at an inn for an early dinner.

'What did you buy?' he asked, gesturing to her stack of parcels.

'Some cloth. Some soap. Other—' Something caught her eye and she broke off. 'My goodness.'

He looked to see.

An older gentleman and lady entered the room with a younger man who leaned heavily on a cane.

'Fowler.'

The man who was once Captain Fowler and had once made Amelie's face light up in joy was every bit as dashing as he had been in uniform, even though his civilian clothes showed him to be much thinner. He also had the vacant eye of someone struggling simply to take a step. He and the two people Edmund supposed were his parents were walking directly towards their table. Amelie had frozen, a look of distress on her face.

Fowler, though, walked right up to her. 'Forgive me, ma'am, but did I once know you?'

Edmund stood. 'You knew my wife as Miss Glenville. I am Lieutenant Summerfield.' He used his army rank without thinking.

'How are you, Captain?' Amelie said, although it was obvious he was not well. She turned to his parents. 'Lord and Lady Ellister?'

They nodded, but their expressions were less than pleased.

She continued. 'I never had the opportunity of meeting you.'

'We know who you are,' Lady Ellister snapped. 'We read of your marriage.'

Fowler still peered at Amelie. 'My memory is not

what it ought to be.' He looked apologetic. 'I was wounded in the head. When did I know you, then?'

'In—in Brussels,' she said.

'Ah, that explains it.' Fowler still had his charming smile. 'I remember nothing of Brussels.'

Amelie glanced at Edmund before again turning to Fowler's parents. 'It was my brother who found your son on the battlefield at Waterloo. My husband helped bring him back to Brussels.'

Fowler, obviously, did not remember. 'Did you help rescue me, sir?' he asked Edmund.

'Yes,' Edmund replied.

Fowler hooked his cane over his arm and extended his hand. Edmund accepted the handshake.

'Thank you, sir,' Fowler said. 'Are you taking a holiday as well, enjoying the scenery and the fresh mountain air?'

'We live here now,' Edmund said.

Fowler's brows rose. 'Do you?' He looked at Amelie again. 'Why do I think of London when I see you?'

'I do not know,' she answered.

He smiled again. 'A faulty memory means a great deal of frustration, I assure you.'

'Come, my son,' his father demanded. 'We need to find a table.'

Fowler shook Edmund's hand a second time. 'I

hope we meet again.' He turned to Amelie and smiled. 'Ma'am.'

His parents hurried him on.

'He recovered. He seems to be what I thought he was,' Amelie murmured as they were out of earshot.

At this moment, if it were not for his cane, he made the perfect picture of what sort of husband she ought to have married.

Her brows knitted. 'His parents do dislike me, though, do they not?'

'Disagreeable people,' he admitted. He supposed they would have heard of him, as well. The bastard son of Sir Hollis Summerfield.

Reid leaned over to him. 'Who was that, laddo?'

Sally's eyes were wide. She knew who he was.

'A gentleman my wife once knew,' Edmund told him.

'It was a long time ago,' Amelie said.

It had not been more than four months, but it did feel like a lifetime ago.

'Were you at Waterloo, then?' Reid asked.

'Yes.' It was easier to talk of Waterloo. 'I was in the 28th.'

'My brother fought there,' Reid said. 'In the Con- naught Rangers. He made it through.'

'I am glad of it,' Edmund said.

Amelie became quiet and seemed miles away.

The encounter with Fowler put a pall over the meal that had begun so cheerfully.

By night back at the house, Amelie still felt affected by the encounter with Fowler. As Sally helped her get ready for bed, all she could do was think of that night. Of what had happened. Of how completely he'd deceived her.

Was Edmund remembering that night, too, and how Fowler's deeds had set in motion all that had happened to them since?

Seeing Fowler reminded her once more that she was not like other society misses. She heard his voice again, telling her she was wanton, shameful, no better than Haymarket ware.

How totally deceived she'd been. Even today he had seemed so sweet and gentle. If she'd met him for the first time today, she'd have been equally deceived.

'It was a surprise seeing Captain Fowler again, was it not?' Sally said, pulling the brush through her hair.

'Yes. It was.' Amelie was not inclined to elaborate.

But Sally looked puzzled and about to burst with questions. 'May I ask you something?'

'Of course,' Amelie said, although she did not want to talk of this.

'Why were you with Mr Summerfield that night in Brussels instead of Captain Fowler? I remember seeing you with Mr Summerfield in his uniform and all, but it was Captain Fowler who went with you to the ball.'

This was an impertinent question for a lady's maid to ask her mistress, but it had been Amelie who had encouraged a closer relationship between them.

'I will tell you.' Amelie met her eyes through the mirror. 'Captain Fowler walked me home from the ball, but we quarrelled and he left me on the street alone. Lieutenant Summerfield rescued me from a ruffian who tried to accost me, and he walked me safely back to the hotel.'

Sally's eyes grew starry. 'And that is where you fell in love with him?'

Yes. It was probably then, although she had not realised it. He'd been the finest man she'd ever met from the moment he saved her on the street.

She did love him. It hurt how much she loved him, because she still felt uncertain about him. He'd told her he did not regret marrying her, but was that the truth?

She'd been fooled before.

Sally stood waiting for her answer.

'Yes, I believe that was when I fell in love with him,' she told her.

'So it is easy to fall in love very fast, do you think?' Sally asked.

The subject had turned to Sally, apparently. 'I do not know about it being easy, but I suppose I am proof that it can happen.'

'Even if you thought you were in love with another man,' Sally went on.

Yes, even so. 'It happened to me.'

Sally put her hair in a plait and stood back, wiping tears from her eyes. 'But it won't work the other way around, will it? He won't love me, not with another man's baby in me and me lying about being married!'

Amelie rose, ready to put her arms around Sally and comfort her, but Sally backed away.

'Is there anything more you need from me, ma'am?' Sally asked, wiping her face with her apron.

'No, but—'

'I'll bid you good-night then.' Sally rushed out the door.

Amelie sat back in the chair.

Had she been wrong to convince Sally to lie about being married? It seemed she was as capable of deceiving as she was of being deceived.

And now she had to face Edmund. The encounter with Fowler had affected him, too, she could tell. It had created a distance between them, when these past few days and nights had been so happy. Would he want her tonight? There was only one way to know. She must walk to the connecting door and ask.

And face the fact that he might say no.

Edmund stripped down to his shirt and drawers. Somehow, tonight, he did not want to be naked, even though the thin cloth could not be any sort of armour.

He flopped into a chair and waited for Amelie, then wondered what he would do if she did appear.

Her bedchamber door closed and footsteps hurried down the hall. Sally had left. If Amelie was to come it would be soon.

He waited. He rose and paced and took a step towards the door, when it opened.

He loved the way she looked at night in her white nightgown draping her curves and tantalising his senses. He'd undo her plait and free her curls with his fingers. Then the picture would be complete. He'd kiss her and carry her to the bed.

But she remained in the doorway. 'Do you want me tonight?'

She'd not asked before. 'Why? Do you not want to come in?'

'I want to know if you want me.' She spoke louder.

Did she want him to say no? 'Only if you want to be here.'

'That is not my question!' she cried. 'You never say! You never tell me what you want.'

'I do tell you,' he protested. He did tell her, didn't he? 'But it should be as you wish it, not me.'

'Why can I not know?' Her voice turned shrill. 'Why hide the truth from me?'

Now she was being unfair. 'I never lie to you.'

'No, you never lie, but you never really tell me, do you?'

'Tell you what?' Did he want her to hear that he felt she deserved a better man than him? That she deserved a man like Fowler. Or rather how Fowler appeared to be. Gentle. Refined. Devoid of scandal?

'I asked you if you wanted me to share your bed tonight. Tell me if you want that.' She placed her hands on her hips.

'Only if you want it.' How much clearer could he be? Would it not be contemptible of him to require her to bed him if she did not desire it?

She made a frustrated sound.

'What is this all about, Amelie?' he demanded. 'Why tonight must I be put to this test? Is it because you saw Fowler?'

'Yes!' she cried. 'Because he reminded me that I can never know if you—or anyone—is telling me the truth!'

He softened his voice. 'Have I given you any reason to doubt what I say to you?'

She glanced away.

He extended his hand to her. 'Come to bed, Amelie. We will just sleep. It has been a long day.'

She hesitated but finally took his hand. He did not kiss her, nor did he gather her in his arms. When they reached the bed he did lift her onto it and climbed in next to her, spooning her against him as they'd spent their other nights here. One difference was he still wore his shirt and drawers.

Sally was too restless to retire to her little room on the second floor. She wanted the fresh air in her lungs. She wanted to gaze up at the stars and wrap herself in the darkness of the night. She grabbed her shawl and a candle and walked downstairs and outside through the conservatory door.

She ran to the middle of the lawn and lay down on the grass to gaze up at the stars, still in their place. She searched for the groups of stars she and Calvin used to find. Lyra and Perseus. Pegasus and Andromeda.

'What do you see up there?'

She sat up. His voice startled her, but it did not surprise her that he also was outside at night.

'I am watching the stars,' she said.

He lay down on the grass beside her. 'Do you know the names of the stars?'

'I do.' She pointed. 'There is Perseus, holding the head of the Medusa. See the square? That is Pegasus.'

She glanced over at him, but he was not looking at the sky. He was looking at her.

She felt blood rush to her face. 'You should not look at me like that.'

'Why not?' he asked. 'Ye're prettier than stars.'

She sat up. 'Please don't.'

He sat up, too. 'Don't what?'

'Do not talk like that!'

His face turned serious. 'Why do you repel my attentions, Mrs Brown? Are they so objectionable to you?'

'Mrs Brown.' She felt as though those words were sin itself.

His brow creased. 'Do you object to my calling you Mrs Brown?'

She could not hold the lie inside any longer. 'I am not *Mrs* Brown!'

He continued to stare at her. 'Who are you, then?'

She wrapped her shawl around her tighter. 'I am *Miss* Brown. Miss Sally Brown and I've never been married.'

'Why say you are Mrs and a widow, then?' he asked, but his voice was low and even.

'Oh, Mr Reid!' she cried. 'Can you not guess?

He kept his gaze on her but finally shook his head.

She rose to her feet. Dropping her shawl, she pressed the cloth of her skirt against her belly. 'Can you see now? It is starting to show. I am going to have a baby and I am not married.'

He stood, too.

She turned away from him. 'It was Mrs Summerfield's idea to tell everyone I am Mrs Brown. A widow. But I cannot like lying to—to you.'

'Can you tell me about it?' He spoke calmly.

'About the father, you mean?' She swiped at her tears. 'It was in Brussels. He was going to marry me, but he was killed in the battle.'

He said nothing.

'I do not want you to think that I—I did what I did with just anyone! I knew him a long time. We grew up together in Hampstead.'

'Then it is a sad thing he was killed,' he said. 'I am sorry for it.'

'I do not know what will happen to me!' she cried. 'What will happen to my baby? Mrs Summerfield says not to worry, but I do. Surely I can't pretend to be a widow for ever! And what will happen to my child if someone finds out! Will he be shunned? We both will be shunned.'

'It cannot be as bad as all that if Mrs Summerfield will help you,' he said.

'I do not know how. I cannot keep working as a lady's maid if I have a baby, can I? Whoever heard of such a thing?' She took several deep breaths to keep from falling apart entirely.

He picked up her shawl and wrapped it around her. 'You should go inside now. But do not worry. Your secret is safe with me. I will not tell anyone.'

He was being very kind, and it endeared him to her even more than before.

But he was still sending her away.

The next morning the wall that had risen between Edmund and Amelie was still intact. In the next few days they went through the motions of rising, conversing with each other, talking over the events of the day, as if that cocoon of closeness still bound them.

Curse Fowler, Edmund thought. *Why did he have to show up again?* Their marriage was built on shaky ground to begin with. Why did he have to put cracks in the fragile foundation they had been building, day by day? Night by night? Now, again, it seemed in danger of crumbling.

Their days were busy, though, so busy that the only time they spent together was at the dinner meal and afterward. They made love, but almost sadly, as if they were both remembering a giddy pleasure of the past that could be no more.

Edmund rose early and tried not to wake Amelie.

As he was picking up his boots to leave as quietly as possible, she spoke. 'Are you off, then?'

'Yes.' He and Reid were bound for another market day in another town. 'What do you do today?'

'I am going to visit the tenants' and farm workers' homes,' she said. 'I think I ought to, don't you?'

He walked back to her and leaned down to kiss her on the forehead. She seemed to stiffen at his touch. 'I think it will be a good thing to do.'

'I'll ask what they need. See if anything is amiss.'

'I have heard no complaints through Reid, but perhaps the wives will tell you more.' It was an inventory he'd not yet had time to do. He was glad she'd taken the interest.

'My father will expect some sort of report about the tenants and workers, will he not?' she said.

'It is likely.' He kissed her again, still savouring her lips. 'I'll be late, I suspect.'

She nodded.

He left feeling as if he were being crushed by grey clouds.

Chapter Twenty

The sheep auction kept Edmund too busy to think much about Amelie. Today there would not only be sales, but also a show to offer prizes for best sheep. Edmund was beginning to understand what made certain sheep better than others. Some of it was pure theatre—keeping the best sheep out of sight until the judging, then trying to get them in the best position to be seen. Some of it was personal opinion and some the fashion of the moment.

The show was meant to generate excitement for the sales to follow, as well as to show what the judges believed were the highest standards and how well or ill the other sheep met them. The sheep were walked into the judging ring by their breeders, who each tried to get their animal to stand out from the others, by their proud stance or, as Reid was skilful in doing, by getting the sheep on the highest ground so as to be the most visible.

The ribbons won and the prize money awarded were incidental to the showing off of the stock. When the sales began in the afternoon, excitement reached a fevered pitch. All the breeders wanted to buy the best at the lowest price and to sell their best at the highest.

This market scene had become familiar enough to Edmund that he could pay attention to more of the details. The prices bandied around began to stick in his head, and he began to know the probable worth of the ewes and tups by their appearance.

He carefully watched Reid's dealings with the other sheep farmers and paid particular attention to the amounts Reid spent and how much he earned. The transactions were quickly made, but Edmund was able to take them all in, unlike those first market days when it had all been a blur.

He stood next to Reid as he sold a ewe. Edmund heard the price and saw the money change hands. The transaction was quick, but Edmund saw Reid record it in his pocket book, only he put in a smaller amount. He glimpsed the receipt that Reid gave the other breeder, and it was for that same smaller amount.

'Did you write down the wrong amount?' he asked Reid.

Reid's eyes flashed at him, but he soon seemed

to recover. 'Don't be daft,' Reid said. 'You misheard, is all.'

On a purchase, Edmund watched closely. Reid listed the amount he spent as more than he and the man agreed upon. The receipt the man wrote was for the larger amount, even though that was not the amount they'd spoken about.

This time he did not question Reid, but he caught him in similar irregularities throughout the afternoon. It looked to him that Reid made more than he documented and paid less than he documented. Where was the extra money going? In Reid's pocket?

He did not want to believe this. He liked the man and had come to trust in his honesty.

Before he left the market, Edmund spoke with several of the breeders, asking them how the costs of the sheep had changed in the last year. He was lucky that, to the man, they could tell him what they paid for sheep and how much they'd sold them for a year ago. He memorised the amounts.

They rode back on the Cumbrian heavy horses that all the farmers owned in this part of England.

'How would you say the sales went today?' Edmund asked Reid.

'I'd say very well. It's been a good year for the farm,' Reid spoke with pride in his voice.

'How did the prices compare to last year's?' Edmund asked. 'What prices were you seeing last year?'

Reid hesitated before answering much more tentatively than the other breeders had done, but Edmund noted what he'd said.

He could still be wrong. He prayed he was.

When they reached the farm, it was dark. Edmund bid Reid good-night and went into the house.

One of the new footmen was attending the hall. 'Evening, sir. How was the sale?'

Everyone had an interest in the sale of sheep. Their livelihoods depended upon it, if only indirectly.

He handed the man his hat and gloves. 'It went well. Mr Reid was pleased at any rate.' He removed his coat. 'Would you brush out my coat, as well?'

'Aye, sir. I will do it and be glad for the work.' He grinned.

These Lakeland servants knew nothing of the decorum of their London counterparts, but it was a difference Edmund found refreshing.

'Thank you.' He added, 'Do you know where Mrs Summerfield is at the moment?'

'I believe she retired to her bedchamber,' the footman answered.

Edmund reached for a taper from a candle box and lit it from one of the lamps. 'I'll be in the library for a little while. I won't need you further, though, if you wish to leave the hall.'

'Thank you, sir!' The man grinned again.

Edmund carried the taper to the library and lit the lamps on the table where the ledger books were stacked. He opened the book from last year and turned the pages until he came to the recordings for the market a year ago.

The figures were roughly what Reid had said. The problem was, they were different from the numbers the other breeders had given him and in a pattern that was becoming sickeningly familiar. Reid recorded the sales low and the purchases high.

Edmund rested his elbows on the table and hung his head in his hands. It looked as if Reid was systematically embezzling from the farm, taking money from Amelie's father, who had given Edmund the right to act in his behalf.

How he must act was now something he dreaded.

He'd misjudged Reid, apparently. He did not misjudge people often, and he hated the idea of being deceived.

He rubbed his face. How would it be if Amelie knew of this? She liked Reid. She hoped Sally would finally allow Reid to court her. She believed Reid to be a good man. Amelie's trust in Edmund was shaky at present. He just could not yet tell her that another man with the appearance of honour had deceived them all.

Not until he confronted Reid.

Edmund finally closed the ledger and lit the taper again before extinguishing the lamps. He left the library and made his way up the stairs to his bedchamber. He could see no light under Amelie's door. Did that mean she was asleep in her own bed? He feared that would be the case. It seemed to him the only connection that still held them together was sharing a bed. Making love.

He opened his door and was not surprised to see a lamp burning. The servants would have left one burning for him, knowing he was coming home late. He blew out the taper and left it on the table inside the door. As he walked into the room, he unbuttoned his waistcoat and untied his neckcloth.

'It is late,' he heard Amelie murmur. 'Did the market last so long?'

'I've been home a while,' he said.

She was in his bed and he was grateful for it. He crossed the room and gave her a kiss. On the lips this time. She accepted it but held back anything in return.

'I've been in the library. I needed to see something in the ledgers,' he explained.

'What did you need to see in the ledgers?'

He could almost hear what she did not say—what did you need that could not wait until morning?

'Last year's figures for this market,' he said.

'Whatever for?'

He wanted to tell her, wanted to pour out his anger and disappointment at being so deceived by Reid. He wanted to say that he still could not believe Reid could do such a thing.

But he didn't. 'I did not want to forget what I was told at the sale. I thought I'd forget if I waited until morning.' This was all true. It was also true that he needed to know right away if his suspicions would be borne out.

'It was that important?' Her tone of voice was disapproving.

He pulled off his boots and trousers. 'It was.'

'Why?'

'So I would not forget.' He walked over to the washbasin, washed his face and hands and brushed his teeth. As he walked back to the bed, he threw off his shirt. He collapsed onto the bed, suddenly exhausted.

Amelie rose on one elbow. 'You are not telling me something.'

That was so. 'Amelie, let us not debate this. I am tired.'

'Very well.' She pulled the covers up to her neck and rolled onto her side, facing away from him, not touching him at all.

Sally waited outside until Mr Reid and his men had placed all the sheep into pens and finished their work while everyone else on the farm was likely asleep. She figured that he would be the last to leave, and she was correct.

He took one long glance back towards the house before turning and starting to walk to his cottage.

She ran to catch up to him. 'Mr Reid!'

He stopped. 'Miss Brown? What are you doing here?'

'I waited for you,' she said, but she halted. 'Unless—unless you do not wish for my company any longer.'

He took quick strides to reach her side. 'It is not that. It is just that it is cold out tonight and you should not get a chill, especially in your condition.'

'It is not that cold,' she said, although she had been shivering while waiting for him.

'Why did you wish to see me, lass?' he asked.

'Today Mrs Summerfield and I went round to all the tenants' houses and the farm workers', and the wives all said the same about you. That you took care of their needs. That you were a good man, and one of the maids said that many of the young women around here would like you to be their husband.'

He dipped his head. 'I never knew that.'

'She said it was so.'

'And why did this make you wait for me?' he asked.

'I want to know why you picked me. You wanted to court me. At least you once wanted to. I want to know why.'

'Why?' He paused to think. 'I am not sure why. You are pretty and sweet-tempered. You do not come from here and I find that captivating.'

She felt her cheeks burn. 'But you changed your mind about me, because of the baby, correct? I want to know for certain, and I promise I will never trouble you again if you tell me the truth.'

He looked directly into her eyes. 'I never said I lost interest in you, because I have not.' He touched her arm. 'I still want to court you, and I hope in time you will want to marry me.'

'You would marry me knowing I carry another man's child?' She could not believe it even though she had come to this place to hear those very words.

'Of course I would,' he said. 'I figure I can give the poor bairn my name and there would be no one to question it. If you want to pretend you are a widow and the baby is your dead husband's, no harm done. It is very nearly the truth.'

Her eyes widened. 'That is what Mrs Summerfield would say.'

'Come to my cottage,' he said. 'I'll make you some tea and warm you up. You do not have to answer me now, but let me show you what sort of house I have and what sort of life you would live.'

She was too shocked to say anything, but she walked with him to his cottage.

The next morning Amelie woke at the first light of dawn, filled with regret. She'd intended to welcome Edmund home from the market. She'd planned to erase these days of her foolish insistence that he tell her each and every feeling he had towards her, but then he'd been so evasive and secretive that her temper had been piqued. Imagine checking figures when he'd been away all day and when matters had been strained between them.

She resolved to turn over a new leaf and stop being so high-handed about trifles.

But a return to sleep eluded her. She slipped out of bed and went into her bedchamber for a wrapper. She put it on and decided to get some fresh air to clear her mind and to help her rid herself of these worries. She wanted things the way they were on those few days of bliss when she'd begun to believe they might eventually be happy.

Amelie left her room and descended the stairs.

She could hear the faint sounds of the house stirring, servants rising to begin the day. She had no wish to meet any of them and feel compelled to explain her early morning wanderings, so she hurried through the hall to the conservatory, still empty of plants.

She noticed that the conservatory door was not locked, an oversight she must mention to Lloyd and Mrs Wood.

Not that it mattered much. In London, perhaps, or even in the country where Northdon House was, but not here. There was nothing much worth stealing in the house and even if there were, the farm's people were not so hungry they had to steal. On the contrary, they were well cared for.

She crossed the lawn and took one of the paths that led up a hill. On her way she noticed a man and a woman walking toward the house. As they came closer she saw it was Sally and Mr Reid.

Sally saw her and blanched. 'Mrs Summerfield! I can explain!'

'It is not how it appears, ma'am,' Reid said.

She ought to be appalled. She knew ladies of the *ton* who would fire a maid for less. Certainly those ladies would have fired Sally long ago. Amelie did not even care if it was exactly how it appeared, that they had spent the night together.

She was merely happy for them.

'Nothing happened, I swear it!' Sally cried.

Amelie directed her gaze at Mr Reid. 'Tell me only what your intentions are toward Sally, sir.'

'Why, to marry her,' Reid said. 'That has been my intention nearly from our first meeting.'

She turned to Sally. 'Will you marry him, then?' If Sally said no, Amelie still would not desert her. Sally and her baby would be secure; she'd see to it.

A rapturous look came over Sally's face as she glanced at Mr Reid. 'Oh, yes, ma'am. I will marry him. We'll have the banns called as soon as we can.'

Amelie smiled. 'Then you need say no more. I wish you happy.'

'Oh, Mrs Summerfield!' Sally hugged her, behaviour unheard of in a maid. 'It is all going to be fine now!'

How lucky Sally was. She would have a devoted husband…and a baby…and a good life, like the rest of the tenants' and farm workers' wives.

Amelie hugged her back, feeling a thousand years older, although Sally was probably very close to her age. 'I am happy for you both.'

Chapter Twenty-One

Amelie walked the rest of the way back to the house with Sally, leaving Mr Reid whistling as he headed to the farm building.

Sally rattled on about their plans, about how they had stayed up all night discussing them, about how lucky she felt to have met this good man.

'His house is just what it ought to be,' Sally said. 'Very cosy and neat, but I think it will be very pretty with new curtains and such…'

Amelie only half listened to her.

She was happy for Sally, happy that Sally would get what Amelie had not. A respectable marriage. A baby. A home that was hers alone. A man who adored her.

They entered the house and walked together up to Amelie's bedchamber. Sally kept talking, all the while helping Amelie to dress. When the girl finally left with instructions to get some sleep, Amelie walked to the connecting door to Edmund's room.

She leaned her forehead against the cool wood and prayed she could somehow make amends for all her foolishness.

She promised herself she would trust Edmund. He'd always done right by her.

She took a deep breath and knocked on the door.

'Come in,' she heard from the other side.

She opened the door.

Edmund was almost dressed. The footman who had been assigned valet duties was helping him on with his coat. Edmund looked over at Amelie guardedly.

She placed a smile on her face. 'Good morning!' she said cheerfully.

The footman greeted her with a smile and a nod before leaving the room.

'Good morning,' Edmund said then.

'I have so much to tell you!' she said. 'Some of it I must tell you before breakfast, because it is a secret.'

He waited.

She told herself not to be daunted by his reserve. She'd brought it on herself, after all.

'It is exciting news!' she went on. 'Sally and Mr Reid are to be married.'

His face turned stony. 'Mr Reid?'

'Yes.' She turned to the window, because Edmund's demeanour disturbed her and she did not want to give in to discouragement the way she had before. 'Mr Reid took a fancy to her almost at first sight. And he knows about the baby. He even knows that Sally is not a widow.' She glanced at the door, turning nervous because he was not at all acting as she expected. 'Shall we go to breakfast?'

He nodded and moved to escort her.

'But you mustn't tell anyone, because they will decide when to announce it.'

'I will tell no one.'

She peered at him. 'Are you not happy for them?'

He shook his head as if to rid it of a thought. 'Forgive me. I was thinking about something else. I hope they know each other well enough.'

What an odd thing for him to say. 'We did not know each other at all,' she murmured.

'No,' he said. 'Of course we did not.'

'Do you know something about Mr Reid that means he and Sally should not be wed?' Sally should not be surprised the way she'd been surprised about Fowler.

'I know nothing for certain,' he said. 'But if I hear something, Sally should know I will say so.'

Amelie told herself to be contented with that response as they walked down the stairs to the dining room. Edmund seemed a world away. Sunlight streamed in the sparkling clean windows of the sitting room next to the conservatory, where the breakfast buffet was set out. Bread for toasting, slices of ham, kippers, eggs, butter and jam. Such a contrast to their first morning. There was even a footman in attendance.

They selected their food and Amelie sat across from Edmund at a small table she'd found in the attic. The footman poured coffee for Edmund, tea for Amelie and retired from the room.

Edmund was lost in his own thoughts.

Amelie disliked the silence but was determined not to ask about it. Instead she said, 'Would you like to hear about my visits with the tenants' and farm workers' wives yesterday?'

He at least looked up at her and almost smiled. 'Yes. I do want to hear it. Did it go well?'

'I think it did mostly,' she responded. 'Some of the wives were cautious and polite, but no one had any complaints to speak of or anything they required that was not provided them. They credited Mr Reid with managing their needs very well.'

'Mr Reid,' he repeated almost in a whisper.

'Mrs Peet absolutely sang his praises, and the maid we took with us agreed with her.' She lowered her voice. 'I cannot help but feel Sally is fortunate. Indeed, we are all fortunate he is here.'

'Yes.' It seemed he turned distant again. 'Fortunate.'

She had to speak. 'What is it, Edmund?' She

leaned toward him. 'Something is troubling you. Can you tell me what it is?'

'A problem I need to sort out,' he said. 'I cannot speak of it yet.'

It must involve her in some way. Why else not tell her? 'I—I am sorry for my ill temper lately.'

He reached over and clasped her hand. 'It is not that. I will work through this problem, I promise.'

'Is it with the farm?' she asked.

'Not with the farm precisely, but do not ask me more. It is too soon for me to talk of it.'

In other words, it was a secret.

'What will you do today?' she asked.

'I need to meet with Reid,' was all he said.

Edmund found Reid in the sheep pens.

'Good morning, Summerfield!' Reid looked particularly cheerful this morning. And why wouldn't he? He'd become betrothed. 'We are preparing for the tupping—the mating—that is next on the schedule. There is always something.'

'I need to speak with you, Reid,' Edmund said. 'Alone.'

Reid's happy mood fell, Edmund could tell, but he tried to cover it over with a false cheer. 'Aye! As you wish. Give me a moment.' He gave some instruction to the men in the sheep pen and climbed over the fence. 'Shall we go in my office?'

Reid kept up the light pretence as they walked to the building where he kept his office. In the sunlight Edmund could see the dark circles under his eyes and the worry lines on his forehead.

Once there, Reid asked, 'Would you care for tea? I can build a fire and put the pot on.'

'Do not go to the trouble.'

'Will you sit at least?' A hint of testiness entered Reid's voice.

'I'll stand.' Edmund knew from the army that a man had more authority when he stood.

Reid rested against his desk. 'What is it?' he asked in a serious tone.

'I think you know,' Edmund said, watching the man carefully.

Reid laughed drily. 'I do not know. I have no idea.' He paused, then asked. 'Unless it has something to do with Miss Brown? I assure you my intentions are honourable towards her. I want to marry her, and she has agreed to have me.'

'My wife told me,' Edmund responded. 'This does not concern Miss Brown.' Although it would seriously affect her.

'What is it then?' Reid could not quite pull off a guileless expression.

'It is about the money you are embezzling from my wife's father.'

Reid tried to appear outraged. 'Embezzling? That is absurd.'

'You pay less for the sheep than the receipts state and you sell sheep for more than you record. Those profits go into your pocket.'

Reid straightened. 'I told you yesterday that you were mistaken. You heard wrong is all.'

'No,' Edmund said. 'I know what I saw, what I heard. The figures in the ledger do not fit with what the other breeders told me about last year's prices. Yours were consistent. You sold high and bought low. Every time. Do me the honour of not taking me for a fool.'

'I deliver a profit from the farm,' Reid said. 'Lord Northdon makes good money from it every year, and each year we do better.'

'You also steal profit from the farm, do you not?'

Reid glared at him. 'You saw the books. Before I came the farm was making a pittance. One bad year and it would have gone under. Now it makes him money.'

'Explain what I saw, then. Those are profits you are not recording.' This was a card he hated to play. 'If you do not explain this, Reid, I will have to let you go.'

'Before the tupping?' Reid's voice rose. 'I need to be here!'

'Then explain about the money.' Edmund insisted. 'Or leave today.'

Reid turned away and waited so long to speak that Edmund thought he would actually leave.

He finally turned back. 'When I came here the farm was a shambles. It was in danger of failing. Worse, its workers were living in deplorable conditions. Roofs leaked. Fuel was scarce. In winter their children were getting sick from the cold. Grain stores were infested with vermin. Deplorable conditions!' He shook his head. 'If the farm failed the effects would stretch further than the farm. The village depends on us. The other farms on the estate depend on us. There would be a lot of people put in dire circumstances. So the farm had to prosper.'

'How does this lead to embezzlement?' Edmund demanded.

'Do me the courtesy of letting me explain in my own way,' Reid snapped.

Edmund inclined his head. 'Go on, then.'

'I applied to Lord Northdon several times for the funds to put things on a solid footing. I sent all the details. Every time I was refused.'

'Lord Northdon refused you?' Northdon did not seem to lack generosity or good sense.

'So his man of business, Mr Frye, said. It was he who proposed this plan—'

'The man of business devised the plan?' Could this be true?

'Aye,' Reid said. 'It was not the solution I thought best. Mr Frye said to skim off the top in all transactions. He said he could keep Lord Northdon from knowing about it for the price of forty pounds per year.'

'You went along with this, though,' Edmund accused.

Reid threw up his hands. 'What choice did I have? I knew if we poured more money into the farm and its tenants and workers, we would reap the rewards of it. And I knew if the farm prospered, the village would prosper and the other farms would not be hurt. I knew in the long run Lord Northdon would make more money.'

'But it is embezzlement just the same, Reid,' Edmund said.

Reid made a sweeping motion with his arm. 'But look what we've done. Everything on the farm is in good repair. The workers' needs have been attended to. As a result they work hard. Everyone goes along with this, because they know everyone benefits. How could I not do this?'

Edmund sank down in a chair. This was even worse than he thought. If he exposed the scheme, many people would be hurt.

Reid looked down at him. 'I can prove to you

that I kept none of it for myself. I have another set of ledgers that show where every penny has gone, all back into the farm or to the workers when the need was legitimate.'

'How many people know about this?' Edmund asked.

'Everyone,' Reid said. 'That is why you received such a cool welcome, you know. We all expected you had come to cause trouble. To change things. To go back to the way it was when everyone struggled. But then you didn't do anything. Nothing but work and that put you in good stead. When Mrs Summerfield helped harvest the hay, that was even better. We thought we were safe.'

Edmund rubbed his face. 'What is to be done now?'

Reid sat, as well. 'Might we not merely go on as before?'

Edmund looked at him. 'I do not see how. The money belongs to my wife's father. How can I turn a blind eye to it?' And how could he allow that man of business to extort money from a scheme he'd devised?

'You must find a way, or these people will suffer.' Reid looked defeated.

What was Edmund to do? He did not exactly have any clout with Amelie's father. In fact, he was quite sure his father-in-law would do the opposite of whatever Edmund recommended.

Edmund stood. 'Let me think about this. Go back to the sheep. Do what needs to be done. I will tell you first what I decide.'

Reid nodded and rose to his feet. The two men walked back to the sheep pens, but there Edmund left him and continued to the house.

What was he to say to Amelie about this? He could not put her in a position that required her to act against her father.

From her bedchamber window Amelie watched her husband and Mr Reid walk from the direction of the sheep pens to the building where Reid had his office. Even from this distance she could tell something was wrong. There was tension in both their gaits, and they were not speaking.

Her guess was the tension had something to do with whatever had upset Edmund the night before and preoccupied him this morning.

That he would not tell her bothered her. It must have to do with the sheep or the sale or perhaps with Mr Reid himself. Edmund had avoided answering her when she'd asked if it was about Mr Reid.

Amelie watched them until they disappeared into the farm building. She rubbed her forehead and turned around quickly to stride into Edmund's room. Even though one of the footman acted as his valet, she liked to straighten his room and fold his clothes.

She heard a sound from outside and glanced out the window. A carriage passed through the gate and was making its way towards the house. She watched it come closer, and as it went around a curve in the road she gasped.

The crest on the side looked like her father's.

She took off her apron and dropped it on one of the chairs. Her father would not like her looking like one of the chambermaids. She ran down the stairs to the hall, where the new footman sat, waiting for something to do.

'There is a coach coming!' she said.

He stood. 'A coach? What do I do?'

'Come outside with me to meet whoever it is.' She opened the front door herself, and he followed her outside.

'It is my father's carriage, I think, but I don't know why he would send it.'

'Your father?' the footman said. 'The lord that owns the farm?'

'Yes.'

The carriage pulled up, driven by the same two coachmen who had brought Amelie and Edmund here only a few weeks ago. She could see that the passengers were men, but she could not tell who they were.

The footman glanced at Amelie, looking uncertain.

'Put the steps down, open the door and assist the passengers,' she told him. 'You will do splendidly.'

He nodded.

The first man out of the carriage was her father's valet. Her father must be one of the passengers, then. The valet glanced at the house and shivered with disgust. He sighed, looked heavenward and waited to assist her father.

The next man was Mr Frye, her father's man of business, a short, portly man who always creaked when he walked from the stays he wore under his clothes. He spied her and bowed.

'Miss Glenville,' he said with a flourish.

She curtsied. 'Mrs Summerfield, sir, as well you know.' The man was more pompous than the highest society matron. She'd never liked him.

Last came her father. Amelie ran up to him and he gave her a big hug. 'Amelie, my dear,' was all he said.

'Why are you here, Papa?' she cried. 'Did something happen to Maman? Or Marc or Tess?'

'Nothing like that.' Her father patted her hand.

The footman was looking disoriented again. She

stepped closer to him. 'Gather their baggage and carry it in.'

He nodded.

She spoke to the coachman holding the horses. 'You remember where the stables are, do you not?'

'Yes, ma'am,' the man said.

'The stablemen should see to your needs nicely.' She hurried over to her father and the other two men. 'Come in, please. The footman will see to your bags.'

She led her father and Mr Frye into the drawing room. 'Please sit, Papa. I'll see to refreshments.'

She stepped back into the hall, where the valet was looking around disdainfully.

The footman came through the door juggling three bags and a basket.

She hurried up to him but spoke in tones low enough that the valet would not hear. 'Leave these and run to find Mr Summerfield and Mr Reid. I saw them walking to one of the farm buildings. Tell them my father and his man of business are here.'

'Man of business,' the footman said in disapproving tones. 'Do you want Mr Summerfield and Mr Reid to come here?'

She did not know. 'Just tell them the men are here. They will know what to do. But hurry!'

'Yes, ma'am!' He ran off.

She turned to the valet. 'Come with me.' She

led him through the servants' door leading to the kitchen. 'Mrs Wood!' she called. 'I need you.'

Mrs Wood appeared in the hallway.

Amelie spoke right away. 'My father and his man of business have called unexpectedly. Please see we are served refreshment in the drawing room and see to Hines, here. He is my father's valet. We will need rooms prepared for them.'

'Your father.' Mrs Wood frowned. 'Very good. We shall attend to it.'

Amelie hurried back to the drawing room.

'I am sorry. I was delayed,' she said. 'We shall have refreshments in a few minutes.'

Her father remained standing and was looking around the room. 'I had forgotten how austere this place was. More like the house of a tenant farmer.'

It was good he'd not seen it before they'd hung the paintings.

'It is plain,' she agreed.

'Where is your husband?' Her father said the word *husband* with great disdain.

'Out tending to farm business, of course.' Her brows knitted. 'Papa, why are you here? And why is Mr Frye with you?'

He walked over to her and put his hand on her arm. 'It is about business, Amelie. It is nothing for you to trouble yourself over.'

She was already troubled over it.

'Something your husband should have been alerted to,' he said scathingly.

Her father never gave Edmund a good word.

She lifted her chin. 'He already knows about it.' It must be whatever was disturbing Edmund.

'He does?' Mr Frye looked surprised. 'He knows about the fraud and embezzlement?'

Amelie felt the blood drain from her face.

Chapter Twenty-Two

At that moment, Lloyd brought in a tea tray, and they stopped talking. He set it down on the table and left.

Amelie poured the tea. 'How do you take yours, Mr Frye?' she asked.

'Three teaspoons of sugar and milk,' the man said, reaching for one of the biscuits Mrs Stagg had included.

Amelie sat, but mostly so they would. Her mind was spinning. What fraud? Who was embezzling?

Her father was restless in his seat. He finally stood again. 'Perhaps you should send someone to find Summerfield and summon him here.'

'I already did,' she answered. 'He will come unless he is involved in something that demands his attention.'

Mr Frye also stood again. 'What could be more important?' He mirrored her father's tone and demeanour.

Amelie fixed a gaze on him. 'You do not know the workings of a farm, do you, sir? Some tasks cannot wait.' She turned to her father. 'Edmund is handling the matter, do not fear.'

'He sent for the magistrate, then?' Frye asked.

The magistrate. Who was to be arrested? 'I said he is handling it, Mr Frye.' She faced her father again. 'Tell me what you know.'

He shook his head in dismay. 'I cannot believe he worried you over this ramshackle business, but since you know, maybe you can tell me what he plans to do about it.'

'Tell me what you know,' she repeated. 'And perhaps I can.'

Her father pointed to his man of business. 'Mr Frye discovered it.'

Mr Frye eagerly took up the tale. He cleared his throat. 'When I learned that you and Summerfield would be coming here, I carefully examined the records.' He smirked. 'To make certain I was prepared in case I was needed.'

As if Edmund would need the likes of Mr Frye, Amelie thought.

'Some anomalies made me suspicious, though,' Mr Frye went on. 'I have convincing proof that Mr Reid is embezzling significant sums of money every year.'

No. Amelie felt this blow deep in the pit of her stomach.

Not Mr Reid. Please, not Mr Reid.

Her father's eyes flashed. 'If he knew about this, why did he not write me immediately?'

She met his eye. 'Why should he write to you, Papa? You gave him permission to act in your stead. Let him act. He will resolve the matter.'

'Resolve the matter?' Frye scoffed. 'Arrest the fellow and send him to the gallows.'

'Arrest who?' Edmund walked through the door, followed by Mr Reid.

Amelie's heart pounded in her chest.

He stood tall and faced her father and Mr Frye with boldness, but Amelie noticed the stiffness of his shoulders.

Edmund inclined his head to her father. 'Good day, sir. I hope you are in good health.'

'Of course I am in good health,' her father snapped. 'What has that to do with anything?'

'This other gentleman is Mr Frye, my father's man of business,' Amelie told him, not trusting her father to have the courtesy to make introductions.

'I met Mr Frye when we made the marriage settlement.' Edmund said. He looked Frye up and down. 'Good day, sir.'

Frye turned red and sputtered, 'We shall see if it is a good day.'

'I am surprised you came, Frye,' Edmund went on. 'Given all we know.'

'I insisted he come,' her father said.

'Papa—' Amelie did not want to ignore Reid standing there '—may I present Mr Reid, the steward?'

'Humph. I am surprised *you* came, sir,' her father said to Reid. 'When you must know we are here because you have been embezzling funds from me all these five years.'

No! Amelie could not have misjudged Reid so completely, could she? Could she not trust the character of any man she met? Poor Sally. Amelie had practically thrown Sally at Mr Reid.

'Yes!' Frye pointed a finger at Reid. 'Mr Reid defrauded you and embezzled from you.'

'What did he do, precisely, Mr Frye?' Edmund asked.

Mr Frye looked smug. 'It appears he made it look as though the sheep sold for less than they really did and that he purchased new stock at a lower price than they really were. I believe he used that principle in buying and selling everything.'

'I wonder how you could tell that from your records,' Edmund remarked in a casual tone.

Amelie stood straighter. How would that show up on records?

'Mr Reid has a tale that is a bit more detailed than

Frye's,' Edmund said. 'And he has the records to prove it.'

A panicked look flashed through Frye's eyes, but he lifted his chin. 'You cannot tell me anyone will believe a hill farmer over me.'

'A hill farmer with good records.' Edmund turned to her father. 'You are a reasonable man, sir. Listen to him.' He nodded to Reid.

Reid cleared his throat. 'Sir, five years ago I repeatedly asked for more funds to improve the farm. When I came on, it was in a poor state. I appealed to you through Mr Frye, who said you refused. I indicated how dire the situation was, and it was he who suggested the scheme he described—'

'I never did!' protested Frye.

'Go on,' her father said.

'I felt I had no choice, sir,' Reid said to her father. 'If the farm failed, all its people would be out of work. The village would suffer. The other farms, too. I could not let that happen. You had good land. Good buildings. You had the foundation of good stock.'

Perhaps Amelie had not misjudged Reid. Whatever he'd done, he sounded as though he'd done it for the farm and its people.

As he talked she stole glances at Edmund, who looked in total command of the situation, unless you saw the stress at the corner of his eyes.

Shame on her for doubting him, for not trusting him. He never failed her. Never.

Reid went on. 'If you want to inspect the books, sir, I will show you everything. Where every penny went, including the forty pounds per year paid to Mr Frye.'

'Paid to Mr Frye!' Her father swung around to his man of business.

'It is not true,' Frye said, but his voice turned weak.

'Will your books show where every penny went?' Edmund asked Frye.

Frye returned a panicked look.

Her father frowned. 'I believe I would like to see these books, Reid.'

'They are in the library,' Edmund said.

Her father swiftly crossed the room to the door. Reid followed him.

Edmund walked up to Amelie. He touched her arm. 'Would you wait here with Frye? I'll have Rogers stay in the room with you. I want someone to watch him, and you are the only one—'

She covered his hand with hers. 'You do not have to explain.' She smiled at him. 'Not this time.'

He touched her face and walked out.

By the time the three men returned to the drawing room, Mr Frye was seated in a chair, quivering in fear and muttering to himself that he could not go to prison, that he could not die on the gallows.

Her father walked up to him directly. 'Here is what you will do, Frye, if you wish to avoid the gallows.' His voice vibrated with anger. 'You will return to London. You will get my affairs in order so they can be turned over to a reputable replacement. You will pay back the money you have stolen in payments from Reid. Then you will leave London, and I had better never hear of you or see you again. The only reason I spare your life is to avoid the scandal that would surely ensue.'

Frye rose from his chair with difficulty, but he nodded vigorously.

Edmund added, 'I'll have a man drive you in the wagon to Keswick. You can get a coach back to London from there.'

Edmund glanced over at Rogers. 'Can you manage it, Rogers?'

Rogers smiled. 'Oh, aye, sir. I'll see to it.' When Frye reached the doorway, Rogers seized his arm. 'Stay with me, sir.'

'Would you like to see the farm now, Lord Northdon?' Reid asked her father.

'I would.' He started for the door but turned. 'Are you coming, too, Summerfield?'

Edmund glanced at Amelie before he followed her father.

She watched him leave the room, wishing for just a moment or two alone with him, enough time for her to tell him she loved him.

After the tour of the farm, Edmund and Lord Northdon left Reid at his office and walked back to the house.

'The farm is well-run, do you not think?' Edmund said. There was nothing like showing it to make the point that Reid's money had been well spent.

'Impressive,' Lord Northdon said. 'But do not suppose this changes anything.'

Edmund went cold inside. 'What is your meaning, sir?'

'Reid still embezzled money.'

Had Northdon not seen the sense of everything? Reid's acceptance of the embezzlement scheme had saved the farm. Northdon had made money instead of losing the entire estate.

He halted. 'Sir, you can't jail Reid. Think of the farm. Breeding is about to begin. You would be throwing away the profits Reid has produced for you.'

Northdon started walking again. 'I agree. Reid ought to stay.' He paused for a long time. 'You should go.'

'What?'

'I want you to go,' Northdon repeated.

'You wanted us here, now you want us to leave?' He and Amelie did not need to be uprooted again. They needed time together.

'As you know,' Northdon went on, 'I have no liking for you and the way you ill-used my daughter.'

'Much has happened since then,' Edmund said.

'This is not a suitable life for my daughter!' Northdon threw up his arms. 'In such a house. Managing servants who would do better working in the fields.'

'This is your property.'

'I did not remember how rustic it was.' Northdon waved a hand. 'And I did not want to send Amelie here. I wanted her to stay with her mother and me. She may have been ruined for a good marriage, but she can at least enjoy a pleasant life.'

Edmund's anger grew. He was a villain in this man's eyes—a bastard—and there was no changing that. 'Speak plainly, sir.'

'I mean I want to take my daughter home. Alone. I want you to leave her. And if you do not, I will call the magistrate and have Reid prosecuted, jailed and hung.'

'No.' Edmund could manage to say no more.

'I am absolutely determined.' Northdon's voice was firm.

'This is impossible.' Edmund fumed. 'Either I ruin the lives of all these people or I hurt Amelie.'

'She will recover well enough when she is back home.'

No, she would not recover. She'd never trust anyone again.

'You cursed contemptible scoundrel!' Edmund shouted.

He strode off, making haste to put distance between himself and Northdon before he put his fist in the older man's jaw, but he waited for Northdon at the door to the house.

When Northdon came near, Edmund crossed his arms over his chest. 'I call your bluff, sir.'

Northdon's brows rose, but his smug expression did not change.

Edmund stared him straight in the face. 'I am going to wager on you being a decent man. I'm going to wager that only a decent man would have produced a daughter like Amelie, a son like Glenville. Only a decent man would have defied society to marry a woman like Lady Northdon. I wager that you will not ruin a good man like Mr Reid; you will not impoverish this farm and its people and its village's people just to hurt me. I wager that, even though you detest me, you will not hurt others merely to revenge yourself on me. So I defy your threat.'

Northdon pursed his lips, but Edmund thought he saw a moment of acquiescence, even respect, in his eyes. 'It is a great risk you take.'

'I do not need this farm,' he said. 'I do not need you and your money or even Amelie's dowry. I can well support my wife myself. I can and will prosper.' He leaned forward for more emphasis. 'But I need Amelie. I need her the way I need air to breathe. I will not leave her, not unless she wants me to go.'

Northdon tilted his head. 'Ah, but suppose she does want you to go. Suppose she would prefer to return to the comfort and loving arms of her family. Would you let her go then?'

The idea of it was like a fresh sabre cut, straight to his heart. 'If Amelie wishes for me to leave her, I will leave, but only if it is what she desires.'

'Then let us ask her.' Northdon pushed past him and walked into the house.

They found Amelie upstairs in the bedchamber that the maid was readying for Lord Northdon.

'We need to speak to you, Amelie,' her father said.

Amelie glanced at Edmund with a questioning expression. He had no answer for her.

She turned to Jobson. 'Are you finished in here?'

The maid glanced at Lord Northdon with a

scornful expression. Edmund supposed the servants already knew Northdon had come intending to arrest Reid.

'I'm done, ma'am.' Jobson curtsied and left the room.

Amelie's eyes slid towards Edmund again before she turned to her father. 'Well?'

It was Edmund who answered. 'Your father wishes you to make a choice.'

'What now, Papa?' Amelie said, exasperated with her father.

Her father's eyes twitched. 'I had forgotten this house was so ramshackle. Like living in a tenant's hut. The servants are deplorable. You've been used to finer things, better service and more comfort. You certainly have not been required to work in the fields.'

Someone told him she'd helped with the haymaking? How unfortunate.

'What is this choice?' she asked impatiently.

He responded, 'Come back to Northdon House with me and resume the life you were born to.'

'Edmund does not wish to live at Northdon House.' Why was he bringing this up again? 'That was settled back in London.'

Her father gave her an intent look. 'I meant for *you* to come home.'

Her stomach clenched. 'Without my husband, you mean.' She turned to Edmund. 'Do you want me to leave with my father?' She quickly added. 'And do not answer by asking me what I want. Just answer me.'

He held her gaze but did not speak right away. Finally he said, 'No, I do not want you to leave me.' His voice was low, but she felt it pulsate inside her. 'I will not prevent you, though, if you desire to leave.'

She closed her eyes and inhaled. Edmund always told her the truth. *He did not want her to leave him.* She could trust that.

She swung back to her father. 'What are you about, Papa? Why are you trying to separate me from Edmund? I love him, Papa.'

Her father lifted his chin. 'How can you say that? He defiled you.'

'He did not defile me, Papa. Why can you not understand that? That night was a beginning for us—a lucky one, Papa.' She stole a glance at Edmund but could not let her gaze linger lest her emotions spill over. She turned back to her father. 'Are you making me choose between here and Northdon House? Because I want to stay here. Or are you forcing me to choose between Edmund and you and Maman?

That would pain me to the quick, but my choice must be Edmund. Do you know why? Because Edmund would never force me to make such a choice.'

Her father's head bowed.

She lowered her voice. 'Make yourself comfortable, Papa. Hines will come to tell you of dinner. We keep country hours here.' She walked out the door, hearing and feeling Edmund following her. Her feelings for him were raw and acute, and she feared she would burst if she let them loose.

He seized her arm and pulled her into an embrace. They held on to each other as if a violent whirlwind threatened to blow them apart. Perhaps that was what had almost happened.

'Amelie,' he murmured. 'Do you truly love me? Do you want to stay with me?'

She hugged him close again. 'Of course.'

He released her but only enough so he could gaze into her face. 'I have not said it to you, because I thought you would not want to hear it, but I love you, too, Amelie. I believe I started to love you the instant we met, but I knew I was not good enough for you.'

'Good enough?' she cried. 'You are the best man I know, the most honourable man I know. You are always there when I need you. You never lie to me. You always do what needs to be done.'

The door to her father's bedchamber opened, and he stepped into the corridor.

Edmund's grip on Amelie tightened, and she braced herself for whatever her father would say next.

'Wait a moment,' her father said in a quiet voice.

He approached them as they stayed rooted to the same spot.

He looked directly at Edmund. 'Summerfield, my daughter is correct—my son even tried to tell me—you have behaved honourably ever since that—that one transgression. I, on the other hand, have behaved abominably. I am not going to have anyone arrested. I'm not making anyone choose between one thing and another.' He extended his hand. 'I apologise to you, sir.'

Edmund released Amelie and hesitated only a moment before accepting the handshake.

'Oh, Papa!' Amelie had feared her father might never see Edmund's worth.

Her father lifted a hand. 'I need to make amends—'

Edmund interrupted him. 'Your apology is enough, sir.'

What other man would be so generous? Amelie's heart swelled with pride.

Her father shook his head. 'An apology is not nearly enough. I almost drove away my daughter! You stopped me. So, I want to give you something.

I want to deed you this farm, if you would like it. Or its worth, if you would prefer. Call it a wedding present.'

His valet appeared in the corridor carrying folded clothing. He halted, brows raised.

Amelie pulled Edmund away. 'Thank you, Papa! We will leave you to Hines and talk about this at dinner.'

Her father smiled wanly. 'As you wish, Amelie. It should always be as you wish.'

Amelie led Edmund to his bedchamber.

Once inside he put his arms around her. 'I knew your father was a decent man.'

She hugged him tight. 'What do you wish to do, Edmund? Do you want the farm?'

'Your father and I agree on one thing,' he said. 'It should be as you wish.'

'I should like to stay here,' she said. 'But if you prefer, I will go to Brussels with you, Edmund. I will go anywhere with you.'

'We stay here, then.' He kissed her forehead. 'It will be our home.'

She sighed. 'Our home.'

He held her again. 'Ah, Amelie. If it weren't for the baby, I would say my life is perfect. With you.'

'We will have more babies, Edmund.' She pulled away and made him look at her. 'We will be a family.'

Epilogue

August 1816—Brussels, Belgium

Edmund found Brussels much the same after a year, but also much altered. The buildings stood as majestically as before; the *parc* was as beautiful, but no soldiers in varied-colour uniforms walked down the streets or strolled through the shrubbery. There was no tension in the air, no fear of what was to come.

Edmund and Amelie had just left Lady Summerfield and Count von Osten, Edmund's stepmother and her lover. The visit had been a pleasant one. Lady Summerfield greeted him as warmly as ever, as if he were her son instead of her late husband's bastard. She also welcomed Amelie and genuinely seemed to delight in her, taking her aside for a tête-à-tête. Edmund and Count von Osten talked over their investments, and Edmund had the chance to tell them both about the farm. They left, promising to come to dinner in two days' time.

The afternoon was brisk and sunny, so they walked back to the Hotel de Flandre from rue Sainte Anne, where Lady Summerfield lived.

'I liked her, Edmund.' Amelie held his arm and they strolled down the street. 'She is very charming but without pretence. I admire that.'

'I'm glad.' He put his hand over hers. 'I wish my sisters would let themselves know her.'

'In time perhaps,' she said.

They walked past familiar buildings, crossing familiar streets.

'Oh, my goodness.' She suddenly stopped. 'Do you know where we are?'

They were at the entrance of an alley. 'This is where that ruffian dragged you,' he said.

She clung to him tighter. 'Where you rescued me.'

He slipped a kiss onto her temple. 'I should like to thank that fellow.'

'Thank him!' She gave him a playful shove. 'He was horrid! I am grateful you came along when you did!'

'As am I.' He hugged her. 'We have had an eventful year.'

'Most of it lovely,' she agreed.

They resumed their stroll.

It, indeed, had been a lovely year for the most

part. After Amelie's father's unreasonableness forced them to admit their love for each other, their days and nights had been more splendid than he could have imagined.

'Who would have thought we'd end up on a sheep farm!' she cried. 'Or that I would love it so.'

'I dare say Reid will keep it running well without us for a couple of months.'

She rested her cheek against his shoulder. 'I miss it.'

'I miss it, too,' he admitted.

She squeezed his arm. 'We did rather well this year, with all that happened, did we not?'

'We did, indeed.' Who would have believed a bastard son would earn the love of a viscount's daughter? Or live on a sheep farm and be happy over it?

She stopped suddenly and turned to him with an odd look on her face. 'I need to tell you something.'

He held his breath. Their life had become so perfect he'd worried that it might all come crashing down. 'What is it?'

'I'm not sure yet.' Now she was being cryptic.

He braced himself. 'Not sure of what?'

A glimmer of a smile tinged her lips. 'Of—of whether I am to have a baby. I think so, though. I haven't been sick but I feel different and—well—I counted the weeks since—'

He cut her off. 'You think you are with child?'

She nodded, smiling widely now.

He uttered a whoop of joy, picked her up and swung her around. Who cared if they were on the streets of Brussels?

'But I am not sure yet!' she cried.

'You are sure enough to tell me.' He could not contain his grin.

'Do not set your hopes on it,' she said more soberly. 'I might be wrong.'

He tilted up her chin and placed a kiss upon her lips. 'Then if you are wrong, let us see if we can still make it happen.'

She laughed. 'Shall we make haste?'

Their leisurely stroll became a dash past the Cathedral of Saint Michael and Saint Gudula, through the Parc de Bruxelles and on to the hotel where their love truly began.

* * * * *

*If you enjoyed this story,
don't miss the rest of Diane Gaston's*
THE SCANDALOUS SUMMERFIELDS
miniseries!

Read the first in the quartet:
BOUND BY DUTY

*And look out for two more captivating
stories still to come!*

MILLS & BOON®

Why shop at millsandboon.co.uk?

Each year, thousands of romance readers find their perfect read at millsandboon.co.uk. That's because we're passionate about bringing you the very best romantic fiction. Here are some of the advantages of shopping at www.millsandboon.co.uk:

✳ **Get new books first**—you'll be able to buy your favourite books one month before they hit the shops

✳ **Get exclusive discounts**—you'll also be able to buy our specially created monthly collections, with up to 50% off the RRP

✳ **Find your favourite authors**—latest news, interviews and new releases for all your favourite authors and series on our website, plus ideas for what to try next

✳ **Join in**—once you've bought your favourite books, don't forget to register with us to rate, review and join in the discussions

Visit **www.millsandboon.co.uk**
for all this and more today!